"Are ~~ed,~~
hold ~~ong~~
before releasing her.

She decided to be honest. "Not really. I'm confused and a bit unsettled."

"I'm sorry."

"If you really were sorry, you'd leave town."

"Ah, you know I can't do that."

Somehow Jade had suspected he'd say that. "Can't? Or won't?"

"Good point." As they climbed over another rocky patch, he once again took her arm. And once again, she had to pretend her skin didn't tingle from the contact. Funny thing that. She hadn't realized she could be capable of such tangled emotions. She both wanted the man gone and to wrap herself around him and never let him go.

TEMPTING
THE DRAGON

KAREN WHIDDON

First Published in Great Britain 2016
By Mills & Boon, an imprint of HarperCollins*Publishers*
1 London Bridge Street, London, SE1 9GF

© 2016 Karen Whiddon

ISBN: 978-0-263-92177-9

89-0716

Our policy is to use papers that are natural, renewable and recyclable products and made from wood grown in sustainable forests. The logging and manufacturing processes conform to the legal environmental regulations of the country of origin.

Printed and bound in Spain
by CPI, Barcelona

Karen Whiddon started weaving fanciful tales for her younger brothers at eleven. Amid the Catskill Mountains, then the Rocky Mountains, she fueled her imagination with the natural beauty surrounding her. Karen lives in north Texas and shares her life with her hero of a husband and three doting dogs. You can email Karen at KWhiddon1@aol.com or write to her at P.O. Box 820807, Fort Worth, TX 76182, USA. Fans can also check out her website, www.karenwhiddon.com.

To my father, Charles J. Corcoran. He fell ill right before I started this book and sadly passed away when I was about a hundred pages into writing it. I will always miss him. Love you, Dad. Always.

Chapter 1

"A lake monster?" The elderly man peered at Rance Sleighter as if he'd shown up drunk at church on Easter Sunday. Never mind that they were standing in front of Rex's Hardware store on Main Street in the small town of Forestwood, New York. Upstate New York, which Rance understood as anywhere north of New York City.

"Yes, a lake monster," Rance repeated patiently, mentally wishing, as he still did several times a day, for a beer. The craving never went away, but at least now he knew he was strong enough to resist it. He hadn't been once, right after his wife, Violet, had died. His drinking had cost him too much for him to ever go back.

Meanwhile, he had to think of Eve. As usual, the thought of his tiny stepdaughter made his gut clench. He'd loved her since the moment he'd met her, when he and her mother had started dating. Luckily for all of them, Eve's human father, Jim, and her mother had remained on civil, almost friendly terms. Rance and Violet had even invited Jim to their wedding.

Now Violet was dead and Eve lay seriously ill in a hospital bed in Houston, silent except for the steady beeping of the machines. Though Jim had taken custody, he'd allowed Rance full visitation. The two men had remained friends, sharing Eve's love.

She couldn't die. She wouldn't die. He wouldn't let her. The thought strengthened his resolve. Eve was why he'd come here. No matter what, he refused to let her down. He'd do anything for his little girl. Even find a lake monster.

"The story has traveled all over the country. It's the reason I'm here. You can't tell me you haven't heard about it."

The old man puffed up at that. "Harrumph. I might have heard nonsense, but you won't catch me discussing it. You want to talk lake monsters, go talk to the witch's family."

"The what?"

"You heard me." Pointing a shaky finger north, the codger grimaced. "Burnett family. Daughter is a witch. I'm sure they'll be delighted to discuss lake monsters with you."

And then, while Rance struggled to formulate a reply, the old-timer stomped off, heading across the street toward a restaurant titled Mother Earth's Café.

As small towns went, Forestwood had a picturesque, holiday-postcard-type of appeal. The brilliant reds and orange of the fall leaves helped. In Houston, where Rance was from, they didn't have much of an autumn. When the trees did shed their leaves, they just sort of turned yellow and fell off.

He took another glance around him, charmed despite himself. It almost felt as if he'd stepped back in time. Fully restored old buildings lined Main Street, and all of the houses surrounding downtown were large and beautiful and…old. Painted and pretty, but from another era.

Not his thing. Rance grimaced. Give him a sleek modern condo downtown in any large city any day. Much less upkeep, especially for a guy who lived the way he did—constantly on the move in search of the next story. If he were to be perfectly honest, which he usually was, a guy who stayed on the run from his internal demons.

Dramatic, too, he supposed. Guess that was what investigative journalism and losing his family had done to him. Lifting his camera, he snapped a few shots of the street with the beautiful trees in the background. Nice to get a sense of place to go with the story.

His stomach growled, reminding him it had been a while since he'd eaten. What the hell, Mother Earth's Café sounded as good as anything else. He could go for a juicy hamburger right now.

As soon as he stepped inside, Rance took note of how many diners were crowded into the small room. That might have been due to the restaurant's relatively tiny size or the fact that he hadn't noticed any other eating establishments in the immediate vicinity. Whatever the reason, the scent of good food—beef and fried chicken among other things—made his mouth water.

Taking a stool at the lunch counter, he checked out the place's leftover-from-the-seventies vibe. Perfect. Surely someone in here would have no problem telling him about the region's very own mythical beast. A local Loch Ness monster would be a great way to attract tourists to this out of the way town. He'd think someone would have gone out of their way to promote it already.

The waitress came over, smiling. "What can I get you today?" she asked, batting her false eyelashes so much he wondered if Forestwood also had a shortage of single men.

He smiled politely back, placing his order for a burger and fries, along with iced tea. If his lack of flirting disappointed her, she didn't show it. Instead, she jotted down his order, nodded and disappeared. Listening to the hum of chatter and clink of utensils, he decided to wait to ask anyone anything until after he'd eaten.

His food arrived a few minutes later and he dug in. The aroma of the place hadn't lied. The juicy burger tasted great—one of the best he'd had in years. The fries were perfect, too—crisp and flavored with a hint of seasoning spice. And the tea—sweet tea, without him asking—tasted like it had been made in Atlanta rather than up north.

A meal like this deserved him taking his time. He tried, but hunger had him scarfing it down. He considered it a tribute to the cook that he completely cleaned his plate.

As soon as he'd finished, the waitress reappeared, asking him if he'd saved room for dessert.

"I don't think so," he told her, genuinely regretful. "Maybe next time. Listen, I'm wondering if you can tell me how to find the lake monster."

Just like that, the smile vanished from her pretty face. "I don't know what you're talking about," she said, no longer batting any eyelashes. She thrust a paper at him. "Here's your check. Pay the cashier on the way out." And she took off without a backward glance, her shoes making slapping sounds on the linoleum floor.

Stunned, he stared after her. Wow. Two for two. People in this place were awfully defensive about a thing that was supposedly nonexistent.

What about asking the witch's family? Seriously? This had him shaking his head. They'd admit to the existence of a witch, but not admit the possibility of a giant lizard living in their lake? Made no sense. A witch. Whatever. The man earlier had called them the Burnetts. Maybe he'd have better luck asking around how to find them. He guessed it couldn't hurt.

After leaving a five for the waitress, he headed toward

the cashier. Evidently, word of his questioning had preceded him since the pink-haired woman eyed him warily.

"I'm wondering if you could help me," he began. She started shaking her head before he even had a chance to finish.

"I don't know anything," she answered, taking his ticket and his twenty and giving him back change. Her long fingernails were painted black with white tips.

He couldn't help but find the way everyone wanted to stonewall him amusing. Did they not realize doing so piqued his interest more than if they'd simply laughed off his questions?

"I haven't even asked you yet. You have no idea what I'm wanting to know."

She shrugged, looking anywhere but at him. "Thanks for visiting," she chirped. "Come again."

"Where can I find the Burnetts?"

This got her attention. "The Burnetts? Which one?"

"Any one," he responded.

Clearly unsure of how to react, she met his gaze and swallowed hard. "Are you in town at their invitation?" The way she said it let him know it mattered if he was. Sort of like being invited by royalty.

He wished he could lie, but he refused to start out on that kind of footing, so he shook his head. "No. But I need to ask someone about your local lake monster. You know, the one no one will admit is here. Someone else told me the Burnetts might at least be willing to talk to me."

Her loud sigh let him know she'd rather be rolling her eyes. "Urban legend, sir. Nothing more. However, if you still want to find the Burnetts, three of them are having lunch at the booth near the back door. Their usual place."

That was all he needed to hear. "Thank you," he murmured, already turning and heading toward the back. He spotted them, three women, apparently all older. The two who faced him looked up as he approached their booth. The one sitting with her back to him, long silver hair streaming in luxurious waves over her slender shoulders, did not.

"Excuse me, ladies. My name is Rance Sleighter," he began. Then the third woman glanced up, and he completely lost his train of thought. Desire slammed into him with all the force of a tornado. Whatever he'd expected, it hadn't been this.

She was stunning, simply gorgeous. And younger than her hair color would make one think. Her brilliant emerald eyes, slightly upturned to give her an exotic look, were fringed with long lashes. Not false. Silver, like her hair. He took a moment to register the unusual color, still dumbfounded. Unable to help himself, he let his gaze travel over her, aching to touch her creamy skin with his mouth, to trace over the curve of her luscious lips, before claiming her with a kiss. A necklace with an unusual purple stone nestled in the hollow between her perfect breasts.

Women didn't affect him so suddenly or powerfully. Not ever. Still marveling at the heat of his desire, he had to admit she might be the most exotically beautiful woman he'd ever met. The metallic glimmer of her hair added rather than detracted from her appeal.

His. Something clenched in his gut. *His.*

Even as the knowledge settled deep inside him, their gazes locked. Jumping slightly, she actually gasped. "You," she said faintly.

He couldn't respond. Or move. All he could do was stare and battle the urge to haul her up against him and claim her as his.

Something of his thoughts must have shown on his face. The two older ladies tittered. "Don't worry, sonny," one said. "Most men have that reaction when they meet Jade."

Jade. The exotic name suited her. Pushing down his strong and almost violent arousal, he collected himself and managed to nod in what he hoped might be a passable semblance of a greeting. "Nice to meet you."

"And I'm Amber," the middle-aged one continued. She had fiery red hair and similar colored eyes. "Jade's mother. And her—" she pointed "—she's Opal. My mother. Three generations of Burnetts right here at one table."

He nodded at Opal, the oldest woman. Her red hair had faded to gray and red tinted the short, spiky tips. Yet the eyes were the same vibrant green.

"What can we help you with?" Jade asked, her mouth curving in a sensual smile so delectable he knew he had to taste it as soon as possible.

"I…" Once again he found himself at a loss for words. This irritated the hell out of him. He earned his living with words and he'd traveled the world covering stories, for Pete's sake. In the course of his work, he'd certainly met tons of beautiful women, all sexy, and photographed most of them, too.

Yet none had knocked him off his game. He shifted his stance, hoping his arousal wasn't apparent to them.

"Yes, the Burnetts. I was told to talk to y'all," he began, his voice coming out a bit more raspy than normal. "I was hoping you could answer some questions for me."

The three women shared looks and smiles, as if his simple words reminded them of some private joke. "Oooh. I adore a man with a Southern accent. We can definitely try, honey," the oldest of them replied. "What do you need to know?"

Judging by the way everyone else he'd talked to had reacted, he figured they'd shut him down really quickly. He braced himself and went ahead with the rest of his request. "I'm trying to find out information about the Loch Ness–type monster reported to be living in your lake."

Again that shared secret glance among them. "Have people been talking about her?" the middle-aged woman asked.

Her. He made a mental note to file that information away for later. Even though Jade sat silently, every fiber of his being vibrated with awareness of her.

"No," he admitted. "And that's the problem. Every time I mention her, people shut down. They act like I'm crazy or overly familiar."

At this, Jade looked down. Her mother and grandmother continued to smile benignly.

"Why exactly do you want to know?" Opal asked. "And think carefully before you answer. This is important."

"All I can do is give you the truth. I'm a fairly well-known photojournalist. I even have a couple of books under my belt." Despite having appeared on various national news programs as well as several late-night shows, rarely did anyone recognize him. He preferred it that way. "Currently I've been traveling the world checking out stories of beasts like yours."

"And have you found any you could report on?"

"Not yet."

"I can't quite place that accent," Jade put in, her green gaze meeting his and sending another jolt straight to his groin. "Like my grandmother said, I can tell it's Southern. Where exactly are you from?"

"Texas." Which might be a short answer, but actually said everything there was to say. He'd learned people up north had some strange ideas about his home state. So far, he'd done as little as possible to disabuse them.

"Really?" Interest showed in Jade's expression. "I spent a couple of summers there when I was younger. What part are you from?"

"Houston."

"Oh. I spent more time in Dallas." The soft lilt in her voice had him leaning in to hear her speak.

Just then the waitress arrived with the women's lunches. This one stood short and was built like a truck—all muscle with a no-nonsense air about her. "Excuse me," she said, bumping his shoulder with the edge of her tray. "I need to serve these ladies their food while it's still piping hot."

Of course he stepped aside. Five more seconds. If he could have had five more seconds, he would have found out if Jade was actually willing to talk to him about the lake creature.

Once their meals had been served, the waitress gave him a quizzical look and strode off.

Taking a deep breath, he stepped back from the table. While the polite thing to do would be to excuse himself and let them eat their meal in peace, no one had answered anything.

"Really, I don't think you want to be interrupting our lunch," Opal said, her mild tone nevertheless containing a hint of reproach.

"I agree," Amber chimed in with an arch look and a frown.

"I'm sorry," he began, focusing his attention on the woman he most wanted to speak with. Jade.

Face once again downcast as she cut up the chicken on her salad, Jade didn't acknowledge his presence. The rigid set of her delicate shoulders spoke volumes of her disapproval.

He didn't exactly blame her. Still, time was short and courtesy warred with necessity. "Darlin', I just need a few seconds," he began. "One quick question. Maybe two."

"Please go." Jade's request, though delivered in a voice as smooth as silk, made the other two women freeze. "You may come by the house later if you'd like, but right now, we're going to have our lunch. And you're going to leave. Now."

"I'm…" To his complete shock, he felt his body begin to back away without him moving it. His legs and feet were not under his control. Like a puppet maneuvered by invisible strings, he traveled toward the doorway, his hand even coming up to grasp the handle to open the door before continuing outside. It was the damnedest thing.

Witch. Now the elderly man's words made sense. Sort of. He wasn't entirely sure he believed in witches. At least, he hadn't until this.

Finally, once he'd traveled half a block down the sidewalk, the compulsion released him and he nearly fell. Heart pounding, he stood stock-still, examining his hands and stomping his feet, just to be certain he could.

"A witch, huh?" Mystified and more than a little intrigued, he knew he'd definitely stop by their house later. As soon as he found out where exactly it might be. This witch angle might make an even better story than a fictional lake monster.

With her heart still beating way too fast, Jade Burnett took a deep breath. She reached up and took her Guardian necklace in between her fingers, a gesture that never failed to bring her comfort. "It was him," she said, full of both giddy anticipation and, oddly enough, a nameless sadness. "The photographer who interrupted our lunch. I don't know how, but I knew I'd meet that man someday. I kept seeing him in my dreams." She blushed, aware she couldn't tell them the sexual nature of those dreams. "I'd know him anywhere."

Both of the older women simultaneously raised their elegant brows.

"He was a handsome devil," Opal mused. "Those eyes—gray? Silver? They were unusual. He seemed a bit cocky and maybe even overconfident, though I like them that way myself."

Jade could feel her face heat. "Me, too," she admitted. The curse of her family's uncommon beauty meant she'd need a man who could be strong enough to resist her. Plus with all the silly (and hurtful) rumors about her in town, any man who'd be willing to date her would have to have enough self-assurance to ignore them.

Her mother and her grandmother exchanged amused glances.

"You want him, don't you, dear?" Opal asked.

Jade nodded. "Inexplicably, I do. I have, ever since I saw him in my dreams."

"Then why'd you send him away?" Amber complained. "You know I want grandchildren. So far, you've done nothing to make me think I'll ever have them."

Though this was an old argument, Jade's blush deepened. Children. She wanted kids of her own someday, too. Ruthless, she quashed down the quick flare of hope at the thought. "Please," she murmured. "I just met him. Let's enjoy our lunch. I'm sure he'll show up at the house soon enough."

Her mother nodded. "I hope you've been practicing your flirting skills because you'll need to do something to keep him distracted." It went without saying that Jade must protect Libby, the shape-shifting beast who lived in Forestwood Lake, from the prying eyes of outsiders. Especially a photojournalist.

Flirting skills. Right. Miraculously, Jade managed not to snort out loud. Instead, she dug in to her salad.

Finally, silence reigned while everyone focused on eating.

The house. Her home... Jade tried to picture the handsome man who'd visited her numerous times in her dreams actually being there physically. The thought made her shiver. She wondered if the house would accept him, then shook off the thought. Sometimes she thought of her family's ancestral home as a living entity rather than just a building.

Stranger things had certainly happened. Hers was a family of shape-shifting werewolves who were Guardians to a mystical lake creature named Libby. Jade was the current

Guardian, and ever since she'd been chosen, she occasionally happened to have the odd magical power. Her family turned a blind eye to these, preferring to pretend they didn't exist, unlike the townspeople, who loved to watch and gossip.

Almost all of the town knew about Libby. Forestwood was made up of both Pack—shape-shifters who became wolves when they changed—and humans. The shape-shifters, like the rest of the Burnetts, preferred to ignore the magic. The humans, who had no idea that such a thing as shape-shifters even existed, accepted the fact of Burnett magic and considered Jade a witch. They appeared to be well aware that only Libby's current Guardian had small magical powers.

They apparently were surprisingly okay with that. Sure, there was a lot of gossip and rumors. Women hated her due to her beauty, while men desired her. And made up odd, hurtful stories about her imagined sexual prowess.

None of it mattered, or so Jade told herself when a particular rumor caused her pain. The only matter of any importance was the way the entire town of Forestwood had silently pledged over the years to keep their lake creature a secret from outsiders. Jade more than anyone else appreciated that, since as Libby's caretaker it made her job easier.

Except someone had apparently broken their pledge. Otherwise, how would the photojournalist have heard about her?

After lunch, everyone piled into Jade's bright green SUV and they headed home. The sunlight shone through the vibrant green trees, dappling the ground with yellow. As she drove the winding roads heading home, Jade found herself holding her breath the same way she always did as she waited for the first sight of her family home.

Burnett House sat perched up on a hill, high enough to appear sitting sentinel over the entire town. Ancient trees cradled the Victorian-style structure and the corner lot had been fenced long ago with wrought iron. The original house had been built in 1803 by one of her ancestors, Floyd Burnett, who'd made it big in the steel industry. The Burnett family had lovingly occupied and taken care of the place, keeping it freshly painted and updated with the latest plumbing and wiring, not to mention granite countertops and modern appliances. The house had been featured in several magazines over the years.

Despite having lived there her entire life, the sight of the huge two-story home never failed to take Jade's breath away.

"Almost there," Amber chirped. Aware of Jade's admiration of their home, the entire family always watched for her reaction. They found it fascinating, Opal had once told her. The rarity of a Burnett with such strong ties to the house could only be a good thing, especially since ancient lore believed the Guardian's powers came from there.

Jade wasn't so sure about that. She tended to believe power came from within. Also, she felt it had something to do with Libby, her charge. Otherwise, why would only the current Guardian be gifted?

One more curve, and there it was. Bathed in yellow warmth from the sun, at this time of day the house appeared to actually glow. Smiling dreamily, Jade sighed with pleasure as she pulled into the driveway. It was a good thing she loved this place so much. Because she, like all the women who'd been given the title of Libby's caretaker, had been cursed to die if they ever tried to leave. Only the Guardians had to remain—the other women were free to come and go as they pleased.

Or so legend had it. There had been numerous stories over the years. Jade wasn't entirely certain she believed them. Mostly, she tried not to think about it. While she didn't like the idea of being trapped, she couldn't imagine herself making a life anywhere else but Forestwood.

"Here we are," Jade said as she parked, ignoring her

family's delighted expression as they watched her. Her heart skipped a beat as she wondered when she'd see the handsome stranger from the café. Unable to help herself, she furtively looked around for another car. Seeing none, she relaxed a little, though she still felt on edge.

She couldn't shake the sense that things were about to change. Her life, most specifically. She could only hope this would be a good thing.

Chapter 2

Once inside the large house, her mother and her grand-mother scattered. One of the other reasons Jade loved her home so much was its size. Not only the various hallways and rooms, but the hidden compartments and tunnels had always ensured the one seeking solitude had a place to hide.

Jade had taken advantage of that when she'd been younger. These days, her younger twin sisters, Pearl and Sapphire, were the ones who often hid from the constant noisiness of the family.

Currently, there was only one man in residence—Sam Burnett, Opal's husband and Jade's grandfather. These days, due to his worsening dementia, he mostly stayed in his room with the aide the family had hired to look after him. On his more lucid days, Sam would announce to any-one who would listen that he considered himself lucky. He'd always claimed Opal's first name, which followed the Bur-nett tradition of naming their women after gemstones, had been a sign that she was his mate.

He was lucky to find her, the rest of the family had always thought. Lucky to have been one of the few men who'd managed to live in the house. Probably because he'd been born a Burnett. Men who'd married into the Burnett family frequently died an early death or the marriage ended in divorce. Most couldn't deal with the Burnett women's amazing beauty. More than one bitter divorce had resulted from a Burnett female attracting far more attention than her husband could handle.

And then there were those, like Jade's father, who hadn't even attempted to marry a Burnett.

Her aunt Emerald, never named Guardian, had married and moved out, though she and her husband, Jack, and their daughter still lived in Forestwood. Jade saw her cousin Di often enough, though Di's brother, Jack Jr., had moved to California as soon as he graduated high school. He'd never returned, not even at Christmas or Thanksgiving.

The only ones who couldn't leave the house were the Guardians. Or so Jade had been told. Like her mother before her, as long as Jade took care of Libby, if she were to marry, her husband would have to agree to reside here. Jade didn't know too many men—okay, none, other than her grandfather, who was related—who would agree to live in a rambling old house with a bunch of women.

Travel could be prohibitive for those chosen. Even before she'd officially assumed the title of Guardian, but after Libby had named her Amber's successor, Jade had only gone away once, back in high school during spring break with her friends. In two days she'd become violently ill, and not from alcohol consumption. Her mother had been dispatched to collect her. Once Jade had arrived back home, she instantly felt better. After that, Jade simply stayed put.

These days it was Pearl and Sapphire who were chafing to go on a grand adventure of their own. They were only seventeen, the same age as Jade when she took her ill-advised spring break trip. Since Libby hadn't mentioned wanting Jade to pass on the mantle to either of them yet, Jade figured they were safe. At least for now, until Libby decided she needed a new Guardian.

The only thing missing, as far as Jade was concerned, was a dog. Her grandmother claimed to be allergic to all pets, so they'd never had any. The longing for a dog was one of the reasons Jade had opened her business, a doggy day care called Dogs Off Leash. DOL, for short.

Jade headed for the kitchen, which was one of her favorite rooms in the house. Her aunt was visiting and, as she often did because she claimed to enjoy the feel of dough under her hands, she was baking bread. The heavenly smell made Jade's mouth water. Emerald was one of the few talented cooks in the family. When her husband and kids got on her nerves, she frequently showed up and worked out her frustration by baking. Jade loved to be around when Auntie Em visited.

"Hello, dear." Her aunt held out her arms, wrapping Jade in a mist of perfume and flour. "Did you ladies have a nice lunch?"

"We did." Jade smiled. "Do you need any help?" she asked. Auntie Em never did, but simply asking was enough to earn a bit of whatever treat she'd made.

This time was no exception. Beaming, her aunt handed her a slice of fresh-baked bread with a dot of creamy butter. After giving her thanks, Jade carried her prize from the warm kitchen and out to the front porch, where she could enjoy it in peace.

She sat down on the wooden swing—her favorite place to sit and watch the world pass by, and took a bite of bread. Soft and fragrant, the white bread contained hints of cheese, onion and herbs and melted on her tongue. She chewed slowly, wanting to savor every single bite. She might even have let out a quiet moan of pleasure.

"You eat that like you're making love to it," a dry, masculine voice drawled.

Instantly, she froze, even though every nerve ending flared to life as his voice and words resonated with her. *Him.* Just like that, her entire body felt energized and taut. *Making love.* An ache seized her as she dared to let herself imagine—for a second—what it would be like to make love with him.

Damn.

Refusing to let him see how much he rattled her, she concentrated on her bread and took another bite while she tried to do her best to pretend he hadn't startled her. She chewed deliberately, ignoring him until she'd swallowed.

Slowly, she let her gaze come up to meet his. Again, she felt the sting of desire, a sharp tug of attraction, immediate and undeniable. Her breath caught in her throat, but she let herself study him, aware she needed to size him up unclouded by memories of those dreams.

And what dreams they had been. Her blood heated as she remembered the sensual and provocative images.

Mouth curling in amusement, he stood there while she let her gaze slowly drift over him, up and down, from the top of his dark and shaggy hair to his worn, faded sneakers. His insolent gray eyes gleamed with amusement, and maybe a hint of desire. He had a craggy, handsome face, rugged and masculine. Muscles rippled under his flannel shirt, making her mouth grow dry. The confidence he wore like a shield gave him a powerful, nonchalant appearance. Despite his quiet manner, he radiated sensuality, making her feel a bit like a helpless moth drawn toward a flame. Even so, she sensed an air of isolation around him.

"Are you done?" he drawled. "Because now it's my turn."

Instantly, her face heated. She pretended a sudden interest in taking another bite of bread, chewing and managing to swallow even though she felt his gaze like a whisper-touch on her skin.

Normal, she reminded herself. She had to appear normal.

"You didn't come up the front path," she commented once she'd swallowed, her voice overly bright. "There's no way you could have or I would have seen you."

"I did, but after I knocked on the front door and got no answer, I went around to the back. The lady baking bread in the kitchen directed me back up front here to find you. And yes, she did let me try a taste of her bread."

Surprised, she glanced up. As she did, he smiled at her. The masculine power of his smile made her entire body tingle. This struck her momentarily speechless and all she could do was stare.

Luckily, she had a little left of her slice of bread to focus on. She took another bite, a big one, the last one, intending to savor it. Instead, the soft bread stuck to the roof of her mouth when she swallowed and she nearly choked. Still, she managed to get it down.

He quietly watched while she coughed and wiped her eyes.

"Are you all right?" he finally asked, the husky drawl in his voice making her think of the overwhelming heat of Texas summers.

She continued to cough, trying not to snort or hack too much, until she could catch her breath. All she could do was wave her hand at him to wait. Finally, she had herself back under control. Gathering what was left of her shredded dignity around her, she stood and met his gaze. "I swallowed wrong. You can be a bit overwhelming."

He grinned, making her regret her admission. "Coming from a woman who looks like you, I'll take that as a compliment."

Her own lips curled up in the beginning of a smile. "Touché. Now tell me, why are you here?"

"Because you invited me," he replied.

"Only to keep you from peppering us with questions at lunch," she countered. She should have been annoyed, but wasn't. And he knew it, she could tell. The glint in his gray eyes told her he was accustomed to using his charm to get his own way.

"My apologies." That Southern drawl had a way of reaching inside her and curling around her entire being. "Speaking of lunch, what exactly did you do to make me move?"

Briefly, she considered batting her own eyelashes. Instead, she went for a steady gaze. "I have no idea what you're talking about."

"You do realize I'm a photojournalist, right? I told you that earlier, didn't I?"

She nodded.

"Well, when a journalist has questions and everyone stonewalls him, that only intrigues him even more."

He had a point. Disconcerted, she swallowed. "All right. You said you had questions. What exactly do you need to know?"

"First, start by telling me how you made me move outside of the restaurant. It felt sort of like being pushed by an invisible hand."

For some reason, she found this amusing. From the intent way he watched her, he'd see if she tried to hide a smile, so she didn't bother. "Around town, they call me a witch. Maybe now you can understand why."

"I've heard that. Are you? A witch, I mean?"

To his credit, he didn't sound at all disconcerted.

"Not really," she finally admitted. "But you know how people talk. I have a few…abilities. Occasionally. Not many, and they're unreliable, so I can't really count on them."

As a shape-shifter, he shouldn't be surprised. He knew

magic existed—otherwise every shape-shifter would be in trouble. But he'd never met a real life witch before.

"I can tell from your aura that you're a shape-shifter," she began.

"Ditto." He narrowed his eyes. "Look, I'll cut to the chase. I'm here because I'm doing a report on lake monsters. You know, like the Loch Ness monster, but in North America. There have been several reported around the United States and Canada. The one in Forestwood Lake came up several times, so I took a chance and traveled here to find out what I could learn."

Monsters. Libby despised that word. And for good reason. Resisting the urge to defend her charge, Jade tilted her head, wishing she had one more bit of bread left. She felt confident no one in town would have told him anything. They were all united in protecting Libby. "And what did you find out?"

"Nothing, nada, zip. Like I mentioned at lunch, no one will talk to me. The only response I got was to ask the Burnetts. Which would be you, right?"

"That would be me," she agreed, flashing her sweetest smile and feeling a swift stab of pleasure in his quick intake of breath. Might as well fight fire with fire. She knew how to use charm, too. "Honestly, though. If I did know anything—and I'm not saying I do—what makes you think I would confide in a total stranger?"

He shook his head, appearing unimpressed. "Honey, answering a question with another question isn't going to make me forget I asked. If you won't tell me about your lake monster, can you please point me to one of your relatives who will?"

Ignoring the thrill at his no doubt unintentional endearment—with a Southern accent like that, he probably called everyone *honey* or *sugar* or something—she shifted uneasily in her seat. While there wasn't some kind of rule forbidding talk about Libby, her family also had a kind of tacit understanding the topic was off-limits to strangers.

Which this man, no matter how handsome, was.

"I'm a photojournalist," he reminded her. "The fact that everyone keeps putting me off just makes me want to dig deeper."

Nodding, she considered. Since they were both shifters, though she had no idea what he became when he changed, he'd know there were rules governing not revealing anything like this to humans. In other words, he couldn't do it. As a shape-shifting wolf, she was Pack. The Pack was the largest group of shape-shifters and their wolves outnumbered all the other animals combined.

Pack Protectors policed this policy and the repercussions were severe. Maybe he reported for some internal magazine or newspaper, meant only to be viewed by their own kind. Though she'd never heard of such a thing, it could exist.

Still, she needed to know. "You say you're a photojournalist. Who do you work for?"

A flash of surprise registered in his handsome face. "You've never heard of me?"

Tilting her head, she studied him. "Apparently not. What was your name again?"

"Rance Sleighter."

"Nope, I haven't heard of you. Should I have?"

He grinned. "I guess I deserved that. I used to work for *National Geographic* magazine. These days, I freelance."

"For the general public?" she persisted.

"If you mean humans, yes. I also have done photo spreads for shifter magazines as well as a few vampire ones. Basically, whoever is willing to pay me."

"And this story? The reason you're here? Who is it for?"

A shadow crossed his face, so quickly she might have imagined it. "A friend," he said. "Someone very close to me."

Then maybe, just maybe, this wasn't so bad. Yet shifter

or not, she wasn't sure she wanted to share Libby with outsiders.

"Let me speak with my family," she said, merely to stall him. She'd have to call a family meeting to figure out how to best deal with this. "Can you come back another day?"

He eyed her. "Tomorrow?"

"I don't know. I'm not sure I can round everyone up that early."

At this, he took a step closer. Close enough for her to smell the light masculine scent of whatever soap he used. "You make it sound like you need to call a board meeting. I'm just asking questions about a lake monster, not wanting to purchase stock in the town's largest business."

Chin up, she nodded, keeping her tone as dignified as she could, especially with the way her entire body heated every time she looked at him. "I completely understand. But I still need to speak with my family."

"Fine, but you know what?" He crossed his arms. With his wide-legged stance, he was the picture of virility. "Until now, I pretty much figured this lake monster wasn't real, like all the rest of them. A legend, a story, something the good people of Forestwood, New York, invented to help with tourism. But the way you—and everyone else in this town—are acting has got me to wondering what exactly you're hiding."

To that, she had no reply. "Check back with me tomorrow," she finally said, even though she had no idea if she could pull together a family meeting by then. "Hopefully I'll know more."

Though she'd pretty much dismissed him, he made no move to leave. Instead, he reached into his backpack and pulled out his camera, fiddled with the controls and held it up to his eyes as if testing the light.

"Okay?" she prodded.

He snapped a couple of shots, startling her. Impulsively,

she stuck out her tongue, instantly regretting it when she heard the click of the shutter. "Stop," she ordered. "No more photos. That's rude, taking my picture without asking."

Lowering the camera, his intense gaze pierced hers. "I'm sorry. Sometimes I take pictures out of habit. Especially when I see something worth photographing, like you."

"Compliments don't work on me," she declared, even though his words made her feel all warm and fuzzy. "You'll still need to check back with me tomorrow."

He grinned, a sexy, savage lift of his mouth that made her insides twist in response. "Since you give me no choice, it'll have to do. In the meantime, I think I'll head out to the lake myself and check things out."

She would have expected no less. "Just be careful," she said, her standard warning as she turned to head back inside. At least she didn't have to worry about him seeing anything. Libby always somehow sensed the presence of strangers and remained in the deepest part of the water. The only reason rumors had floated out of town had to be because someone had talked when they shouldn't have.

Back straight, she walked away. As she did, she felt him watching her. She halfway expected him to stop her and felt faintly disappointed when he didn't.

Once inside, she barely had time to take a deep breath before her twin baby sisters barreled around the corner. Blond ponytails flying, tall and leggy, they both had the all-American girl look going on. Except Pearl dressed exclusively in black while Sapphire favored vintage seventies attire, the more colorful, the better.

"Who was that?" Pearl demanded, grabbing at Jade's arm. "He's rock-god material."

Amused and secretly in agreement, Jade glanced at Sapphire to see if she'd echo her twin's sentiment. "He's pretty cute," Sapph finally allowed. "Who is he?"

"My new boyfriend?" Jade answered, ruining it by turning what should have been a statement into a question.

"Ewww," Pearl squealed. "That would mean he's old." She shuddered, as if their visitor had taken out his dentures before asking for his cane.

Sapph, always the more thoughtful one, frowned at her sister. "Jade's not old."

Pearl shrugged, her expression unconvinced. "Fine. If you want to snag every gorgeous man in town, don't let me stop you."

The heavy layer of sarcasm in her voice made Jade smile. "He's here because of Libby. He wants to do a story on her."

At her words, both teens' mouths dropped open. "Seriously?"

"Yep."

The twins exchanged looks.

"So what are you gonna do?" Pearl finally asked, seeming worried.

Jade made a show of checking her watch. "Call a family meeting. That's the only thing I can do."

Family meetings in the Burnett clan were frequent, noisy and fun. Usually a potluck, everyone brought a home-cooked dish or two. Tons of delicious food, free-flowing wine and lots of talk made the meetings occasions to be looked forward to.

Even the twins and their teenage cousins attended without complaint. The abundance of food was enough of a lure.

"A family meeting!" Pearl brightened. "Oh, I so hope Auntie Em brings her fried chicken."

"Oh, me, too!" The twins hurried off, heads together, planning what they'd eat first.

Watching them go, Jade sighed. Sometimes being around her younger sisters made her feel really old, even though she only had twelve years on their seventeen.

Jade made three calls, which meant those people would

make calls of their own until the entire family had been notified. Due to the urgency of the situation, the meeting would be that evening at seven. Unless life-threatening, all previously made plans would be canceled. The family meeting always took precedence.

Opal and Amber took to the kitchen, intent on cooking whatever culinary delights they'd decided to team up and make this time. Jade barely suppressed a shudder. The pair's creations were legendary, and not in a good way.

Finally, as the hour neared seven, cars pulled up in front of Burnett House and parked. People brought food—some in ice chests, boxes or bags, or casserole dishes they carried in their hands. Redheads outnumbered brunettes and blondes since almost all of the Burnetts and their offspring were gingers. Jade's flame-colored mane had turned silver immediately after taking on the mantle of Libby's caregiver. At first, this change had horrified her, making her fret about appearing old. But in the years that had passed, she'd come to love her moonlight tresses. She knew once she passed that task on, her normal color would be restored and the new caregiver would immediately go gray, like what had happened when Amber passed the title on to her.

Wonderful smells drifted out of the formal dining room as Jade made her way downstairs. She could hear the low hum of conversation, which meant the family had already begun to gather.

Stepping into the room, she stopped. It looked like it always did—a packed room, with the long mahogany table groaning under the weight of food that would soon be demolished when everyone descended on it like sharks on a feeding frenzy.

Her eyes watered at the competing smells of the older ladies' perfumes and the men's cologne. Jade had tried once to get everyone to agree to attend fragrance free, but she'd been immediately shot down by the elders. Despite the fact that wolves had super-sensitive noses, those ladies loved their scents, so Jade had to let it go. Even though every time she hugged her aunt Agate, Jade's eyes would water and she'd have to stifle a fit of coughing, the overabundance of scent thrived to this day. Jade countered this by trying to stand as far away from the worst offenders as possible.

Since she'd called the meeting, she would have to do the majority of the talking. She remembered the first family meeting at which she had to speak, immediately after her mother had announced her retirement and Jade had been assigned the chore of looking after Libby, the popular and mysterious lake shape-shifter who resided in Forestwood Lake. Libby despised the term *monster*. Jade couldn't blame her.

Since then, Jade had grown accustomed to giving speeches. She found she did better with little or no preparation. Winging it seemed well received.

But first, everyone had to eat. A line had already started forming at one end of the table, where someone had placed two stacks of sturdy paper plates. She watched, amazed even though it was always the same, as relatives took their places at certain dishes, filling their plates as high as they could, before carrying the mound of food over to their respective seats at the table.

Jade waited until just about everyone had gotten what they wanted before going over to check out what remained. Waving at a couple of her cousins on the other side of the room, she stepped in line. As she eyed the half-empty pans of pasta salad and fried chicken, her stomach growled. She made herself a small plate, wondering which dish her mother and grandmother had made. Amber and Opal had been holed up in the kitchen for hours, shooing away anyone who attempted to enter. They'd refused to say what they were making, only claiming it would be the best surprise ever.

Jade only hoped it would be edible. Separately, her grandmother was a good cook, but Amber wasn't. And together… They ended up competing, each adding just another pinch of something, and the end result always, without exception, turned out terrible.

What astounded Jade was that no one could tell from looking at it. No, it wasn't until you took the first bite and gagged that you realized what had happened.

Ladling a little bit of everything on her plate, she tried to spot Amber and Opal's latest concoction. Since she couldn't, she knew she'd find out once she started to eat.

The desserts had been placed on a side table. There were the usual cakes and pies, and a beautiful peach cobbler. Jade knew which one she'd be having. That is, as long as her mother and grandmother hadn't made it. Unfortunately, without tasting it, there was no way to tell.

Taking a seat next to her aunt Agate since it was the only one available, Jade hoped the overwhelming scent wouldn't ruin her taste buds, and dug in. Every single morsel she put in her mouth tasted delicious. Which meant, she realized after she'd cleaned her plate, that one of the desserts would be awful. But which one?

She caught Aunt Agate's eye, aware she—and just about everyone else in the room—was thinking the exact same thing.

A few people had already gingerly approached the dessert table, selecting two or three things to be on the safe side. Jade did the same, helping herself to a slice of chocolate cake and the peach cobbler. Praying neither of her choices would be the one, she took her seat and dug in. The chocolate cake tasted moist, with just the right amount of airy sweetness.

She polished that off and turned her attention to the cobbler. Just looking at the peach slices swimming in a syrupy glaze and the perfectly browned mixture of crumble made her mouth water. Someone should have taken a photograph of the entire thing when it had been undisturbed. Surely, this couldn't be the dessert item Amber and Opal had managed to ruin, could it?

Jade glanced up to find Aunt Agate watching her, spoon poised over her own mound of cobbler.

"You first," her aunt said, grinning.

Taking a deep breath, Jade plunged her spoon down, scooping up a good-size bite. It appeared juicy and moist, and the fragrant steam whet Jade's appetite. She swallowed, then shoved her entire spoonful into her mouth.

Her taste buds exploded with flavor. Slowly chewing, she let out her breath and swallowed. "It's good," she began, letting her relief show in her voice. "I'm not sure who made it, but neither Mom nor Grandma was the cook."

As she reached for another bite, her tongue began to burn. Eyeing her aunt, who was happily tucking in to her own helping of cobbler, Jade tried to blurt out a warning. Instead, she only managed a croak.

Chapter 3

Tears filling her eyes, Jade grabbed her water glass and began chugging, too late to help Aunt Agate, who had just begun to feel the burn. What the heck had they put into that thing—peppers?

One glass of water wasn't even close to enough. Jade jumped up, sprinting for the table where plastic cups had been stacked near water pitchers and ice. She filled two glasses, drinking one down and refilling it, before carrying them back to the table. Handing one to her aunt, she watched while the older woman drained hers before giving her the second.

"Oh, my," Aunt Agate finally gasped. "Guess we know who made that, after all."

All around the room, people were digging into the gorgeous cobbler. "It seems we never learn," Jade commented, her voice as dry as her still-burning throat. All around her, people gasped, reaching for their water glasses and shooting murderous looks at the oblivious pair of cooks, who continued to eat and chat happily.

Finally, Jade figured everyone had eaten—and suffered—enough. Taking a deep breath, she tapped her fork on her water glass for attention. "As I'm sure most of you know," she began, well aware how fast gossip traveled in this town, "a photojournalist is here asking questions about Libby."

Her mother and her aunt exchanged knowing looks. "The *handsome* stranger," Amber put in. "And I could tell by the way he looked at you that he found you attractive, as well."

Both Pearl and Sapphire glowered at her. Several of the other relatives whispered behind their hands to one another, which reminded Jade her lack of a man in her life had been a topic of conversation for quite some time.

She used to find the pointed comments hurtful. These days, she simply ignored them.

Jade managed to shrug. "I don't know about that, but we're not here to discuss my love life." Or lack of, she amended silently. "I need direction as to what to do about Libby. If he finds out about her and does a story, we can say goodbye to our privacy and hello to a wave of tourists."

Another standing argument in both town and her family. People were equally divided. Some wanted to capitalize on the monster in their midst, while others insisted on leaving things the way they'd been for centuries.

"That old debate again?" Jade's uncle Jack, Auntie Em's husband, huffed. "Why do you want to go and ruin a perfectly good family get-together with that nonsense?"

"Yeah," her cousin Coral, who hated her name, seconded. "Can you just finish up whatever you have to say so we can go?"

"This is important, everyone. A photojournalist is asking about Libby. I need to know what, if anything, to tell him."

This time, her grandmother spoke. When Opal addressed the family in her matriarchal voice, everyone paid attention. "In all my years of taking care of Libby, not once did word about her existence leak beyond this town."

The accusation seemed clear, at least to Jade. In fact, everyone in the room swung their heads around to stare right back at her, accusation in their expressions.

As if she'd already failed.

And it didn't matter that she'd never asked for this job. It had been expected of her from the moment she'd been born.

The last thing Jade had ever wanted was to be put in charge of taking care of Forestwood's resident lake beast. Libby had resided in the cool, deep depths for as long as anyone could remember, and the Burnett family had always been her caretakers. Libby personally chose whom she wanted and when. Since Jade's mother, Amber, was still young and vibrant, Jade had figured she'd had at least ten more years before being asked to take on the task.

Thus when Libby gave her approval for Amber to retire from her duty and pass the chore down, Jade had been completely unprepared. Worse, Amber had said nothing other than a terse "Good luck." Evidently, training wasn't one of the perks of the job.

Jade had been caretaker since she'd turned twenty, nine years now. In the beginning, she'd often resented that fact. These days, she felt more comfortable, more at ease with her role, which mostly consisted of being Libby's friend. Maybe in the beginning, when Libby had first come to Forestwood, the role had been one of a protector, Jade wasn't sure. Every decision, even those made by the Burnett family in a family meeting, had to be run by Libby before being implemented. In truth, Jade privately thought the family meetings were all for show. And an excuse to get together and eat.

"I'm doing the best I can," she muttered to herself through clenched teeth, while she tried to figure out what to say. "I think I've done well considering my age when I assumed the role of Guardian."

Unfortunately, Opal's hearing was the one thing that hadn't declined with age. "Life is not fair, honey," Opal drawled. "And since Libby specifically requested you, there wasn't much choice in the matter."

Ever since the first time Jade had heard Opal make that statement, she'd grit her teeth and wondered how anyone had actually known what Libby wanted. In the prior years when Jade had accompanied Amber to take care of Libby, not once had Libby—whether in human form or not— ever said two words to her. Not once. Jade had begun to sincerely doubt she could talk. Of course the minute Jade had stepped into her mother's role, all that had changed. She and Libby had sat down several times and shared a meal and chatted. These days, Jade felt as if she and Libby could easily become close friends.

Once, the knowledge that Libby had requested her had filled her with resentment. Now, she felt a little glow of pleasure.

Belatedly, she realized everyone was staring at her, waiting for a response.

Jade dipped her chin at Opal to show she understood. "That may be," she continued, addressing the entire family. "But the fact is, someone did talk to an outsider. Word traveled, far enough to attract that photojournalist's attention."

"Then deal with it," her mother said tiredly. "Distract him. You're pretty enough. Pretend to be helpful. You know as well as I do that Libby stays deep when a stranger comes around. That journalist will learn nothing, unless you tell him. And I know you won't do something that foolish."

And there she had her answer. She wondered why part of her had hoped...what? That they'd let their secret finally out in the open, for the rest of the world to marvel at and share? Or at least the shape-shifter world. Humans could never know.

"Are we finished?" cousin Coral demanded, sidestepping closer to the food table. "Because if we are, I'd sure like to eat my dessert."

Jade glanced at her grandmother, who dipped her head yes. Then at her mother, who did the same, except with a smile. "Then I guess we're done."

The instant the words left her mouth, chairs scraped on the wooden floor as they all rushed, en masse, toward the bathrooms. All except Coral and a few others who clearly hadn't yet tried the peach cobbler. Watching as they approached the dessert tables, Jade considered warning them, then decided not to. She snagged another slice of the chocolate cake and carried it out of the room, across the yard and into the main house. There, she took a seat at the kitchen bar and ate it slowly, needing to wash the taste of the cobbler out of her mouth. She had to plan a strategy. From what she could tell of the handsome photographer, he wouldn't be easily distracted or put off.

"Are you about ready?" Amber asked as she entered the kitchen. "We've got a full moon. It should be a perfect night for hunting."

The shape-shifting wolves were called Pack for a reason. There was nothing they loved more than changing into their lupine selves and hunting together. When a younger Jade had shown signs of reticence, preferring privacy over too much family togetherness, her mother had told her, "A solitary wolf is a lonely wolf." As far as Jade had been concerned, a little loneliness could be a good thing.

These days, Jade relished her family hunting times. Sometimes, family meetings were called just so everyone could change and hunt together after.

"Of course." Blotting her mouth with a paper napkin,

Jade carried her paper plate over to the trash bin. "It's been a while since I've changed."

"Then this hunt will do you good." Patting her arm, Amber wandered out toward the dining room to gather up any stragglers. Though technically, Grandpa Sam had been designated Pack leader years ago, his worsening dementia had made him unable to even attend the family hunts. Now, Jade's grandmother, Opal, led.

The woods in back of Burnett House stretched back several acres and the boundaries had been clearly marked on certain trees. Behind that, lay forest preserve, protected from hunters. A bounty of wildlife thrived there, and the Burnett Pack did their part to keep rabbits, squirrels, foxes and other smaller mammals from overpopulating.

Already the family had begun gathering on the back lawn, talking excitedly. With their full bellies, not too much hunting would likely take place tonight, but there were always a few who so loved the thrill of the hunt they attempted to do a sort of catch and release. Of course, once most shifters gave over to their animal side, the term *catch and release* lost all meaning.

Jade joined her aunt Agate and Coral. A second later, Sapphire and Pearl joined them. The twins seemed especially keyed up tonight, judging from their flushed faces.

"How long has it been since you changed?" Jade asked them, concerned.

Both girls giggled, but neither answered. Jade let it drop, since they were about to rectify the problem any moment now. Still, she resolved to have a chat with the teens later and reiterate the dangers of remaining human too long. Shifters who neglected their need to shape-shift often went insane or became ill. She didn't want anything like that to happen to her baby sisters.

The hum of voices quieted as Opal appeared on the back patio, followed closely by Amber. She led the way through the crowd, and they all followed her, their eagerness palpable.

An unpaved winding path led into the forest. Autumn's fallen leaves provided a colorful carpet beneath their feet. The evening breeze fell off here, muted by the shield of the ancient trees. This was as sacred and holy a place as Jade had ever been.

In the deepest part of their land, they passed the large maple tree that marked the edge of the preserve. Here, the family fanned out. Each, whether individually or as a small group, had their favorite spot they liked to go to shed and store their human clothing before initiating the change into wolf.

Ever since she'd first shifted, Jade had claimed a little glade rimmed by sumac and pine trees that had been mere saplings all those years ago.

Slipping into her own private leafy enclosure, Jade quickly undressed, placing everything into a weatherproof plastic box she kept chained to a rock. And then, with the scent of the damp earth surrounding her, she dropped to the ground and began the change.

Some shifters rushed this, anxious for the change to wolf to be over. There were a few who claimed they found it excruciatingly painful, but the vast majority took pleasure in the act. Jade liked to take her time, enjoying the feeling of her bones lengthening and changing, her body going from human woman to female wolf. Each time, she treated this act with reverence, like the miracle she considered it to be.

Finally, she blinked to clear away the sparkling pricks of light that always accompanied the shape-shifting. Wolf now, she used her nose before her eyes, sniffing the air and recognizing the individual scents of her family.

Bounding from her clearing, she greeted them with play bows. And they were off. Running, tumbling, stretching out their lupine forms until they were more used to being in this shape.

This—wild and free—was when Jade felt happiest. The damp leaves under her paws, catching the tantalizing scents of rabbit and fox, the feel of her powerful muscles under her fur as she ran.

Often, the Burnett clan would stay out all night, only changing back to human as dawn neared. Sometimes the elders, tiring easy, would leave early, but often they, too, reveled in the freedom from human aches and pains.

This night, Jade took the opportunity to make sure when she returned home as human she'd be exhausted. She hunted, but killed nothing, enjoying the sport. She played and rolled, teased and ran. And finally, as the sky began to lighten, she returned to her little grotto and began the change back to human.

Then, aroused as she always was, the way all shifters were when they changed back to human she found herself longing for a certain man. Rance. Glad her fatigue kept her from thinking too much, she dressed and began the long trek home. Ahead, she saw a few others doing the same thing.

Once she reached the house, she headed upstairs to her room and slid into bed. Closing her eyes, she fell into what she hoped would be a deep, dreamless sleep.

Of course, the next morning she slept in. Bright yellow sunlight streamed in through her bedroom window. Immediately, she knew she'd dreamed of him again. Rance. Sensual dreams, the kind she'd never had until recently. Rance. The man she'd craved when she'd returned to her human form. From the instant she first opened her eyes, she could see his face. They wanted her to distract him, but she needed to be careful. Nervous with anticipation, she put extra care into her appearance, styling her long silver hair into a mass of curls and applying eyeliner and mascara as well as powder and blush. And gloss. As she smoothed that over her mouth, she couldn't help but imagine Rance tasting her lips, lingering over the slightly sweet flavor.

The instant the thought occurred to her, she blushed. All over. Glad no one else was around to notice, she reminded herself she needed to distract him, nothing more.

Pearl and Sapph came running into her room, both talking excitedly at the same time. "He's here. Or not here yet, but walking up the street toward the house. He's got a camera with a huge lens and he's taking pictures of everything. I saw him…"

"No," Sapph interrupted, grinning. "I saw him first. So I get dibs."

Dibs?

"No one gets anything," Jade reminded them, keeping her voice stern while she hid a smile. "He's too old for you both, anyway."

"Staking a claim?" Amber lounged in the doorway, her gaze sharp, her expression interested.

"I'm the distraction, remember?" Jade summoned up a sweet smile. "Unless you want to do it?"

Amber laughed, the sound deep and throaty. "Don't tempt me. That man is easy on the eyes."

This made Jade snort.

"Ewww." Pearl said, grimacing. "Mommmm. Don't be a cougar. That's disgusting."

Inspecting herself in the mirror, Jade decided she looked presentable enough in her faded jeans and light green T-shirt."

"You're wearing that?" Amber asked, perfectly shaped brows raised. "How are you going to be a distraction dressed like that?"

Jade eyed her mother patiently. "Don't you think he'd find it a little strange if I met him on the front porch wearing a miniskirt and six-inch heels?"

Both Pearl and Sapph snickered.

"You could put a little effort into it," her mother began. "At least wear a dress. Even a nice blouse."

Jade stared at her. A blouse. She wasn't even sure she owned such a thing. "No," she finally answered. "Now if you ladies will excuse me, I've got some distracting to do."

With that, she swept out of the room, her head high.

In the hallway, her steps slowed. Unlike her heartbeat. So much for bravado. She'd been racking her brain trying to figure out exactly how to distract Rance.

She wasn't sure how far her family expected her to go, but she had no intention of getting even the slightest bit intimate with the man.

Her body's reaction to the idea of seeing him again called her a liar.

"Good morning." Pasting a bright smile on her face, she strode forward, hand outstretched. Tall and broad shouldered, his gray eyes blazed as he looked at her. He took her hand, but instead of shaking it as she expected, he lifted it to his lips and kissed the back, his mouth lingering.

Damn. She thought she might melt into a puddle right then and there. Somehow, she remembered to breathe.

Then, while her knees still shook and she couldn't find her voice to save her life, he released her and flashed that same charming smile. "Hold on, darlin'," he said, lifting the camera that hung around his neck and snapping a few shots of the house, the front porch and her.

When he'd finished, he was still smiling. "How about you and I go visit Forestwood Lake?"

Together? And then she remembered she needed to distract him.

"Okay," she managed. Because she knew he wouldn't see anything unusual there at all. Not once in all the time her family had been taking care of Libby had Libby let an out-of-towner see her.

* * *

How Jade Burnett could manage to look so damn good in blue jeans and a T-shirt, Rance didn't know. But when he turned and saw her sauntering toward him, her long silver hair tumbling in a luxurious fall over her shoulders, his breath caught in his throat. And his entire body went on red alert. At least he'd gotten a few shots with his camera.

Giving himself a mental shake, he focused on what she'd just agreed to do. Go to the lake. With him.

"Do you want to walk or drive?" she asked.

He pointed to the shiny red Mustang convertible he'd rented in Albany. "Let's take that. I'll put the top down so we can enjoy the day."

Most of the women he knew would have immediately protested, claiming the wind would mess up their hairdo or something. Jade appeared supremely unconcerned. In fact, she seemed delighted. "I love convertibles," she said.

"Did they tell you to be extra nice to me?" he asked, suddenly suspicious.

"They? Who is they?"

The perplexed frown didn't fool him. Especially not when she combined it with a mischievous grin. "If by *they*, you mean my family, then no. They did not ask me to be nice to you."

Interesting. "Well, then, what exactly did they decide?"

This time, the blank look she gave him was decidedly fake. "What do you mean?"

He waited until they were both inside the car, seat belts fastened, before answering. "About the lake monster. You were going to call a meeting to find out what you could and couldn't tell me."

"Put that way, you make it sound as if you truly believe there *is* a lake beast," she quipped, well aware of how much Libby hated the word *monster*.

He shook his head and pressed the ignition. The engine

came to life with a powerful rumble. When he glanced at her, she grinned. She dug a hair-thingy from her pocket and expertly put her hair up in a ponytail.

"Nice ride," she said. "Too bad it's a rental."

Amused, he chuckled. "If that's your attempt at a dig at me, it's pretty weak."

She widened her eyes, the picture of innocence. "A dig? Why on earth would you think that? It's just that this is such an awesome car, probably nothing like what you drive at home."

Instead of responding, he had the strongest urge to kiss her. This didn't surprise him, not in the least. Jade Burnett was gorgeous, with her long sexy hair and those amazing green eyes. Not to mention the lush curves of her body. Rance liked women, all women, but until today he'd never really figured he had a type. But now he knew. That type would be Jade. Slender and perfectly shaped, gorgeous creamy skin, with a tiny dusting of freckles across her nose. Lips that were made for kissing and a body that begged for his touch.

Yep. Jade was his type. He had the awful feeling that, forever after this, he'd be comparing other women to her.

Astounded at this thought—after he'd lost his wife Violet and started drinking, he hadn't ever thought of getting close to any other woman—he concentrated on the drive. He'd already taken a solo trip to Forestwood Lake, walked the trails, stood on top of the marbled stone cliffs. With the wealth of leafy trees and undergrowth all over the rolling hills, the area was pretty, but then so was every other lake or hiking trail in the Catskill Mountains. This part of the earth called to something primal, deep inside him.

In fact, in his previous life, Rance had thought if he ever wanted to become a country guy, he'd buy some land and build a house here. Now, he knew he never would. He needed the fast pace of the city to distract him from everything he'd lost.

"Take the next right," she said, startling him out of his reverie.

He did as she asked, turning onto the unmarked dirt road. Though there were occasional ruts and bumps, for the most part it seemed to be well maintained. As he drove, he noticed with a sense of amusement the way it wound through the forest in an apparently nonsensical pattern. Then they made one more turn and he slowed, awed despite himself.

The lake spread out below them. From this vantage point, higher than any of the others he'd been to, the sparkling expanse of water was a dark, vibrant blue. He let the car coast to a stop, even though the road continued, and got out, grabbing his Nikon D4S out of the bag on the backseat. While he had several cameras and lenses, he liked this one the best for everyday use.

He walked to the edge of an area that had apparently been set up for viewing purposes and stood still, marveling. A sense of rightness settled low in his chest. He'd only had this feeling a few times in his life—once in a remote area of Alaska, another on Vancouver Island and now here, on the opposite coast.

Lifting the camera, he lost himself in his art.

Jade came and stood by his side, silent, as if she understood. He appreciated that she didn't feel the need to fill the silence with meaningless chatter.

Once he'd taken his fill of pics, he lowered the Nikon and drank the scenery in with his eyes.

As he soaked in the strange feeling of contentment, he reminded himself he'd come here for a reason. "The only thing that could make this better would be if the so-called lake monster would make an appearance," he joked.

She snorted, but when he cut a sideways glance her way,

her intent expression as she stared at the water seemed far too serious.

For maybe the eightieth time, he caught himself wondering if there really *was* such a creature. In his world, where shape-shifters walked the streets unnoticed alongside humans and vampires, who was he to even think to discredit such a possibility? Just because he'd never seen one—not Nessie in Scotland or any of the others reported to have been sighted—didn't mean they didn't exist.

Hell, he could shape-shift into another creature entirely. Judging by Jade's aura, so could she, as well as the rest of her entire family. Pack, he figured. Most of the other shape-shifters he met were wolves. Even though he wasn't, not by a long shot, the aura revealed nothing about what kind of beast they changed into.

He eyed the lake and wondered. A flash just below the surface of a wave caught his eye. As he peered hard at whatever it had been, something big—something huge actually—leaped out of the water as if trying to fly. Or maybe like a whale breaching. Except this was fresh water, not the ocean. Moving fast, its large body arced in a flash of glinting silver scales before it dove back under.

It looked like… No. It couldn't be.

Stunned, he didn't move. Didn't breathe. While he wasn't entirely sure what he'd just witnessed, he felt a sense of awe that he'd been privileged to have seen such a sight. And of course, he hadn't been holding his camera.

Chapter 4

"Did you…?" Turning to the silent woman next to him, one glance at her ashen face told him she had also seen. "So there *is* a Forestwood monster."

"Which never, ever shows itself to strangers," she mused, her voice breaking.

"I guess there's a first time for everything." He glanced from her to the lake and back. "Why do you think that is?"

"Since we've already discussed the fact that we're both shifters, what kind are you?" she asked, staying true to her apparent penchant for avoiding answering questions by asking one of her own. Still, her question surprised him, since an unwritten rule existed forbidding discussing this sort of thing. While everyone recognized one another from their auras, they were specifically forbidden from discussing intimate details unless you were a mated pair.

Which he and Jade definitely were not.

Since he wasn't sure how exactly to answer, he settled on simply staring at her.

Deciding to see where she meant to take this, he waited. When she didn't speak, he finally had to. "You know better than to ask me that."

"Yes. I do. And since you apparently do as well, you're clearly aware of the law," she continued. "We are not to reveal ourselves to humans."

"True." Intrigued, he watched her, waiting to hear what she'd say next.

"So you can't write an article about Libby," she said.

Momentarily confused, he frowned. "Libby? Who's Libby?"

She clamped her lips together tightly before lifting her slender arm and pointing toward the lake. "Her. The so-called lake monster. Except she hates being called a monster. Use the word *creature* instead."

"Libby?" Flabbergasted, he stared at her for so long her face turned pink. "Y'all named it?"

"Her, not it. And yes. She's lived in that lake for centuries. My ancestors' ancestors took care of her, just as I do today."

He lifted his camera, pushing the video option and getting ready to record. Before he did, he was about to ask her if she minded, but the way she froze at the sight of it told him she did.

"I've said enough," she told him, her voice sharp. "If you'd like to see more of the lake, we can continue. Otherwise, I'd appreciate it if you'd take me back home."

He lowered the camera and headed back toward the car. "I'd like to see more."

Her deliberate movements telegraphing her reluctance, she climbed in the passenger seat and secured her seat belt.

"And while we're driving," he continued, "you can tell me why the people in town consider you to be a witch."

A witch. If she hadn't been so upset, Jade would have laughed. For as long as she could remember, people in town claimed to know that the Burnett who took care of the lake monster had magical powers. Jade has always laughed it off. Until she'd been assigned to be Libby's Guardian, and realized quite suddenly she did have powers. The day she'd been given the necklace by her mother, she'd felt the sense of honor the heirloom conveyed. On that day, she'd come into her own powers. Each Guardian's was different. Amber had never said what gifts she'd been given, but Jade didn't doubt that her mother's had been inconsequential just for that reason. Amber was the type to shout from the rooftop.

As for herself, Jade considered her own powers minor, as well. She couldn't do a whole lot, just a bit of telekinesis. Oh, and the occasional bit of prophetic ability. Not entirely reliable, most of it came to Jade in her dreams, usually as a jumbled mess, leaving her to puzzle out the meaning.

No, the only one with actual magical abilities was Libby. A powerful seer and oracle, there were many written accounts of her being asked to help the Burnetts with something. Every single recorded time, her answers were correct.

Still. If Rance wanted to believe Jade had really strong magic, well… Since she needed all the advantages she could take, she decided she wouldn't disabuse him of the notion. Let him think she had true magical powers. Maybe if he focused on that, he'd let his determination to write about Libby fall to the wayside. Being called a witch was the least of her worries right now. Actually, she'd grown quite used to it.

Why had Libby chosen that moment to rise out of the water? Jade didn't know what to think. In all the years her family had been taking care of Libby, she couldn't think of a single instance when the beast had revealed herself to an out-of-towner. Scratch that. The only ones in town Libby had let see her spectacularly beautiful scales were all shifters. Maybe because she knew they, unlike humans, would never betray her.

Forestwood seemed pretty equally divided, as far as Jade

could tell. Her entire family was part of the Pack, which meant they shifted into wolves, as did most all of the other shifters in town. There were a few large cats, but not many as they preferred a warmer climate.

Shaking her head, she tried to clear her jumbled thoughts. Worry and uncertainty had her second-guessing herself. Would it have been better if she'd pretended she hadn't seen Libby jumping out of the water? In her shock, she'd inadvertently revealed the truth of Libby's existence.

And she wasn't even certain she could trust him with that knowledge. As her stomach roiled, she saw another family meeting in the near future.

They rounded a corner and the picnic area sat directly ahead of them. Rance pulled into a parking spot and killed the engine. He glanced at her once with his hand on the door. She pretended not to notice, so he got out and walked down the path that weaved around the little pavilions and picnic tables.

Heart hammering, she followed him all the way to the edge of the water. As she came up beside him, she half expected to find him staring out into the expanse of lake, searching for another sign of Libby. Instead, he looked down at the shallow pools where the gentle waves slapped against the rocks worn smooth.

"It's peaceful," he murmured. "Not exactly the kind of place one would expect to find a monster."

Not a monster. She bit back the words, her automatic defense of Libby hovering on the edge of her lips. She'd already revealed too much. And warned him not to use that word. Anything else she said would only make the situation worse.

"You can't go back, you know." A half smile curled his sensuous mouth. The combination of his deep, sensuous voice and Southern accent made her weak in the knees.

"I don't know what you mean," she lied, aware she

sounded more prim than dignified, even though she'd tried for the latter.

His smile widened. "Pretending you didn't tell me about Libby."

Though she should have known it was coming, she winced at the sound of the name on his lips. "I made a mistake."

"Maybe." He shrugged, turning again to look out at the water. The wind whipped his dark hair, giving him an otherworldly look, and she found herself wondering exactly what kind of shifter he was. If he were wolf, she'd bet he'd be magnificent in his lupine form.

If he were something else… She shook her head. No matter what form of beast Rance Sleighter changed into, he'd be golden and perfect.

"Hey, Jade." The familiar greeting made her turn, smiling. She often ran into Lucas Everett, one of the other sets of twins in town. Lucas and his brother, Monroe, were identical twins and made no effort to help anyone tell them apart. They both wore their dark hair long, brushing their shoulders, and the same blue eyes. The two had been pining after Pearl and Sapphire for as long as Jade could remember. They were one year ahead of Jade's sisters in school and rumor had it that they'd actually considered failing so they could share the same classes. Both brothers loved hanging out at the lake and often one or the other could be found here, making sure the picnic area remained pristine.

Lucas gave her his usual one-armed hug. "How's everything?" he asked. By "everything," she knew he meant her sisters.

"Fine. They're both fine."

He grinned. She grinned back.

Rance coughed. "Aren't you going to introduce me?" he asked.

"Sorry. Lucas, this is Rance. Rance, meet Lucas."

After she finished, she expected the usual handshakes. Instead, Lucas took a step back, his eyes wide.

"Rance Sleighter?" The reverence in his tone was usually reserved for his favorite musicians.

"That's me." Rance held out his hand.

After vigorously shaking it, Lucas exhaled. "I've followed your work. In fact, I even did a report on you last year for journalism class. I dig photography, too, though my camera isn't as nice as yours." He glanced from Jade to Rance and back. "How do you two know each other?"

Jade clamped her mouth shut, making a mental note to do a Google search once she got home.

Rance glanced at her once, then shrugged. "I came here to do a pictorial report on your lake monster, er, creature. Ms. Jade here has been trying to convince me not to. Says Libby wouldn't appreciate it."

All the color blanched from Lucas's face. "Jade told you her name? Seriously?"

Crap. Jade swallowed hard, hating the look of dismay and condemnation on Lucas's face.

She wasn't sure how exactly to respond—in fact, she wasn't certain she should. This was not the kind of thing she wanted the kids gossiping about in the hallways at school. She could only imagine Pearl's and Sapphire's reactions if they learned what she had done.

When he realized Jade wasn't going to answer, Lucas turned again to Rance. "Why are you bothering with stories about a hypothetical lake monster? I'd think you were famous enough without having to spend time on fluff like that."

Only because she was watching Rance closely did Jade see the kid had scored a direct hit. Though the wince seemed barely perceptible, she saw it.

"Fame is a fleeting thing," Rance responded, a trace of bitterness in his voice. He'd once been famous, but jobs had dried up when he'd started drinking. And then once Eve had became ill, he'd basically quit. "But if you've followed my work, you surely know I've always specialized in photographing offbeat, unusual stories."

"And put your own personal spin on them." Lucas shook his head, clearly disappointed. "But this is different."

Rance's gaze sharpened. "How so?"

Jade placed a warning hand on the teenager's shoulder, just in case he might be goaded to say something he'd regret.

"This is beneath you," Lucas tried, his voice vibrating with the urgency of his conviction. Not for the first time, Jade wondered why her younger sisters refused even to give him the time of day.

"Is it?" Though Rance spoke in a mild tone, his gray gaze blazed. "These sorts of things have long been a personal interest of mine. And I'm finally at a point in my career where I've earned the right to do what I want."

"Even if doing what you want hurts people?" The kid stared intently, perhaps realizing his idol might actually have feet of clay.

Rance tilted his head, his dark shaggy hair glinting in the sunlight. "Explain."

Double crap. "I think that's enough for now," Jade interjected, giving Lucas a stern look. "I appreciate your help, Lucas, but I'll be handling this."

Immediately he dropped his head. "Whatever. I guess you have to since you're the Guardian."

Though she winced inside, she managed to keep her face expressionless. Of course Rance missed nothing. She had no doubt he'd made a mental note and would ask her about this later.

So be it. For whatever reason, Libby had chosen to show herself to him. That had to mean something. Until she knew more, all Jade could do was try and distract him. And hope and pray she could talk him out of writing that article.

"I'd like to walk along the shoreline," Rance said. "Would you care to join me?"

"Of course." She hoped she managed to sound as smooth as he did. Her inner wolf, reacting to her heightened emotions, paced. Snarled, wanting to break free. Even though she'd just changed the night before, her beast wanted more. She'd need to make an effort to shift and have another hunting run that evening. Since she preferred to become wolf in a group, her large family came in handy at times like this. She'd have to see who else might want to go with her.

"Hey, darlin'." Rance's light tap on her shoulder startled her, nearly making her lose her footing. Only his quick grab of her elbow stopped her from falling.

"Are you okay?" he asked, holding on for a heartbeat too long before releasing her.

She decided to be honest. "Not really. I'm confused and a bit unsettled."

"I'm sorry."

She sighed. "You sound like you mean that."

"I do."

At this, she shook her head. "If you really were sorry, you'd leave town."

"Ah, you know I can't do that."

Somehow she'd suspected he'd say that. "Can't? Or won't?"

"Good point." As they climbed over another rocky patch, he once again took her arm. And once again, she had to pretend her skin didn't tingle from the contact. Funny thing that. She hadn't realized she could be capable of such tangled emotions. She both wanted the man gone, and to wrap herself around him and never let him go.

Days like today, Libby felt the full weight of her many years. Her kind did not live forever, but their lifespan far exceeded that of humans or other shape-shifters. She'd constructed the Guardian necklace when she'd first arrived in Forestwood years ago, using an unusual purple-colored stone she'd found deep in the lake. Since then, each Guardian wore the talisman, passing it down to their successors. Libby had a matching one in her jewelry box somewhere, though she no longer felt the need to wear it. She'd learned long ago that a piece of metal and stone couldn't replace an actual connection between living beings.

Sometimes the loneliness made her bones ache. When that happened, she'd go out into the lake, change into her beast and sink to the bottom, holding her breath as long as she could. Long enough to make herself dizzy. Long enough to almost convince herself that she could make herself drown.

Libby hadn't always been alone. Once, a long time ago, she'd been surrounded by others of her kind. Friends and lovers, family and strangers. A vibrant community, similar to the one Jade and the Burnetts enjoyed here in Forestwood. Like those of the Pack, they'd spent most of their time in human form, taking great care never to allow regular humans to see them change.

Unfortunately, due to their great size, sightings had abounded. Through the centuries, they'd been alternatively revered and feared, worshipped and hunted.

Now there were so few of them they'd become mysterious. The lake creature that might be real. Or just myth.

Libby no longer cared. After years of doing what she should, she wanted a normal life. With friends and a man.

She wished she could discuss this with Jade. She had, at least inside her head, many times. She could picture how the conversation would go, could see Jade shoving her fingers into her thick silver hair to push it back from her face, and demanding to know why Libby didn't have those things she claimed to want so badly.

The sad truth was, Libby didn't know. When she'd been

younger, before the illness killed off so many of her kind, she'd fallen in love. More than once. She'd broken hearts and had her own shattered. And then...so many got sick, so many dying, and her father had spirited her away to this small town and ordered her to stay here, away from her own kind, her own people.

"Only until the illness passes," he said, giving her shoulder a reassuring squeeze. "I'll come for you then."

Except he hadn't. He'd fallen ill, just like a score of others, and she never saw him again.

These days, her aloneness lay gently across her shoulders like a cashmere cloak. She'd long ago stopped wanting more. She even managed to convince herself that she was satisfied—satisfied—with her life.

And then Amber Burnett had asked if her daughter could take over as caretaker. Libby hadn't hesitated to agree, even though she usually was the one who chose the next Guardian. After her agreement, Jade had visited Libby for the first time alone.

At first, a young Jade had been terrified of her. Libby had felt the pain of that like a knife stabbing in her gut. For the first time in her life, she'd hated being considered a monster. Once, her iridescent scales had been considered beautiful. Now she'd been relegated to a thing, a creature or a beast, lurking in the depths of Forestwood Lake.

That hurt more than she would ever have believed possible.

Over the past nine years, she and Libby had grown close. Her relationship with Jade gave her hope. Of all the Guardians over the years, only Jade treated her like a friend or a relative, rather than a creature to be feared. Originally, when Libby had first arrived in Forestwood, she'd done as her father requested and set the whole Guardian thing up. She'd chosen a Burnett simply because one happened to be hiking out near the lake. At first, the Burnetts had been tasked with protecting her from outsiders and making sure she had everything she needed to survive. She'd even used a bit of her very basic magical skills to ensure they wouldn't leave, by making her Guardian become ill if she tried to leave Burnett house.

Since then, Libby had become pretty self-sufficient, except for her crippling shyness that kept her from making friends. After all, if she went to town, she looked like everyone else. Half the time, people had no idea she was actually the "lake beast."

With all of her kind gone, Libby had felt the weight of her aloneness grow heavier. It wasn't until Jade had taken over that Libby had realized she didn't have to live as an outsider. She just needed Jade to help her figure out how to make that happen.

It had been a long day. Rance had seen the panic and condemnation on that kid Lucas's face. The sickly sort of disbelief on Jade's. Though he'd itched to photograph everything, document it for posterity, in that particular instance, he knew better. For the first time since starting out on this quest, he'd felt a faint prickle of conscience, as if the teen might be right and he should focus on other things.

Except he couldn't. Not if he wanted to bring Eve what she'd asked for.

Deliberately forcing his thoughts to other things, Rance remembered the pub he'd seen on the way to Jade's house. The thought of pub food—greasy hamburgers and seasoned fries—made his mouth water. Though as a recovered alcoholic he no longer drank, he'd refused to avoid places that served alcohol entirely, viewing it as a way of testing his fortitude. Tonight, this would be exactly what he needed to get his mind off both his predicament and the sexy silver-haired Jade Burnett.

Since the evening air felt perfect, he left the rental car parked outside his motel and walked the few blocks to the bar. The road climbed and dipped, but the Brew and Chew Pub sat halfway up the first hill, making his walk more of a workout than he'd anticipated. Which was all good. Hiking around the lake had made him realize he needed to get out more. He'd even purchased a nice pair of hiking boots so he could do this.

He also needed to change. But in what he assumed must be a community of shape-shifting wolves, his kind of beast would definitely be noticed, so he had to be careful.

The unhurried pace of the locals as he strode past them made Rance smile. In larger cities, these people would get mowed down by the fast-walking crowds. Even compared to Houston, Forestwood seemed positively bucolic. Here, even though he would have thought they'd take the scenery for granted since they lived here, every person he passed appeared to be engrossed in the picturesque storefronts with blooming flower boxes and towering trees, enjoying one another's company. Inhaling deeply, Rance could smell the scent of hamburgers and fries cooking somewhere drifting on the breeze.

Unable to resist, he got out his camera and snapped a few shots. Then, because he never knew if he might want to take another, he kept his Nikon in his hand, secured by a neck strap.

His spirits lifted. All in all, this began to look like it would be a perfectly great night. The possibility of achieving his goal put a spring in his step and hope in his heart.

Even better, he felt like he might fit in while here, despite having only been in town a couple of days. No one stared at him or gave him sideways glances. No, sir, generally the locals didn't even appear to act like he might be out of place. Which was in stark contrast to the way they'd acted when he'd first arrived in town.

In fact, one might consider them a bit *overly* friendly. Especially the other men. Rance noticed every single guy—

old or young—gave him a broad beaming smile. Sometimes a wink, or a dip of the chin, and even once a thumbs-up. All very convivial and jovial, almost like they were congratulating him for something, though he had no idea what. Maybe word had leaked out that he'd seen their lake creature? Judging from the teenager they'd run into at the lake, he wouldn't have thought that'd be a good thing.

In fact, it was beginning to creep him out.

Ahead, he saw the sign for the Brew and Chew Pub.

Finally reaching the bar, he yanked open the surprisingly heavy red painted wooden door and went inside. As the door swung closed behind him, he blinked, letting his eyes adjust to the dimness.

The inside smelled like heaven. Grilled burgers with onions and fries. No cigarette smoke, for which he felt grateful. In fact, several no-smoking signs were prominently displayed.

One empty bar stool in the middle of the bar beckoned him. Red pleather, he thought as he took a seat. While he waited for the bartender to notice him, he thought about grabbing a menu, but decided he didn't need it. He already knew what he wanted.

When the bartender—a tall, thin guy with a close-cropped head of gray hair—appeared, he slid a tall glass of draft beer to Rance. "Guys at the pool table bought it for you," he said, grinning.

"Why?" Perplexed, Rance eyed the drink, his mouth suddenly dry with longing. He even reached for the glass, feeling the cold sweat on his palm before turning and raising it in a salute of thanks in the general direction of the pool area.

Cheers erupted.

When Rance turned back, he carefully relinquished his hold on the glass and slid it away from him. "I don't actually drink," he said. "Could I get a ginger ale instead?"

"No problem." Dumping out the beer, the bartender, whose nametag read Earl, refilled the glass with a can of Canada Dry. "You're kind of a local hero today. Do you want to see a menu?"

A local hero. Deciding food trumped hearing gossip, Rance shook his head. He'd ask why later. "No need. One burger and fries is what I need."

"Double or triple?"

Since he needed meat, Rance opted for the triple.

"Coming right up." Earl left to go put in the order.

The guy on the bar stool to the right of Rance swiveled around. "Lucky bastard," he said, grinning. "Not sure how you managed it, but every single guy in town wishes they were you."

Now Rance knew he had absolutely no idea what this man meant. He took another pull on his ginger ale and shrugged. "Thanks, I guess. Though to be honest, I have no idea what all of this is about."

The other guy's eyes widened. He opened his mouth to say something, but just then Earl appeared with Rance's dinner.

"Here you go," Earl said, sliding the plate in front of him. "The cook had started making one for my meal, but I'm letting you have mine. Hope you enjoy. And, Ted—" he shot Rance's neighbor a warning look "—let this guy eat in peace, will you?"

Mumbling what sounded like a disgruntled affirmative, Ted turned back to his beer.

Mouth watering, Rance grabbed the burger and dug in. He tried to make himself eat slower, but the food tasted so good and he was so hungry he practically inhaled it. Luckily, he had the soft drink to help wash everything down.

When he'd cleaned his plate and drank all his ginger ale, Earl brought another. "This one's on the two guys at the end of the bar." He jerked his head toward them and they waved.

"Okay." Rance began to wonder if he'd inadvertently wandered into a gay bar. "Listen, Earl. Why is everyone buying me drinks?"

Earl scratched his head. "You really don't know?"

"I have no idea."

Ted snickered.

Ignoring him, Earl leaned on the counter. "Two words. Jade Burnett."

Chapter 5

Since he still didn't understand, Rance took another sip and waited.

"Every guy in this town has been wanting to date her. You've been seen hanging out with her on more than one occasion. Most of the guys are taking bets that you'll be the one who finally breaks through."

Though he knew he shouldn't, Rance had to ask. "Breaks through?"

Earl's grin widened. "You do know she's a witch, right?"

"I've heard that, yes," Rance answered cautiously.

"She has…powers. If you get my drift." And Earl actually winked.

Though Rance now had a good idea where this was headed, he figured he might as well make the bartender spell it out.

"What kind of powers?"

Next to him, Ted tried to stifle a laugh and ended up spewing a mouthful of beer all over the bar.

Earl tossed him a rag. "Clean it up," he ordered, before turning his attention back to Rance.

"Listen," Earl said, lowering his voice. "There isn't a single guy in town who hasn't tried to tap that. And her rumored powers are the main reason why. Sure, she's gorgeous and sexy as hell, but if the stories are true…"

"Stories?" Despite the anger beginning to simmer inside him, Rance deliberately kept his face expressionless and cocked his head. "What kind of stories?"

Grinning, Earl shook his head.

Apparently, Ted couldn't take it anymore. "Sexual powers, you idiot," he said, unable to contain his glee. "And we're counting on you to let us know if it's true."

Rance had to suppress the sudden, strong urge to punch the guy in his face. All of them, in fact. Poor Jade. He couldn't help but wonder where all this had come from if no one had gotten near to her.

"Does Jade, er, know about this legendary power of hers?" he asked, jaw tight. "Is she aware what y'all are saying about her?"

"Y'all?" Earl shook his head. "You ain't from around here, are you?

"No, obviously I'm not. You didn't answer the question. Does Ms. Jade know?"

Earl shrugged. "I don't know. This is a small town, so I imagine she might."

Damn. Rance had to look down at his hands to hide his fury. "I'd like the check, please," he said. Getting into a bar brawl wouldn't do anything to help his position in this town. "And don't ever let me hear you talk about Jade like that again."

The walk back to his motel wasn't enough to dispel the turmoil inside him. Despite knowing the rumor had to be complete and utter nonsense, even the thought of it fueled his already deep desire for Jade.

Frustration coiled inside him. He wanted to claim her as his. Part of him already had. And truth be told, a lot of it was sexual. Jade Burnett's beauty attracted him. His inner beast roared, reminding him of his earlier resolution to change and let his other self run free.

Perfect. Exactly what he needed to do. As long as he took precautions not to be seen. His kind was not only rare, but largely misunderstood among other shifters.

Increasing his stride, he continued on past the intersection where the business part of town gave way to residential. The well-kept houses were fully restored and beautifully land-scaped. As he passed one house with colorful flower gardens, he could smell the heady scent of lilac.

For some reason, this made him think of Jade, with her clear green eyes and uncertain smile. No wonder she seemed a little standoffish. People spreading wild rumors about her would have a way of messing with her self-confidence.

Yet despite all that, or because of it, he couldn't keep himself from picturing her naked underneath him, her perfect skin gleaming in the moonlight.

Aroused and furious, he picked up his pace, heading toward a wooded tract of undeveloped land he'd seen when driving around. As soon as his feet left the pavement, the sound of the fallen leaves crackling underfoot began to soothe his restlessness. He inhaled sharply, pine and earth and wood, continuing on, in search of a meadow or a large enough clearing to accommodate him once he assumed his other form.

Finally, deep within the forest, he found a meadow. The overgrown wild grass rustled in the light breeze, and above, the black night sky twinkled with a thousand stars. Rance made a slow turn, listening, scenting, just to make sure no creatures other than wild ones roamed near. The last thing he needed was for an errant pack of wolf shifters to see him.

Even though the wolves and the dragons were allies, until

their Pack council found a way to announce the existence of his kind, he and all the few others like him had been asked to keep everything low-key.

Sensing nothing other than an owl in one of the nearby trees and a rabbit cowering under a bush, he stripped off his clothing. He dropped to all fours and initiated the change. He couldn't wait to soar into the air, rushing toward the stars. Flying felt so weightless, and the distances he could travel in a few hours, brought its own kind of freedom.

Except flying could be dangerous. His heart sank as he considered his choices. Then, with a rush of excitement, he realized what he'd do instead. The cliffs overlooking the water weren't too far away. The vastness of Forestwood Lake beckoned. There, he could dive deep into the water, unseen by anyone who walked the land. For his kind, swimming felt akin to flying, except for the necessity of holding one's breath.

And if he happened to run into the local lake monster, even better.

The unsettled feeling had come over Jade during the night, startling her wide awake at 3:00 a.m. Lying awake in her bed, desperately wishing for sleep, she'd seen shadowed images. A beast of some kind, flying. At first, she thought Libby was making contact—her charge had done that before—but this felt different. As if someone or something was watching her, hearing every breath, feeling every stuttering pulse of her heart. Her necklace even felt warm, but that could have been because of her rising bodily heat. Now every nerve ending along her skin came alive as she waited, wondering what she was supposed to do.

When she finally fell asleep, she saw his face again. Rance. In her dream, she reached for him as he came in for a kiss. The instant their lips touched, she knew...

Because she shied away from the knowledge, she'd

startled awake again. This time, her clock read five-thirty, which meant she could get up and shower.

Once she was dressed, she snagged a cup of coffee and carried it out to the front porch like she always did. Settling in the large wooden swing, she took a sip and watched the sky lighten as the sun readied itself to come up over the horizon.

Today, she fully expected Rance Sleighter to make an appearance. Her entire body heated as she pondered what she'd do if he tried to kiss her. And then, she wondered if she'd be disappointed if he didn't.

Inside the house, all was silent and still. Her entire family still slept. Her mother, Amber, didn't believe in getting up before sunrise and Pearl and Sapphire were teenagers. Enough said.

This morning in addition to opening up Dogs Off Leash, she'd be helping out her mom by opening their store, Jewels and Essence. Over the weekend Amber and Opal had each taken turns, since they'd given their healthy-oil classes to twenty-two attendees who'd signed up in advance. That part of the business had really taken off. While interest in aromatherapy had blossomed worldwide, Jade had a feeling the popularity of theirs had a bit to do with the way the townspeople believed she had magic.

Opal and Amber weren't bothered by this. In fact, they capitalized on it whenever they could. Pearl and Sapph rolled their eyes and giggled whenever the topic of magic came up.

It appeared the only one bothered by the rumors and gossip was Jade, the so-called sexy witch. When she'd first learned of the tales of her sexual prowess, she'd been mortified. And then, the embarrassment had settled into a simmering anger, which made her retreat from any attempts at dating. Of course, it didn't help that she'd recently turned twenty-nine and, with thirty looming on the horizon, was more than ready to settle down and have a family. With the ridiculous expectation looming over her, all any of the men in this town were interested in was seeing if it was true.

Recently, she'd signed up for an online dating service and was careful only to go out with men from one of the neighboring towns, where they'd have no idea who she was. So far, while she hadn't met anyone she couldn't resist, none of the men she'd dated had any preconceived ideas about her. That had been a relief.

She yawned and checked her watch. Time to finish her coffee and get inside and eat. Her first clients would be dropping off their dogs at 6:00 a.m. sharp.

When she'd decided to open Dogs Off Leash, her mother and grandmother had scoffed. Her aunt and uncle had rolled their eyes and her sisters couldn't have cared less. Only Grandpa Sam had clapped her on the back and told her he thought she had a fine idea. Since Grandpa rarely spoke to anyone since the dementia had taken hold of him, Jade considered his words a high compliment.

In the year and a half since her doggy day care had been open, business had been brisk and increasing in increments. She'd taken her profits and reinvested in the business, adding on to the fenced dog play areas and hiring additional staff.

Even better, she loved her business. Every morning she greeted the day with a smile on her face, eager to get to work. Raised as a child without pets, she adored being around the dogs, often sitting on the floor and rolling around with them. Even Sapph had taken to stopping by to play, much to the amusement of her twin sister.

Once she'd eaten, Jade hurried to her room to grab her watch since today she needed to make sure to be aware of the time. With the timepiece clasped securely around her wrist, she went back to the kitchen, intending to make one more cup of coffee to take with her. When she got there, she stopped short, surprised to find her mother sitting at the kitchen table, her head down.

"Mom?" Jade hurried over, alarmed. Amber never rose before sunrise. "Is everything okay?"

When Amber raised her face, her cheeks were wet with tears. "Your cousin Diamond has gone missing."

Diamond, aka the Wild Child. Still… Jade stared. "But she just came to the family meeting the other day."

"I know." Amber sighed. "My sister says she didn't come home after that. They assumed she went out with friends, but she's not answering her cell. They have no idea where she is and they're worried sick."

This said a lot. Amber's sister Emerald wasn't the dramatic type. If she was worried, this meant she believed she had good reason. Of course, ever since Diamond had started running around with a partying crowd, Jade had been concerned enough for the both of them.

"What are we going to do?" Jade asked quietly. "I assume we're going to organize a search or something?"

"I don't know. Em said something about Diamond's new boyfriend. No one has actually met him, but Di never stopped talking about him."

Which meant, Jade thought privately, he probably didn't exist. It wouldn't be the first time her cousin had made up a boyfriend. Especially since none of her friends had actually seen him.

"It isn't like Di to just disappear," Jade mused. "Unless she's pulling some sort of stunt for attention." Attention appeared to be the one thing Diamond couldn't seem to get enough of. Add to that the fact that several of Di's close friends had done this exact same thing, and Jade figured they considered it a trend or something. Jade had never pretended to understand how her cousin or her friends thought.

Amber's frown deepened. "You do have a point, but I can't see her willingly causing her mother this much worry.

Something must have happened to her." She took a deep breath. "Will you help?"

"Of course. What would you like me to do?" When her mother raised her gaze, Jade knew. It always came down to this. Anytime someone had a problem, the family sent Jade to talk to Libby. To be fair, they had no choice, as Jade was the only person Libby would speak to.

When Libby agreed to respond to Jade's questions, her answers were always correct. Not seventy-five percent of the time, or ninety. But one-hundred-percent, every-single-time correct. Worse, when Libby went into one of her trances, she'd relay to Jade her visions. Often, these were ten times more vivid than any dream.

Of course, the family knew Jade had magic, though they erroneously assumed she could do more with it than she could. And everyone regarded Libby as a Seer as well as a lake creature. Because there was no way any normal person could have all the answers. Only those who had been caretakers before her knew the truth. Amber knew. The magic was real and special. Because Libby wasn't a normal person, or even a normal shape-shifter. She was one of a kind. Maybe the last of her kind. And Jade believed fervently that Libby didn't deserve to be bothered with small stuff.

Jade had gotten to the point of hating to have to ask favors of Libby. She wasn't sure her cousin Di taking off for a few days warranted asking for magic.

"Please," her mother pleaded, correctly interpreting Jade's hesitation. "Your Auntie Em specifically asked me to ask you since you and she are so close. She knows your connection to Libby. If I still had the ability, I'd ask her myself."

And therein lay the problem. No way could Jade say no now. Not to a worried-sick parent and her favorite aunt. Even if her cousin was a little bit…wild. Jade wondered if her aunt Emerald knew that several others in the crowd

Di ran around with had taken off at various intervals for a few days, only to reappear suddenly, acting like nothing had happened.

"Fine. I'll do it." Grabbing her stainless steel coffee mug, she poured one more cup, keeping herself busy as she added cream and sugar, and stirring.

"When?" Amber pressed. "Can you run out there this morning?"

Reminding herself that her mother felt a sense of urgency even if Jade did not, Jade sighed. "Remember, you asked me to open up your store for you?"

"I can take care of that." Amber stretched. "I feel much more rested. So you'll talk to Libby today."

Jade nodded. "Yes, of course. After I get DOL open and make sure my employees show up, I'll head on out to the lake."

"Oh, thank you." Amber gave a wan smile over the rim of her coffee cup. "Let me call Em. She'll be so relieved."

Jade slipped out of the room as her mother turned away to make the call. What was Diamond up to? While of course Jade hoped her cousin was all right, if this disappearance was some sort of prank, Jade would let the younger girl have a stern lecture. The time had come for that girl to grow up and start thinking of others besides herself.

At least they had Libby. Either way, she knew Libby would be able to help.

Pushing away the bad mood that now threatened to ruin her day, Jade took deep breaths and willed herself to return to the calm, serene happiness she'd felt earlier while having her first cup of coffee. She had to get the doggy day care up and running for the day and no one could be out of sorts around dogs. The thought made her smile. It seemed the pups could always sense emotional distress and would work extra hard with wiggles, wagging tails and doggy kisses to cajole a smile or a laugh.

As a shape-shifter, sometimes she thought the dogs sensed the inner wolf inside her. Other times, she guessed they didn't even have a clue.

Arriving at DOL, she hurried inside and unlocked the door. Inside, she went from room to room, flipping on lights as she passed through. She checked to make sure both the indoor and outdoor play areas were clean and ready. After she'd made sure the gates were closed and the toys put up, she was ready. Dusting her hands off on her jeans, she smiled as she heard the sound of a car pulling up. The day had just begun.

Some days, her morning crew barely beat the first of the dogs. People liked to drop off Fido or Lucy before work and pick them up after. After a day of play with the other dogs, by the time the client returned to collect their pet, the animal was exhausted in a happy way. People loved it, the dogs had a great time and everyone won. Jade laughed out loud sometimes when she realized what a terrific job she had.

By the time the sun shone in the cloudless blue sky, Jade had a packed house. Her employees were already outside in the play yards, which were segregated due to dog size. Happiness colored the air, making the place practically sparkle with joy—on the faces of both dogs and people.

She didn't want to leave. How many people could say that about their jobs? Still, duty called.

"I've got to go run an errand," she told Sue, her most long-term employee. "Keep an eye on things until I get back, okay?"

Sue nodded, her short gray pixie cut swinging. "Are you going to…the lake?" Her hushed, almost reverent tone made Jade smile. Everyone acted as if visiting Libby was some sort of sacred duty. Which in a way, it was, she supposed. Though not like the others appeared to think. She didn't bring offerings of food, though occasionally she'd take out a bottle of wine and a couple of glasses for the two of them to share. There were no rituals involved, no magic. Nothing but a little conversation. If Libby happened to be swimming as her beast, she'd emerge from the lake and shift into her human form, heading into the small cabin she occupied year-round. There, she'd put on one of the numerous dresses she owned, some of them reminiscent of years gone by. She'd brew a pot of tea, and she and Jade would hang out.

Hanging out with the lake creature. Who knew what people would think if they realized? She supposed the shapeshifters in town wouldn't be surprised, but the humans would be simply flabbergasted. As far as they were concerned, the lake creature was a myth, like bigfoot or the Loch Ness monster. Long ago, the local shifters had made it law to keep Libby's existence a secret from the rest of the world. This, they reasoned, was the only way to protect her.

Until Rance had shown up, this law had worked for decades.

Today Jade would take the proper precautions to make sure she wasn't followed—Rance Sleighter immediately came to mind—and drive out to the lake to have a chat with Libby. She hated to have to ask the other woman to access her prophetic abilities, but she would. She had to ask about Diamond vanishing.

Until she knew more, Jade decided not to say anything about her cousin's disappearance to anyone outside of the family. News—aka gossip—traveled fast in a town this size.

"Yes, I am going to the lake." Her grin widened at Sue's gasp. "I'll be back as soon as I can."

Though showing up again at Burnett House unannounced would have Jade Burnett considering him a major pain in the ass, Rance hadn't gotten to be an excellent photojournalist by worrying about annoying people. Plus, if he were completely honest with himself, he hadn't been able to stop thinking about Jade and her exotic green eyes. He'd actually caught himself viewing the photos he'd taken of her again and again. Even if he hadn't been chasing a story, he knew he had to see her again.

Checking his watch, he debated whether or not to knock on the door. While he figured everyone would be up by now, he wasn't entirely sure of their schedules. He knew Jade often had a cup of coffee on the porch swing in the morning, so he decided to wait for her there. He internally winced, aware this could be considered a total lack of manners, but he hadn't gotten where he was by being a Southern gentleman, so he stayed put.

A few minutes after he'd sat down, the front door opened, making his heart speed up.

Instead of Jade, one of her sisters wandered out on the front porch, taking a seat near him on another chair. Her flowing bell-bottom pants and tie-dyed shirt made her look like a poster child for Woodstock.

"Hi. I'm Sapphire," she said, grinning. "Jade's baby sister. Or one of them."

"Nice to meet you."

"Jade almost got engaged once, you know." The teen's expression went somber. "She really loved him, too."

Engaged? That had come out of nowhere. Still, he found it intriguing. Though he knew he shouldn't, he couldn't keep from asking. "What happened?"

Jade's sister looked away. "He turned out to be different than she thought."

And that's all she would say. No amount of questioning or cajoling would entice her to say any more. Rance figured he now knew where all the rumors about Jade's supposed sexual prowess had originated. If he ever got his hands on that guy...

The other twin appeared. Unlike her colorful sister,

she wore all black, with matching fingernails and lipstick. "Sapphire? What are you two doing?" she asked, narrowing her eyes in suspicion.

Sapphire grinned again, her moods as mercurial as any teenager. "This is Pearl," she explained before turning back to her sister. "I'm trying to talk to Jade's boyfriend."

"Ewww. He's too old," Pearl responded. And then, just when Rance was trying to decide if he should be flattered to be referred to as Jade's boyfriend or annoyed because these teenagers thought him too old for her, Pearl spoke again. "Don't hurt her," she ordered. "If you do, we'll come after you."

Since he had no idea how to respond to that, he nodded. "Your sister tells me Jade was once engaged?"

"Almost," Sapphire corrected. "Almost engaged."

Pearl shot Sapphire a dirty look. "You told him *that*?"

Sapphire shrugged. "Not in any detail."

"Girls?" Amber appeared, her expression stern. "Did you two get your rooms clean? You know I asked you to do that before you went anywhere."

The identical guilt flashing across both their young faces gave her their answer.

"Go." She pointed. "I'll sit out here and keep this nice man company."

Once the twins had disappeared back inside, Amber took a seat next to him. "Looking for Jade?" she asked.

He nodded. "Would you mind letting her know I'm here?"

Instead of agreeing, she tilted her head and eyed him. "First, why don't you tell me why you're really here?"

Surprised, he cocked his head. "Ma'am? I believe I already did."

"No. I mean why you're in Forestwood." Waving his answer away, she leaned close. "I looked you up on the internet. Plus one of the twins' friends is apparently a big

fan of yours. Like he said, a photojournalist of your cali-
ber doesn't waste time on a fluff piece about a fictional
lake monster. So why don't you tell me why you're really
in town?"

He nodded. She was right. However, she didn't know
about the promise he'd made to a dying child. "I haven't lied
about my purpose," he said. Then, picturing Jade's beautiful face, he sighed. "I may have more than one reason for
staying in town these days, but I promise you, my main
focus is on Libby."

Her loud gasp told him his mistake. "Jade gave you her
name?"

Though her shock appeared palpable, he didn't know
what else he could do but nod. "She didn't mean to, if that
helps any."

"Let me explain something to you." Anger simmered
in Amber's green eyes, so like her daughter's. "If you hurt
my Jade, you'll answer to me."

"The twins just told me the same thing," he mused.
"Why does everyone find it necessary to warn me of this?
Do I look like the kind of man who goes around hurting
women?"

"Not because you want to, but looking the way you do,
with that Southern drawl of yours, I think more women are
hurt than you realize."

He didn't want to dignify her response with words, so
he said nothing.

"Whatever you might have heard…" Amber continued.

"Stop." Interrupting, he touched the back of her hand. "I
know about the nonsense they repeat in town. I don't care.
I'm attracted to Jade—what red-blooded man wouldn't
be?—but I'm not in the market for anything serious. I'm
pretty sure she's not, either."

"But you're not positive. I don't want you toying with
her emotions."

"I can promise you, ma'am. I never toy with any woman."

His words coaxed a reluctant grin. "And there's that accent again. No wonder my daughter has trouble resisting you."

"Does she?" He grinned right back. "Because if that's truly the case, then I'm the last to know."

She laughed. "You know what? I like you. Despite my first impression, I think you're all right." She cocked her head, her grin slightly coquettish as she looked him up and down. "Just go easy on her, all right?"

"You have my word. Now would you mind letting her know I'd like to talk to her?"

"I would if I could, but she's already left for work. As I'm about to, as well. We own a store on Main Street," she pointed out. "We sell spices, essential oils, candles, things like that. We open in half an hour, or as soon as I get there. You should stop by."

A bit confused, but guessing that was her roundabout way of telling him where to find her daughter, he thanked her and got back into his car. With thirty minutes to kill until this store opened, he took the road up to the lower part of the lake, below the wooded forest and cliffs where he'd changed the night before. The experience had been surreal, one of the best in his entire life.

He'd changed in the deep part of the woods, and then walked to the edge of the cliff in his Drakkor form. His heart pounded. He'd let himself fall over and drop into the water, aware an outright dive might not be safe until he knew the actual depth of the water.

The shock of the cold water had made him grin. As a dragon, he enjoyed chillier temperatures, especially since his internal body thermometer could keep him overly warm.

Slicing through the clear, cool lake, he'd been surprised at how deep it actually was. At least sixty or seventy feet, maybe more. The farther down he'd gone, the colder the water temperature. As his huge beast's body had adjusted, he'd marveled at the abundance of healthy plant life and fish. He'd caught a large striped bass and swallowed it whole, musing over the fact that such a fish might be considered a trophy catch if caught by a human angler. For him in his dragon form, it was only a small snack, nothing more. Well fed, he'd surfaced a few times to take in air. Beautiful.

Though he'd kept his eye out for the lake beast, he saw no signs of her. Libby, he remembered. The name seemed so ordinary and out of place for a creature that magnificent. He wished he could have gotten a better look at her the single time he'd caught a glimpse.

Ah, well. Maybe he'd be given another opportunity.

Sitting in his rental car, he ached to experience it all again. But he didn't have time, not right now.

Blinking, he glanced at his watch, noting only fifteen minutes had passed while he sat in his car and relived the night before. Still, by the time he drove back to town, he should be able to catch Jade before she began her day.

Starting the car, he turned around and headed back toward Forestwood.

Chapter 6

As soon as Rance reached the outskirts of the downtown area, he slowed his speed. Once again the picturesque, storybook feel of the place enchanted him. He located the Jewels and Essence shop without difficulty, found an open parking spot right in front and, after snapping a few quick shots, went inside.

The instant he entered, the strong scent of competing perfumes assaulted him. His eyes watering, he covered his cough with his hand, wondering if he'd be able to breathe. How had the smell gotten this bad if they'd just opened? And how did anyone work in here? Maybe the Burnetts weren't wolves, as there was no way any creature who operated primarily with smell, could stand the scent.

Understandably, the place appeared empty. He saw no sign of Jade or her mother or any of her family.

"Jade?" he called out. Unfortunately, this required him to inhale, which brought on another fit of coughing. Wiping his eyes, he pushed through the haze of smoke, locating one of the culprits—a fat stick of incense—which he promptly extinguished. Next he blew out two strong-smelling candles, and finally unplugged a small Crock-Pot of simmering potpourri. Presumptuous, maybe, but he knew if he didn't, he'd have to wait outside. That done, he went back to the front door and opened it, swinging it back and forth so as much of the tainted air as possible would flow out.

As he did, an elderly woman with faded red hair emerged from the back. He remembered her from the Mother Earth's Café. Opal Burnett. Jade's grandmother. He couldn't resist taking a couple of photos of her, too.

"Can I help you?" she asked, her voice sharp. Then, as she studied him, her frown deepened. "You're the one who was bugging my granddaughter at lunch the other day."

"I was," he answered cheerfully. "And I'm here to bug her some more."

"Here?"

"Yes. I went to the house and her mother told me to come here."

"Amber did?" She frowned. "She came and made sure I'd opened the place up and went out to get us doughnuts. But why would she tell you to come here?"

He sighed. "I'm not sure."

Glancing around the shop, she finally noticed his handiwork. "Why did you remove all my lovely scents?"

Figuring if no one had told her, maybe the time had come that someone did, so he lied and said he had allergies and truthfully mentioned all the competing odors were overpowering. "Maybe you should highlight just one scent at a time," he suggested.

Though she narrowed her eyes, she gave a slow nod. "I'll consider it," she told him. "Now why have you come here looking for my granddaughter?"

"Well, like I said, I went to the house and her mother told

me I'd find her here." He looked around. "In fact, when do you expect Amber back?"

Opal chuckled. "When she has the doughnuts." Tilting her head, she peered at him. "You still haven't answered my question. What do you want with Jade?"

Briefly, he considered how to answer. In the end, he went with the truth. "Because I need to talk to her about what I realized when I saw the lake creature, Libby."

The candleholder she'd been holding fell from her grasp, shattering on the wooden floor. Instead of moving to pick up the pieces, Opal stared at him. "You saw… Libby? And how do you know her name?"

"Because Jade told me." Spying a broom in the back room, he retrieved that and a dustbin and then swept up the pieces. Once he felt satisfied he'd gotten them all and deposited them in the trash, he turned to face her. She still stared at him as if he'd suddenly shape-shifted in front of her, or something equally unusual.

"But…" she began.

"Please just let me talk to Jade."

She gave a wordless nod. "Despite what Amber told you, Jade was only going to do us a favor this morning. She doesn't actually work here. She owns a doggy day care up on Pinetree Road. You can find her there."

A doggy day care? He grinned. Perfect.

"Thank you." And once again, Rance took off. Briefly it crossed his mind that not only were the people in the Burnett family closed off and secretive, but he couldn't shake the feeling they found sending him scurrying around like a rat in a maze highly amusing.

He located Dogs Off Leash without any problems. After pulling up in front of the brightly painted wooden building, he parked and stared. Though he hadn't actually thought about it until now, if he'd pictured beautiful Jade doing any kind of job, he would have imagined her dressed to the nines working in some sort of professional capability—like an attorney or a doctor. Learning she ran a dog day care made him realize how little he actually knew about her.

Right then and there he decided to learn as much about her as he could.

The instant he stepped from the car, a cacophony of barking made him grin. He liked dogs—a lot, in fact—and the only thing keeping him from having one was the fact that he had no roots. Someday, if he ever settled down, he planned to have his own minipack of rescue dogs.

Again he brought his camera up. Snapping photos of everything had become second nature to him. At the end of every day, he'd go over the pictures and discard the ones he didn't want to keep.

Inside, it would take a few minutes to get the attention of one of the employees, so he watched them interacting with their charges. Outside in the back, he saw several play yards, apparently arranged by dog size, staffed by two or three employees. The animals ran and jumped and played. Their caregivers played with them, pure joy shining on their faces.

Fascinated, he watched until his fingers itched for his camera and he lifted it to his face. As usual, he took a few more pictures. It wasn't often that he—or anyone else for that matter—witnessed this kind of communication between animals and people.

Of course, most of the workers, as evidenced by their auras, were shape-shifters. Maybe their wolf side enabled them to understand better the dogs' canine nature.

Finally, a woman with short gray hair and a broad, pleasant face came into the reception area. "I'm Sue. How can I help you?"

"I'm looking for Jade." He smiled, curious to see if Sue acted as defensively as everyone else he'd met.

"She's not here."

Though he waited, she didn't elaborate.

He decided to take a lucky guess. "She's at the lake, isn't she?"

Sue started. "Um..."

But he'd seen the flash of truth in her eyes.

"It's okay," he told her as he turned to go. "I was going out there, anyway."

Walking away, he found himself smiling as he got into his rental car. Still smiling, he headed back to the same place he'd seen the lake monster leaping into the sky. He had a feeling he'd find Jade there, too.

Jade couldn't get rid of the nervous, unsettled feeling. The winding drive out to Libby's house made her think of Rance. The picturesque cottage where the shape-shifter lived when she wasn't swimming in the lake was their normal meeting spot. Of course, to be honest, Jade found Rance on her mind a lot these days. She didn't really want to analyze why. Maybe because Libby had actually shown herself to him—Jade made a mental note to ask about that. Whatever the reason, she kept an eye out for his red Mustang, worried that he might be watching her.

Even though she saw no sign of him or his rental car, instead of pulling up in Libby's driveway, she parked in a different spot, near some hiking trails that headed up the mountain instead of down toward the lake. Hopefully, if he "happened" upon her car, he'd assumed that's where she went.

Otherwise, Jade would just have to rely on Libby's stellar instincts to protect them. After all, in her beast form, Libby could tell when an interloper was anywhere near the lake. When she was human, none of that mattered. All anyone would see was two women chatting.

Humming under her breath as she approached the cabin, Jade felt her mood improve. Despite her unwillingness to ask Libby any sort of favor, she looked forward to seeing her. They enjoyed each other's company, especially when they talked about nothing and everything, the two of them sharing a simple appreciation for life's many nuances.

She scanned the water as she went but saw no sign of the gigantic scaled animal Libby became. Which meant most likely the other woman was in her human form and at home.

Since she usually arrived by car and parked right in front of the house, Jade inhaled the pine scented air and took the time to appreciate the hike down. The narrow stone path wound near water and through clusters of trees. Occasionally the undergrowth had grown over the stones, and Jade stopped and took the time to trim them back with a sharp knife she kept sheathed on her belt. This she usually always wore, though sometimes she wore a leg sheath, when she truly needed to keep her weapon undetected. The knives had been passed down from caregiver to caregiver and were rumored to be gifts from one of Libby's ancestors, though none of them was as old as the necklace.

Once the plants had been cut back, Jade continued on. Rounding the last grove of trees, she stopped, admiring the sturdy cottage. Giant trees appeared to cradle and protect the wooden A-framed structure, and with the ancient stone trim, the place seemed timeless, as old as the lake itself. The scene could have been in any holiday card or movie about faeries or elves. This last made Jade grin. Though the Fae most certainly existed, Jade had never met one and wouldn't know how to act if she did.

Movement caught her eye. There. Libby. With her silver-white hair bound in a long braid, she worked bent over, weeding her vegetable garden. Her movements were graceful and unhurried, projecting the same sense of peaceful serenity Jade got when talking with her.

For all her mystery, the woman truly was a marvel. She'd always seemed an old soul.

Jade watched her for a moment, wondering as she always did, exactly how many years Libby had lived. Jade's grandmother's mother had taken care of her, and if there were others before her, Jade wouldn't be surprised. Yet despite this, Libby's pale skin bore few wrinkles. Her bright purple eyes remained clear and unclouded. And she moved with the grace of a woman Jade's age.

"Greetings," Libby called, waving. "Come see my crop of tomatoes! I'll be having a lot this year."

Smiling, Jade strolled over toward her friend. Libby appeared as radiant as ever. And the same sorrow lurked in the depths of her gaze. Jade figured being the last of your kind would do this to one.

They chatted about vegetables and the weather while Jade tried to figure out how to broach asking Libby why she'd revealed herself to Rance Sleighter. On top of that she still had to ask about her missing cousin Diamond. Just thinking about that made her stomach hurt. She'd seen what it cost Libby in terms of energy to use her psychic powers. Still, a missing cousin certainly warranted a request.

"You seem troubled." Libby placed a slender hand on Jade's arm. "Come inside. I'll make some tea, and you can tell me what's bothering you."

Inside the cabin felt cool. The fragrance of lilac drifted in through the open windows.

Libby hummed while she filled the teakettle and put it on the stove. "Tell me about your visitor," she asked, her tone casual. Since she had her back to Jade, she didn't see Jade start.

"So you did know he was there," Jade commented.

"Of course. I always do."

Again the unhurried serenity. Jade wondered if this ability had to do with the years Libby had spent on this earth.

The kettle whistled and Libby poured two cups, using

tea bags like she always did, something Jade found interesting. She'd figured Libby would use loose leaf tea, but the other woman had chuckled and said she liked to take advantage of modern conveniences.

Once they were both seated with their steaming cups of tea, Libby smiled. "Now tell me what's bothering you."

Instead of answering right away, Jade dunked the tea bag a few more times. One thing Libby had taught her was the value of taking the time to speak carefully. "Yesterday, I was at the lake with a man from out of town, the one you asked about, and…"

"He saw me."

Jade nodded. Rather than sounding worried, Libby's voice had been…pleased.

"I intended him to," Libby assured her, leaning forward and patting Jade's knee. "I am actually thinking about asking to meet him. Something about him calls to me."

Shocked, Jade couldn't find words. She took a hurried sip of tea, nearly burning her mouth. The pain stung. When she could finally speak again, she raised her head to find Libby watching her.

"Are you saying you…have a romantic interest in him?" she asked, surprised at how much the notion pained her, as if Libby had reached inside and twisted Jade's stomach.

Libby laughed. Until today, the pure joy in the sound had always brought an answering smile to Jade's face. This time, she could only eye the other woman, thoroughly perplexed.

"No, honey," Libby assured her. "He's much too young for me. The important question is… Do you like him?"

Immediately, Jade felt her entire body blush. "No," she answered, much too quickly. "I don't. But, Libby, he's dangerous. He wants to write a story about you. With pictures," she added. "I know you understand how awful that would be for you and for this town. Promise me you won't let him see you again in your other form. Please."

Libby's clear gaze studied Jade's face. "I promise I won't let your man see me as my beast," she finally said, each word concise. "At least, not until you ask me to."

Relieved, Jade took another sip of her tea. "Thank you."

A peaceful silence fell while they enjoyed their drink and Jade tried to figure out the best way to ask Libby to use her psychic abilities.

"Is there more?" Libby finally asked. "My promise should have dispelled your worry, but I still sense it wrapped around you in a shroud."

The vivid imagery made Jade shudder. "I promised my mother I'd ask you about my cousin Diamond. She seems to have disappeared and now everyone's worried."

"Except you," Libby observed. "You're more anxious about asking me to use my abilities than about your cousin. Why is this?"

"Because Di is a bit of a wild child. Among her friends, it seems like one is always vanishing for a few days. Right when everyone is getting all wound up, the missing girl reappears, acting like she'd never even been away." Jade shrugged. "I'm guessing Di felt like it was her turn."

Tilting her head, Libby sighed. "If you feel this way, why do you want me to seek?"

Seek was the word Libby used when she sought to use her psychic abilities to find a person or a thing.

Slightly embarrassed, Jade swallowed. "Because I promised my mother and aunt."

"Amber! How is she doing these days?" No rancor colored Libby's voice, despite Amber's claims that the two had never gotten along. Much of that might be due to the fact that Amber had wished to marry Jade's father, but the caretaker's inability to leave Burnett House had nixed that idea. Jake had taken off soon after Amber became pregnant. He came back a few years later, which resulted in Amber having Pearl and Sapphire. The idea of twins had so horrified Jake that he'd hightailed it out of Forest-wood and no one had seen him since.

Despite this, Jade had grown up blissfully unaware of her future. Libby had always chosen who would be her caregiver and when. Since Amber had been only eighteen when Jade had been born, Jade had figured the honor (or curse, depending how you looked at it) would go to one of the twins.

Instead, Amber had come to Jade on her twentieth birthday and told her Libby had requested her and that her time had come to take on the mantle of caregiver. Despite Jade's shock, Amber had been unable to hide her glee at the potential of again being able to have a life outside of Forestwood.

And so, with very little training or ceremony, Jade had taken over Libby's care from her mother. Since then, to her knowledge, her mother had never come back to visit.

"She's fine. She stays busy with my younger sisters, the twins."

While they chatted, Libby made them each a second cup of tea. She never could be rushed—Jade knew this and understood she had to exercise patience. She figured this one trait of Libby's had been the thing that had gotten under Amber's skin. Amber had zero patience for anything or anyone. Waiting for Libby must have driven her crazy.

Only when they'd both drained their second cup of tea did Libby rise and cross over to the yoga mat she kept near the window that looked out over the lake. Jade excused herself while Libby got comfortable. She headed to the restroom, planning to take her time before returning. Watching Libby enter a trance felt uncomfortably intimate, and Jade hated to intrude.

In fact, after emerging a few minutes later, Jade took a detour to avoid the kitchen and went outside to sit on the deck. The breathtaking view never failed to soothe her spirits and today was no exception.

Below, on the narrow ribbon of road encircling the lake, she saw a flash of red. Heart skipping a beat, she leaned forward, waiting for it to emerge from under the tree canopy. A moment later, she saw it again. The bright red Mustang that meant Rance was headed this way.

Aware he'd recognize her vehicle parked near the hiking trails, she hoped this would be enough of a distraction to keep him from coming here. Just in case, it would be better if she left as soon as possible.

Fidgeting, she hesitated. She still needed to find out what Libby had been able to learn about Di. If she failed to do this, Amber and Auntie Em would be upset. And even though Rance was a bit pushy, she hoped the remnants of what was left of his Southern manners wouldn't allow him to knock on the door of a stranger's house, especially if he wasn't sure she was inside.

Since she didn't want him to spot her, Jade got up and headed back in. Hopefully, Libby wouldn't be too much longer.

To her relief, when Jade returned to the kitchen, Libby had gotten up from her yoga mat. Back to the room, she stared outside with a look of such total concentration that Jade knew not to interrupt her.

"I see your man approaches," Libby said, not turning from the window.

"He's not mine," Jade corrected automatically, flushing.

"Not yet. But he will be. He aches to claim you as his."

His. Jade's throat inexplicably closed. "You know better than anyone how impossible that would be. My father left because my mother could not abandon her duties."

"Your father left because he was a selfish man who couldn't face responsibility," Libby drawled. "And Amber is well aware of that fact."

Jade swallowed hard and remained silent. It would be pointless to argue. Still, she couldn't stop thinking about what Libby had said, especially since she had the gift of prophecy. She hadn't been wrong as long as Jade had known her.

Closing her eyes, Jade allowed herself to envision what it would be like to be claimed by a man like Rance. Despite his sexy Southern drawl and his kind way, the intensity in his gaze told her if he claimed her she'd never have any doubts that she belonged to him.

His. Ah, the thought made her entire body tingle.

"Have you had many dealings with the Fae?" Libby asked, breaking into her admittedly erotic thoughts. Jade colored, glad Libby couldn't read minds.

"The Fae?" Confused, Jade tried to figure out what Libby meant. Had she missed something while she was daydreaming about Rance? "Are you saying Rance is Fae? I don't think he is, mostly because he has an aura like a shifter, and…"

"No." Libby smiled gently. "I'm talking about your cousin Diamond. As you asked, I've located her. She's traveled to the realm of the Fae."

"The land of the Fae?" Jade wasn't sure how to respond. "Why would she go there? I'm not sure anyone in our family has even ever seen a faerie."

"You might not know if you did." Libby seemed unconcerned. "Anyway, Diamond has gone there willingly. Apparently so have several of her friends. There is nothing you or I—or anyone for that matter—can do."

"But why? Why would they want to go there?"

"Fae men are graced with an uncommon virility, as well as an exceptional masculine beauty. Throughout time they have used this to lure unsuspecting females to their realm for trysts."

"Unsuspecting? Are you saying Di might not be aware of what she's doing?"

"She's aware," Libby immediately responded. "Well aware.

What she hasn't thought through are the ramifications of her actions."

"She has to know she's making her mother sick with worry. Di and my auntie Em are really close."

"Time passes differently there. To her, she will believe she's been gone a mere hour or two, when in fact it will have been days or weeks, maybe even a month."

"Did you happen to see when she plans on coming back?" Jade asked.

"No. But wisps of the trance still cling to me. Let me see if I can envision the answer."

"Okay." Jade waited, wishing her cousin would just come to her senses and stop taking foolish risks. At least she'd be able to tell Di's mother that Libby had seen her and she was safe. That had to count for something.

But then, Libby gasped and her body jerked. "No. Oh, no."

Before Jade could ask, Libby met her gaze, her eyes wide with terror. "Your cousin Di is in grave danger, though she doesn't know it. Evil plans are afoot there. You must travel to the land of the Fae and save her."

"Me? But I can't leave. I'll get sick." Not only that, but Jade had never saved anybody in her life. She wasn't trained in martial arts, didn't own a gun or know how to shoot, and her magical skills were dismal at best.

"Not this time. Since you'll be in another realm, the tie between us will remain unbroken. I think."

"You think?" Jade peered at her. "Don't you think you should actually know?"

"I'm relatively certain," Libby allowed. "And this is important enough for us to take a chance."

"What could I do?"

"You must hurry," Libby responded, conveniently avoiding the question.

"Hurry where? I have no idea how to get to Fae." She had a sneaking suspicion Libby was about to tell her.

"There's a portal in the forest, up near the ancient burial mound." Libby fixed her with that no-nonsense stare she'd begun to recognize. "You've got to go there and find it. You will be able to sense the energy it puts off. And bring your man with you. Otherwise, you may find yourself in need of saving, too."

"And then do what?"

"You'll know."

Great. Libby had slipped in and out of the trance, and Jade didn't know what else to say. Clearly, any specific questions weren't going to be answered. On edge, she watched Libby for the telltale sway that always followed her trances. If she wasn't quick enough to grab her, Libby would fall to the floor.

The instant Libby staggered, Jade grabbed her arm and helped the older woman over to a chair. Though her mind raced with the news about her cousin, she needed to focus on the more immediate need to care for Libby. "What can I get you? I know how draining your trances are for you."

"I'm fine." Libby gave her a wobbly smile. "Now you'd best go. Your young man awaits you. He's sitting in his car outside."

Jade started to protest, but a sharp look from Libby silenced her. "Remember, you have to take him with you," she said. "Otherwise, you might end up as lost as your cousin."

Aware he'd think her nuts and wondering if she could even convince him to go, Jade nodded. "I'll try my best," she said, ducking her chin in parting. "I'll see you soon."

Libby didn't respond. When Jade glanced at her again, she saw the other woman had fallen fast asleep.

Jade braced herself and swallowed hard before heading outside to face the man she couldn't seem to shake, even in her thoughts.

* * *

Rance had just rounded the curve when Jade appeared, heading straight for him, her long hair swinging and her hips swaying. The second he caught sight of her, his inner beast stirred.

Mine.

Again the primal need to claim her. He rolled down the car window, wondering if she needed a ride back to where she'd left her own vehicle, a bit down the winding road. Judging by her determined stride, she was seriously annoyed to find him there.

He couldn't blame her, even if he had gotten lucky in spotting her. After seeing her car, he'd decided against hiking after her and had decided to drive up to the cliffs.

"Following me?" she asked, her green eyes blazing as she stopped about five feet from his open car window.

He had to fight to keep himself from jumping out of his car and hauling her up against him. Gripping the steering wheel to keep from touching her, he pushed back the rush of desire and swallowed.

"No. But I have been looking for you," he managed, trying to push away the erotic images that ran through his mind any time he got near her. "I went by the house, then by your grandmother's shop, and finally the dog day care. When I couldn't find you, I decided to head out to the lake. That's how I wound up here."

She stepped closer. For one heady moment, he thought she might lean in the car window as if she, too, felt compelled to be as close to him as possible.

"What do you need?" she asked, her tone as frigid as the ice in her green eyes.

"You." Startled, he realized he'd spoken out loud.

She didn't even crack a smile. "I got that the first time. You came looking for me. You found me. Now tell me what you want."

"Darlin', will you please get in?" He indicated the passenger seat with a jerk of his head.

To his surprise, she stomped around to the other side of the car and slid into the seat. "I'm in. Now what's up? Why are you searching for me?"

Befuddled, bemused and aroused, he let his gaze rake over her. Damn.

"I want you." Once said, he couldn't take the words back. Hell, he didn't even want to.

She stared at him, her lush lips slightly parted, her chest heaving. "You…" she began.

Before she could finish, he knew he couldn't resist the temptation she presented.

Leaning over, he cupped his hand around the back of her head, slanted his mouth over hers and kissed her.

Chapter 7

The kiss felt like falling into the deep, dark depths of the lake. Even more fiercely aroused, Rance sank into the kiss, grateful that she didn't push him away and reject his raw act of possession.

Incredibly, she made a sound, low in the back of her throat, a moan of pleasure, as he deepened the kiss. Mindless with need, he damn near pulled her over the console to nestle in his lap, but he didn't want their first time to be in the front seat of a rental car, near the road where anyone could happen along and see.

Their first time. As if he knew there would be others. What the hell?

When he broke it off, they were both breathing hard.

"What the…?" Green eyes blazing, she stared at him, clearly furious, even more gorgeous in her anger.

Despite that, or because of it, he only wanted more. With every fiber of every cell in his body, he wanted more. Instead, he managed to take a deep breath so he could attempt a semblance of calm.

But then, his inner beast roared, fighting to break free. Dimly he realized he warred against himself. If he wouldn't claim Jade as his while human, his dragon intended to.

Mate.

"No," he growled, gritting his teeth, aware of Jade eyeing him as he struggled to subjugate the other half of himself. Not many were strong enough to meet the fierceness of his beast. For this reason, Drakkor had to be extremely careful when they chose their mates.

Mates? Again that word. Seriously? He'd already had a mate, and lost her. The chance of finding another was unbelievably small.

While he fought to get himself back under control, he saw that Jade had her own inner battle. Her beast—whatever kind that might be—had sensed his conflict and reacted.

Rance used a technique he'd learned when photographing in war zones. He'd had to learn not to give in to the fear, or his photos would be no good. One, two, three...focus on his breathing and regain control.

"Are you...?" Raspy voiced, Jade sounded as if she'd swallowed a handful of rusty nails. "Are you all right?"

Mates. He met her gaze and knew he'd do whatever he had to do in order to make her his. It was a foolish thought. He didn't need a mate. He didn't want a mate. What he needed was a lover, nothing more.

"I am now." Gaze still locked, again he felt that incredible pull of attraction. "How about you?"

Instead of answering, she shook her head and pushed the car door open. "Don't ever—and I mean *ever*—do that again."

And then, her back ramrod straight, she strode off. Not in the direction of the trails that would lead back to her car, but simply up the road, as if she felt the need for a brisk walk to clear her head.

He waited for a moment, just in case she reconsidered and came back. But she didn't, so he started his engine and turned around, driving in the opposite direction, back toward her parked SUV.

While he didn't have a plan, he figured he'd wait for her there, so they could have that talk he'd wanted before the kiss.

Furious, Jade took off, not caring or even thinking about where she would go. Aroused, confused, but most of all angry, she walked as if someone was chasing her, her Guardian necklace warm against her skin.

Her inner wolf snarled, still wanting out. Maybe that was what she should do. Head up to the forest, past the trails, into the deep thicket where people never went, and change.

But what about her cousin? She stopped, even more agitated.

"Go after him," Libby urged, startling Jade. How she'd found Jade and come up right behind her undetected, Jade had no idea.

Spinning around to face Libby, Jade swallowed hard. "I thought you were resting." In the dappled sunlight, Libby's amethyst eyes had a soft glow. The yoga pants and cream colored tunic she wore fit her well, giving her an elegant appearance without even trying. She looked serene and wise and achingly beautiful.

Jade loved her as much as she loved her own mother.

While she stared, trying to formulate a reply, Libby smiled gently. "You need his help to save your cousin, remember? He's gone to wait by your parked car for when you return."

"Stalker much?" Jade huffed. "These days I can't even turn around without him showing up."

"Oh, stop, child. You want him as much as he wants you," Libby pointed out. "And don't try to deny it."

Jade swallowed back her instinctive retort. "Wanting someone isn't possible for me now. You know that better than anyone."

Because she was the Guardian. Libby's Guardian, who couldn't leave. Which should have gone without saying.

Shaking her head, Libby sighed. "You're wrong, you know. The right man will be willing to stay."

Jade deliberated for a moment before responding. "But in the meantime, I'd run the risk of a lot of heartache."

Libby shook her head. "Sometimes, the pleasure is worth the pain."

Finally, Jade laughed. "You sound like some mystical guru, dispensing sound bites of platitudes."

Just like that, Libby's smile vanished and Jade realized she'd hurt her.

"I'm sorry," Jade said, giving Libby a quick hug. "This is all new and confusing. I didn't mean anything by my careless choice of words."

Leaning forward, she gave Libby a quick—and impulsive—kiss on her cheek. "And please, stay here. He's gone looking for another glimpse of you jumping out of the water."

The other woman froze. She turned her head away, but not before Jade saw the shine of tears in her amethyst eyes.

"I'm sorry." Jade wrapped her in a hug. Still, Libby held herself rigid, as if she thought she might break.

"You'd better hurry." Stepping away, Libby awkwardly patted her shoulder, avoiding direct eye contact. "Go find your young man."

Though Rance Sleighter certainly wasn't hers, Jade couldn't suppress a quick thrill at the notion. Aware Libby often revealed veiled messages of what she saw, Jade briefly wondered what such a thing would be like, to truly belong to someone, like a mate, before pushing the notion away.

She couldn't afford to waste time speculating on impossibilities. Libby was right. Her cousin needed her help.

"I'll see you later," Jade said, taking to the trails and heading toward her car. She turned back and waved at Libby, all the while hoping her face wasn't as red as it felt.

As she hiked down in the direction Rance had gone, she took deep breaths and willed her heartbeat to slow. Though she had to be on guard when around him, she also enjoyed his company.

Which should have frightened the hell out of her.

Libby was right. She found the bright red sports car parked next to hers at the end of the hiking trail. Another trail took off heading up, to more cliffs overlooking the lake. Since Rance's car was empty, Jade could only assume he'd decided to hike up and check out the scenery. Familiar with the territory around the lake, she favored this particular trail, which afforded spectacular views of the clear blue water.

Due to several steep climbs, a sign warned it was not for the beginning hiker. Thinking of Rance's old sneakers, she wondered if he had the right footwear, then shrugged off her concern. A seasoned photojournalist like him most likely would be prepared.

For the first time in his life, Rance had no idea what the hell he was doing. For a man with his drive and sense of purpose, this came as a shock. Originally, he'd come to fulfill a promise he'd made to a dying child, despite the fact that he knew she'd probably never live to see her wish fulfilled. He'd always chased down amazing photographs, loved the stories they told. Some were significant, others pure fluff, but as strange as the idea of a lake monster might seem to his colleagues, he considered this story one of his most important. Because of Eve, the five-year-old girl who wanted nothing more than to see a lake monster.

Again, the familiar pain punched him in the gut.

From the time she could walk, his stepdaughter Eve had been fascinated by the story of the Loch Ness monster. She'd insisted she'd one day meet her. When she'd fallen ill, Rance had hoped she hadn't gotten the illness that had not only killed her mother, but decimated most of his kind. Her human half might be the only thing that could save her. For only the second time in his life—the first being when Violet had fallen ill—Rance had prayed.

Despite not being related to her by blood, Rance had visited with her during her hospital stays. He always made sure he had time to visit. Finally, Jim had tearfully revealed Eve had leukemia, though Rance knew the truth. Even though she was a halfling, she had the plague, the same one that had killed her mother.

Since Jim was human, Rance couldn't tell him the truth. Still, he'd made sure to notify Pack specialists, and one had immediately converged on Houston to try and save the little girl.

Jim had been grateful and they talked frequently. Especially when Eve had taken a sudden turn for the worse. Rance had calmed Jim's fears, and after hanging up the phone, he'd cursed and raged alone in his empty apartment, begging the universe to let him trade places with Eve. The one thing he hadn't done was drink. He felt both angry and proud of this. He knew how close he was to unraveling. He'd worried what Eve's death would do to him and hoped he wasn't close to finding out.

Despite all the doctors' attempts to help her, Eve's illness had marched through her tiny body with all the fierceness of an approaching hurricane. Rance had dropped everything to be by her side, taking turns sleeping in the chair by her bed in the hospital room as Eve drifted in and out of consciousness.

And then one day Eve, bald and wan with blue-black

circles under her brown eyes, had come to and asked him to make her a promise. She wanted him to find a lake monster, write a story and take pictures and bring them to her so she could see.

He could deny her nothing, even if it meant briefly leaving her side. So superjournalist Rance Sleighter had gone in search of the elusive lake monster, not even certain one truly existed.

He'd traveled first to Scotland. After multiple trips to Loch Ness in hopes of seeing Nessie with nothing to show for it, he'd even taken to changing late at night and diving down into the cold depths of the water.

While in Scotland, he'd run into an American from upstate New York who, after a few pints of ale in a local pub, regaled Rance with stories of the Forestwood Lake monster.

Since the clock kept ticking and Eve showed no signs of improvement, Rance decided what the hell and flew to New York.

His unexpected sight of the creature had brought hope to his heart for the first time in forever. Hope was something he'd never thought he'd feel again.

Despite understanding all too well what Jade and her family—heck, the entire town—wanted, his promise to Eve took precedence over anything and everyone else.

Even Jade.

A sound behind him made him turn. Speak of the devil. He watched silently as Jade came into view, her curvy hips swinging as she hiked up the path toward him. His fingers itched to pull out his Nikon and capture a few images of her, but he resisted the urge and watched her with only his eyes.

Gorgeous. He couldn't help but marvel at her sensual beauty, the tightness in his chest mimicking the way he'd felt the first time he'd seen the lake creature rise from the water.

"Hey," she said when she reached him, her greeting brusque. "It turns out I need your help."

He hid a quick flare of interest. Finally, maybe she would give him a bargaining tool. "Help with what?"

She swallowed. "My cousin is missing. I need you to go with me to bring her back."

"Back from where?"

Instead of immediately answering, she looked away, apparently trying to figure out how to frame her answer. As she shifted her weight from foot to foot, he realized she truly was uncomfortable.

"Is this some kind of a trick?" he asked, suddenly suspicious.

Her gaze flashed to his, startled. "No. It's just…awkward. I don't really know where to begin."

"The beginning." And then, when she still hesitated, he smiled. "Try me. I'm a journalist. We're resilient."

This earned a tiny smile. "Okay." She took a deep breath. "How familiar are you with the Fae?"

Whatever he'd been expecting, it hadn't been this. "Faeries? I can't say I've ever met any."

She nodded, lifting her chin and continuing. "If you agree to help me, you will. I need to travel into their realm and rescue my cousin."

His first impulse—to mock even the idea of such a thing—he immediately squashed. After all, he was a shapeshifting Drakkor talking to another shape-shifter, type unknown, though most likely wolf. He'd met vampires and even one being who'd claimed to be an angel. Just because he personally had never seen a faerie didn't mean they didn't exist.

"How do you know your cousin is there?" he asked.

"Libby told me."

"What?" Staring at her, he let her see he was even more incredulous. "You speak to the lake beast?"

"Of course. She has certain…abilities. One of them is the gift of being able to find anything or anyone who has gone missing."

"I see." But he didn't. The matter-of-fact way she answered told him she clearly believed every word she uttered. She didn't seem to think she'd just asked him to take a giant leap of faith.

She watched him closely while he considered, her marvelous eyes narrowed.

When he still didn't respond, she sighed. "Never mind. I'll find someone else to help me. I suppose any man will work."

He took care not to reveal his instant visceral reaction to the thought of her with another man. "I'll be happy to help, but you've got to do something for me in return. I want you to take me to meet Libby."

He had to give her credit. She received his request stone-faced, with only the slight hitch in her breath as her reaction. He didn't elaborate, aware this had to be her choice, though he couldn't keep his heart rate from speeding up at the thought he might be this close to his goal. He could only imagine Eve's reaction. Since time definitely wasn't on her side, the sooner he got what he needed, the better.

"Okay," Jade finally said, startling him. "You can meet Libby. After we retrieve my cousin and at a time and a place of my choosing."

He nodded, afraid to speak in case he revealed his relief. "Are you ready?"

The question confused him. "Ready for what?"

"To go get my cousin."

"Now?"

Cocking her head, she eyed him. "Do you have something else you need to do?"

"Well, no. But… You surprised me, that's all."

"Good." Pulling out her cell phone, she scrolled and found a contact. "Let me call DOL and make sure someone will open and close for me for a few days."

While she talked to one of her employees, he pondered her words. *A few days.* For the first time, he wondered how long this foray into Fae would take.

At least he had his camera. He hoped to get a few good shots and, if he was really lucky, one or two great ones.

And after, he'd finally get to meet Libby, the Forestwood Lake creature.

Things were finally looking up.

"Okay," Jade said, pocketing her phone. "Let's go. Once we get near the portal, we'll find a good place to stash our electronics."

"Wait, what?"

Taking off up the hiking trail, she shot him a quick look over her shoulder. "Yeah, you can't take anything metal into the land of the Fae. Are you coming or not?"

Cursing under his breath, he started after her.

"They wouldn't have cell phone service there, anyway," she added, a hint of amusement in her voice.

"I'm more worried about my camera and lenses," he fired back.

"They'll be fine."

At the point where the trail made a sharp turn toward the cliffs, she stopped and pointed. "We've got to leave the trail and go deep into the woods, away from the lake," she said. "There's a couple of places rumored to be ancient burial mounds. The portal is near there, according to…"

Instantly alert, he eyed her. "According to whom?"

"Never mind. It's enough to know it's there. I'll be able

to sense the energy field. We'll need to hold hands when we step through."

With another woman, he might have made a quick joke. Instead, reading Jade's restless agitation, he kept his mouth shut. The photojournalist in him was fascinated by all this talk of portals and energy fields, not to mention actually traveling to Fae. He could already imagine the article he could write, if he wanted people to think he'd lost his mind and become a nutcase.

The only way he could publish such a story would be in a Drakkor periodical, or maybe something put out by the Pack. A story on Libby, on the other hand... Especially if he treated it all like a huge mystery, the way the Loch Ness monster had been for years and years.

But only after he'd shown Eve. Eve mattered more than anything else. He prayed she'd live long enough to see it.

The deeper into the forest they went, the more they slowed down. In places, the underbrush was so thick they had to work their way through it. Grim-faced with determination, Jade silently plowed ahead. He kept at her side, doing his part. Once or twice he almost asked her to let him clear the way, but something told him she'd never be content to follow.

After thirty minutes had passed, he began to wonder if they'd ever reach this so-called portal. Still, Jade kept trudging forward, undeterred.

He couldn't help but admire her determination. Her dedication to family, which he also shared. Hell, he'd do anything to save Eve, and the two of them didn't even share the same blood. Still, he'd never considered Eve as just his stepdaughter, rather the daughter of his heart.

"Hey," Jade called. "Earth to Rance."

Belatedly, he realized she'd stopped and he'd continued on a few paces without her. Turning slowly to look at her, with the leaf-dappled sun turning her silver hair gold, he marveled again at her beauty.

His. Again the thought, like a virtual punch in the gut. And again, not willing to even consider it, he pushed the idea away.

"We're here," she announced, hands on her hips. "You were thinking so deeply I wondered if you were even able to hear me."

He offered her a sheepish grin. "Sorry, darlin'. I've been known to do that from time to time." Glancing around, he saw nothing out of the ordinary and certainly nothing that even remotely resembled a portal. Of course, he had no idea what such a thing would look like.

"So when you say we're here…" He let a sweeping arm gesture complete his sentence.

"We are."

The certainty in her voice intrigued him. "How do you know?"

"I just do. I can sense the energy."

Lifting one arm, she beckoned him closer. "Look."

Goose bumps dimpled the creamy skin on her arm.

Still, that wasn't a lot to go on. But since he was only along for the ride, he guessed he'd simply have to trust her. "Okay. What do we do now?"

"Take my hand," she ordered, her green eyes clear as she lifted her fingers.

He did as she asked, bracing himself for the jolt of desire even the smallest bit of contact with her brought. This time was no different.

"Are you okay?" she asked. Her direct and frank gaze made him wonder if she saw too much.

"I'm fine." His curt response couldn't be helped. "Lead the way."

"You'll need to take your cell phone, watch, anything modern or electronic or metal, and put it somewhere."

"Somewhere?" Incredulous, even though she'd mentioned this earlier, he made no move to pull his cell from his pocket.

Gently she tugged his hand to get his attention. "Yes. I even had to take off my necklace, which I don't like to ever do. I put all my stuff in that hollow tree over there. Judging by the assortment of other cells and stuff in there, that's a favorite place for people to stash their stuff."

He didn't like it, not one bit, but he let go of her hand and did as she requested. Once he'd finished, she slid her slender fingers back into his, sending yet another jolt all the way through him.

Briefly, he considered asking her if she felt it, too, but knew better than to open that can of worms.

"Are you ready?" she asked. When he jerked his head in a nod, she squeezed his fingers. "Whatever you do, don't let go of my hand."

"Or what?" he joked, only half kidding. "Will I end up floating alone in the void of space, lost forever?"

Her steady gaze didn't waver. "That's entirely possible. I don't know for sure, but I have a feeling you could end up in a different place than me. And then we might have trouble finding each other again."

The sincerity in her voice convinced him. "I won't let go," he promised. And if that inner voice inside him added the word *ever*, he ignored it. Ever since Eve had gotten sick, he'd gotten good at ignoring a lot of things.

She took a deep breath. "Good. Come on, then."

Hand in hand, they faced east, moving in between two slender birch trees. A ghosting of electricity raised the hair on his arms, giving him the first inkling that something had changed. Then the air in front of him shimmered, like the wavy lines heat made on pavement. Beneath his feet the earth shifted and moved enough that he staggered, almost losing his balance. Only his grip on Jade's hand kept him upright.

Just when he thought it was over, all went black, sucking

the air from his lungs. He struggled to breathe, trying like hell not to panic. Jade's hand still gripped his, grounding him. If she could survive this, so could he.

Chapter 8

The darkness felt all-encompassing, contracting. Rance struggled to breathe. And then...the world righted itself again. The pressure on his chest lifted. He blinked, focusing on Jade, his lifeline. She appeared energized by whatever had just happened. She practically glowed, her silver hair translucent.

Awestruck by her beauty, he stared. Finally, he forced himself to look away. He took in the fact that they no longer stood in the forest. Instead, a meadow of lush emerald grass lined with a rainbow of vibrant flowers stretched before them.

"We're here." Her voice rang husky with satisfaction.

Since she made no move to extricate her hand from his, he didn't, either. "What now?" he asked. "Where do we go from here?"

For the first time, her confident expression faltered. "I'm not sure. I've never actually been here before. I'm guessing we'll need to find someone."

It occurred to him to wonder if the Fae were actually

welcoming of visitors. Asking this, he didn't feel reassured when Jade shrugged.

"I guess they are," she said. "Otherwise, I don't think my cousin and her friends would come here so often. Though to be honest, Diamond can be very…pushy. I wouldn't put it past her to go where she wasn't wanted."

"Great. So we don't know if the Fae are friendly and whether your cousin is a welcome guest or a prisoner. Does that about sum it up?"

Now she smiled. Struck momentarily dumb, he concluded wars could be fought over a smile so beautiful. Damn, he had it bad.

"The Fae are a peaceful people," she said. "And Di is gorgeous. I'm sure she's welcome." Though her tone didn't waver, something about her deceptively bland expression indicated that she hadn't told him everything.

Should he call her out on it, whatever it might be? Or play along, figuring she'd eventually reveal whatever she'd left unsaid. He decided to continue in a lighthearted vein. After all, he'd probably find out soon enough. "Gorgeous, huh? Is that a family trait, darlin'?"

She only continued to smile and shook her head. "Come on. Let's go find the city and talk to some Fae." She started off.

Cursing under his breath, he didn't move. "I'm going to need something more from you," he said slowly.

One brow raised, she waited. "What?"

"Since I came here to help you, I need to know exactly what I'm getting into. In other words, complete honesty. What is it that you aren't telling me?"

Silence. And then she nodded.

"You're right." At least she had the grace to wince. "I've been told by good authority that my cousin might be in danger. That's why I need you to come with me."

"Might be?" He kept his eyes locked on hers. "That sounds pretty vague to me."

"It's the best I can do. And yes. Her mother is worried. Better safe than sorry."

"Darlin'," he drawled. "I have to tell you, I don't like the idea of you putting yourself at risk."

She reared back, as though his words had startled her. Only his grip on her hand kept her close. For a moment she went silent, considering what he'd said. Then a slow smile blossomed over her beautiful face, making him ache to touch her. "That's why you're coming along—to protect me."

"Lead the way." Now he pulled his hand free. Instantly regretting the loss of contact, he covered with a mock bow and an insolent grin.

Jade only stared. Then, shaking her head as if shaking off water, she looked away. "I'd rather you stay close to me," she said, her words contradicting her earlier assurances that they'd be perfectly safe.

Again, he had to squash the urge to kiss her. Now was not the time nor the place.

"I will," he promised, meaning it. If he had his way, he'd never let her out of his sight again.

The winding path appeared illuminated ahead of them, a luminous pearly white. The vibrant blue of the sky reminded him of the clarity of a Santa Fe afternoon. Except the colors—the greens and reds and yellows—glowed, as if lit from within.

Jade must have noticed his bemused expression. "I'd heard this place was gorgeous. I guess I should warn you that the Fae's beauty is legendary. Steel yourself, because men have been known to be beguiled and ensnared by it."

"I'm not most men. I'm…" He cut the words off, aware he'd nearly revealed his nature.

"You're what?" She regarded him curiously.

"Different." His lame answer sounded too curt. "Don't worry. I'll be fine. What about you?"

"Me?" Surprised, she turned to face him. "I'll be okay. I can't stay gone too long—my duties won't permit it."

"Duties?" He knew he couldn't let that go. "You mean looking after Libby?"

Immediately her expression shut down. "Yes." She started off again, forcing him to catch up.

Like a mirage appearing in the desert, ahead in the distance a building appeared. Shimmering in the bright sunlight, it looked like a castle, like something straight out of a medieval story. As they got closer, he saw it was indeed a castle, apparently made out of some sort of pearly marble that glowed where the sun touched it.

Beyond the castle, he saw several other structures, constructed from wood and stone. "This is like a village in Europe, built in the shadow of an ancient keep," he commented.

"Except this castle isn't old and abandoned," she pointed out. "It looks occupied and vibrant."

Still, he'd yet to see a single person. "Where do you suppose they all are?" he asked.

Again her lips tugged up into a smile, as if she found his question amusing. Whatever it was about this woman, she beguiled him. He had to fight to keep pulling her close and kissing that pretty mouth.

"They're here," she said, clearly unaware of his thoughts. "When they're ready to reveal themselves, I'm sure they will."

She'd barely finished speaking when three men appeared, striding up the path toward them. If they'd come from the city, he hadn't seen them until now.

All of them were tall and moved with an uncommon grace. They wore their hair long and as they approached they each had aquiline features, perfectly symmetrical, a kind of masculine beauty he hadn't realized even existed.

A quick glance at Jade revealed her thunderstruck expression. Evidently, neither had she. Was that a twinge of jealousy stabbing his chest?

One of them stepped forward. His long, blond hair was streaked with shades of the sun. His eyes were a mixture of cobalt and violet, a shade Rance had never seen before. And those eyes were locked on Jade, his expression indicating he'd never seen a woman as beautiful.

"Oh," Jade murmured, blindly reaching for Rance. Quickly he gave her his arm, and then decided the hell with it and tugged her close. Putting his arm around her in a clear gesture of possession, he stared at the other man, daring him to protest.

Instead, the two companions stepped up in a show of solidarity with the blond leader.

"I'm Cai, Prince of Fae," he announced, his smile both confident and full of charm. "This is my cousin Bradrick and my best friend, Llewyn."

Clearly still starstuck, Jade attempted a curtsy. Only Rance's arm holding her up kept her from falling. Rance hoped the Fae prince couldn't tell.

For whatever reason, Rance had taken an instant dislike to the man. Still, with his amazing bone structure, he couldn't help but wish he had his camera. Faces like Cai's were born to be photographed.

"I'm looking for my cousin." Finally, Jade spoke up. Her voice had a breathless quality that told Rance she still hadn't entirely recovered. The second stab of jealousy knifing through him both irritated and surprised him.

"Her name is Diamond," she continued. "Have you seen her?"

The two men flanking the prince exchanged glances, but didn't speak.

"Yes, I have." His confident tone grated on Rance's nerves. "Come with me, pretty cousin of Di." He held out his hand, a large gemstone winking on one finger of his slender hand.

When Jade took a step forward, Rance wasn't sure whether to tighten his grip or let her go. In the end, he gave in to his instinct and kept her close. After all, he'd promised to protect her, even if that meant saving her from herself.

Jade shot him a startled look, her green eyes slightly unfocused, but didn't fight him.

The prince, on the other hand, shook his head, his gaze sending daggers Rance's way.

"Of course, we'll both be glad to follow y'all," Rance put in, his smooth tone revealing none of his annoyance.

Prince Cai waved his hand and, just like that, they stood at the castle steps.

"Neat trick."

"Magic," Jade whispered in Rance's ear, as if he hadn't just experienced it.

"I get that," he drawled, tugging her closer. Caving in to his impulse, he gave her what he'd intended to be a quick kiss but changed to a searing kiss of possession. Maybe this could drive away whatever Fae enchantment Cai had placed on her.

She shivered but didn't pull away. Meanwhile, Mr. Fancy Prince and his companions made sounds of impatience.

"We understand what you're attempting to make so clear," Prince Cai declared. "I assure you, I have no intention of moving in on your woman."

Now would be where Jade would protest, Rance felt quite sure. She'd say something along the lines of she wasn't anyone's woman. But she didn't. Instead of speaking, she simply nodded.

"Shall we go and locate your cousin? I'm certain she'll be happy to see you."

Rance found himself wondering if the men looked like this, how beautiful were the women?

A few seconds later he found out. A woman strolled into the room, her lustrous inky black hair long and straight. His heart skipped an involuntary beat as he took in her exotically tilted, amethyst eyes fringed by thick black lashes. She walked with a sensual grace, the form-fitting gown she wore swirling around her lush figure.

Belatedly realizing his mouth might be open, he glanced at Jade, who watched him with a narrow gaze and no hint of amusement. In fact, her reaction was an external manifestation of the way he'd felt inside when she'd ogled the Fae men.

He laughed; he couldn't help it.

"What's so funny?" Jade asked, sidling up close so their hips touched.

"I'll tell you later, darlin'." Smiling down at her, he completely forgot about the other woman.

"Excuse me?" The lilting feminine voice exactly matched the gorgeous creature who'd strolled into the room. "I thought you wanted to see Diamond."

"We do," Jade answered. She actually slipped her hand into his—he wasn't sure if she did so for her benefit or his, but he didn't care.

"Follow me," the Fae woman said. Still Rance kept his gaze on Jade, aware at a visceral level that she mattered most.

When Jade started forward, Rance finally glanced away so he could watch where he walked as he went with her. All he could see was the other woman's back. Her glorious curtain of hair swirled and swayed as she walked, almost as if it had taken on a life of its own.

"We've got to be careful," Jade said, sotto voce. "The Fae are very skilled at ensnaring the unwary. I'm worried that's what may have happened to Di."

He hardly thought that would qualify as danger. Whatever or whoever had given Jade reason to believe her cousin was in danger would surely have had a better reason than that.

He figured they'd find out soon enough.

"Don't let your guard down for a second," Jade murmured. "Especially don't eat or drink anything—I've heard that alone can trap you here."

"But why?" he had to ask. "Why would they want to do something like that?"

"The Fae always have their own agenda."

He wondered where she got her information. He'd had a pretty decent education, including classes taught by his own people about the other nonhuman races, but he couldn't remember learning much at all about the Fae.

For now, he'd simply take her word on it.

"Here we are," the Fae woman said. "Di awaits you in here." She stood back and waved her hand gracefully at a set of wooden doors gilded in gold.

Carefully avoiding meeting her gaze, Rance nodded. "Are you ready, sweetheart?"

Jade swallowed and then nodded. "I think so. Yes. Yes, I am."

"Then you may enter."

Since Jade continued to stand frozen, Rance stepped forward and pushed the door open, still holding Jade's hand. He tugged her through the open door.

As soon as they stepped into the room, the double doors closed by themselves behind them.

Rance barely noticed. At the other end of the room, a blonde woman reclined on an overstuffed bed. Four gauzy drapes hung on all four corners, the silver color threaded with gold. The woman eyed the two of them without expression, her emerald eyes marking her clearly as Jade's relative.

She didn't appear to be in any danger, as far as he could tell.

As they got closer, Jade spoke up, clearly thinking the same thing. "Di, are you all right?"

"What are you doing here?" Rather than pleased to see them, Di's voice vibrated with anger. "You're a Guardian. You can't leave and come to Fae."

Jade's tight smile matched the coldness in her gaze. "Well, now, I don't know about that. It looks like that's exactly what I did. I need to know if you're planning to come home or not?"

"What's it to you?"

Rance decided he'd had enough. "Your cousin and I went through a lot to get here. There's no need for you to talk to Jade like that."

Di's emerald gaze touched on him briefly and without interest. "Did my mother send you?" Ignoring Rance, she directed her question to Jade, which made Rance want to shake her.

"She's very worried about you," Jade said, a thread of steel underlying her deceptively soft voice. "So worried, she had me ask Libby about you."

This got a reaction. Di's eyes widened. "What did she say?"

Jade glanced back at the closed doors. "Only that you might be in trouble and I needed to find you."

"Trouble." Di's laugh sounded bitter. "I guess you could call it that."

And then she stood, letting them all see her rounded stomach. "I'm pregnant."

"But…" Jade nearly choked. "You haven't been gone that long. How could you show already? It hasn't even been two weeks."

"Time passes differently here, you know that. What seems like a couple weeks there is months here."

"I thought it was the opposite," Jade said, frowning.

Di shrugged. "Maybe. I don't know. I guess it can be either way. Or maybe Fae babies grow faster. Apparently."

Rance stepped in, deciding to ask the question Jade apparently hadn't thought of yet. "Who's the father?"

Di shot him a disgruntled glare. "Who are you again?"

"He's with me." Jade's clipped tone was a warning. "Now answer the question."

Di sighed. "Cai. My prince. My child will be Fae royalty. I'm not sure they want me to leave."

"Tough. You need to go home and tell your mother."

While Rance knew he should stay out of this, he couldn't help but admire Jade's no-nonsense, take-no-prisoners approach.

"You'll have to talk to the prince." Di's smug tone grated on Rance. "He's always telling me how precious I am to him. I'm sure he won't let me out of his sight."

"I'm sure he can bear a few days apart," Jade insisted. "Let's just find him and ask."

Before she'd even finished speaking, the double doors swung open. The tall blond man who'd met them earlier strode into the room. He spared Jade a lingering smile before turning his attention on the now-glowing Di.

"You can go," he told her. Rance inwardly winced at the disinterest in the other man's voice. "Di, you are free to leave."

At first Di simply stared at him in stunned shock. "But, Cai. What if I don't want to?"

"This is not your place." Cai's tone hardened. "You don't belong here any more than your friends did."

Her friends? Were they pregnant, too? Rance and Jade exchanged a look.

As she stared at the prince, on the edge of tears, Di's mouth trembled. "But what about the baby?" she asked.

"The child will survive a few journeys back and forth

between your realm and mine. After all, your other friends have all returned home."

Di stared at him, dawning horror reflected in her green eyes. "Are you telling me that you're the…"

"Father of their children?" Again he flashed that humorless smile. "Yes. Of course."

Of course? Rance balled his hands into fists to avoid punching the guy. As if she felt the same way, Jade gripped his arm.

One single sparkling tear ran down Di's alabaster cheek. "But why? I thought you loved me."

"I do love you." He stepped forward and gently wiped away her tear. "As I love them. I'm a Fae prince. I love many women. That's what we do."

Rance snorted, unable to take much more. "That's the biggest bunch of BS I've ever heard."

The prince ignored him. Rance clenched his fists, aware he couldn't let his temper rule his actions. He needed to get both Jade and Di out of this place without complications.

Apparently, Cai didn't share this sentiment. He turned to Jade, taking her free hand and kissing the back of it. Rance just about decided if the other man's mouth lingered a second longer, the hell with keeping his temper in check. Luckily, the prince released her.

Jade blinked, her expression confused. Rance squeezed her hand to bring her back to reality.

"We need to go," Rance told her. A quick glance at Di revealed a jealous storm brewing in her eyes as she took in her prince fawning over her cousin.

Jade shook her head as if clearing out cobwebs. Rance squeezed her hand again to keep her gaze from drifting back to the prince. He didn't know what the Fae man was doing, but whatever it was, even Jade succumbed to the pull of it.

"We need to go," Rance repeated. "Now."

"You're right. We do." Jade frowned, glancing at her cousin, who glared at her as if she'd like to set her on fire. "Di, come on. We need to get back to Forestwood."

"I don't want to go." Enunciating each and every syllable, Di crossed her arms in defiance. "I'm going to stay right here until my baby is born."

"My darling, don't overstay your welcome. You know as well as I do, when I want you, all I have to do is call and you'll be back." Voice silky, the prince gestured. All at once, Jade, Rance and Di were no longer inside the palace, but back in the forest, near the portal where they'd entered this place.

Jade swallowed, stunned to see they stood back in the trees near the portal. If they'd walked all this way from the castle, she had no memory of it. She saw that she still clutched Rance's hand, and relief flooded her. Whatever had happened, at least he'd done as she'd asked and had never left her side.

An outraged squeal from behind her informed her that Di was with them, too. A quick glance around verified the prince was not.

"This is ridiculous!" Di declared, stopping just short of stomping her feet. "How dare he treat me this way? I'm going to be the mother of his child."

"You and a couple of others, it seems," Rance drawled. "I think you need to get with your friends and find out how many of you were taken in by this guy."

Jade wondered why he shot her a look as he spoke. And then she remembered how dreamy she'd felt when she and the Fae prince had locked eyes. Damn. She shuddered. It seemed even she hadn't been immune. She'd mistakenly believed her rapport with Libby and her role as Guardian would protect her. And Rance. Grateful, she decided to thank him later.

Meanwhile, Di continued to complain. Loudly.

A headache began brewing behind Jade's eyes. "How are we going to get her back home?"

Oblivious, Di appeared to be on the verge of throwing a very childlike temper tantrum, stomping her feet and all. Any second now, Jade thought her cousin might drop to the leafy forest floor and start kicking and screaming.

"You grab one arm, I'll take the other," Rance said. "We'll shepherd her through the portal together."

And that was exactly what they did.

Libby paced, unable to sleep. This restlessness was new, at least for this decade. She'd been agitated before, in brief spurts, but nothing like now. Deep within her bones she knew her life was about to change irrevocably.

This unshakable certainty kept her up at night, pacing the floor in her tiny cabin, until finally she gave in to the urge to change. This night, instead of diving into the cold, deep waters of the lake, she took to the sky. The simple pleasure of soaring over the hills and forests of Forestwood was a treat she seldom allowed herself. As she spiraled higher and higher, spreading her massive wings to catch the current, she vowed not to let so much time pass between flights again.

At this hour, only the streetlights brought light to the darkness. Libby felt more alive than she had in years. And free, as if she wasn't shackled by invisible chains to a small town in the Catskill Mountains.

She flew for a long time, until she realized the eastern sky had begun to lighten. Slightly regretful, but exhilarated, she dropped back down to the wooded area next to the lake, and began the process of shape-shifting back into her human form.

This done, she grabbed her clothes and hurriedly dressed. Ignoring the sudden pang of longing for a mate's caress, she began hiking through the woods in the darkness and heading for home.

Once there, she considered trying to sleep. Instead, still unsettled, she made a cup of tea and carried it to her porch. She'd watch the sun come up and attempt to pinpoint the source of her restlessness.

She couldn't shake the feeling it had something to do with Jade's man. Rance Sleighter. Something about him felt...familiar. Not in a sexual sense, but as though he might almost be family.

Family. A word so many took for granted. She had, too, once. And now, now that they were all gone, she missed them more than she could express.

Pink ribbons of color began to streak the slate sky, announcing the imminent arrival of the sun. She sipped her tea—Darjeeling this time—and tried to relax, maybe even meditate. She'd long ago learned her clearest thoughts came after she stilled the noise inside her head. She set the timer on her phone for twenty minutes.

Settling back in her chair with the ease of practice, she focused on her breathing. In. Out. In. Out. Each time a random thought tried to interrupt, she noted it and sent it away.

The timer chimed—too soon—and she stretched, quite pleased. The sun had risen above the horizon, and bright golden fingers of light painted the tops of the trees. Her tea had cooled, but she drank the rest of it, anyway.

She knew what she had to do. Talk to Rance Sleighter and find out who he truly was, where he'd come from and who his people were. Maybe then she'd be able to understand why he seemed so familiar even though she hadn't left Forestwood in fifty years or more.

Chapter 9

Trying to tune out her cousin's complaints, Jade shepherded her along toward her car. She was glad to have Rance on the other side and she chanced a look at him to see what he thought of Di's complaints. One glance at his set profile and the terse line of his lips told her he, too, had just about had enough.

"Here we are," Jade said, keeping her tone light and breezy when she really wanted to tell her cousin to be quiet. "My car. Once I get you home, I know your mother will be thrilled to see you. She's been so worried."

For whatever reason, this simple statement silenced Di. Her crestfallen expression told Jade that her cousin had once again managed to forget all about her mother.

"It was probably the enchantment," Jade ventured, mentally bracing herself for a second round of denials or complaints.

Instead, Di bit her lip and looked down. "Maybe," she said, her voice uncertain. "I was so preoccupied with the prince and the baby, I somehow managed to completely forget about my home and my family."

Jade squeezed her shoulder to express sympathy.

"Are y'all good here?" Rance asked.

"I think so." Jade smiled, aware he could see her relief. Even now, that Southern drawl of his made her insides tingle. "I'll take Di home. I really appreciate all your help today. I don't know what I would have done without you."

"Oh, I do." A teasing light danced in his gray eyes. For one heart-stopping moment, she thought he might lean in and kiss her, but instead he dragged his hand across his chin and looked away.

"Okay, then," he said, turning to head toward his car. "I'll talk to you later. Remember what you promised."

I'm not disappointed, she told herself as she watched him climb into the Mustang and drive away. She wasn't disappointed at all. He'd held up his end of the bargain, now she'd have to do as she'd agreed and let him meet Libby. Only she wasn't at all sure how Libby would take to that idea.

"Are we going?" Di asked, managing to sound belligerent and afraid at the same time.

Jade nodded. "Yes, we are. Please get in and buckle up." She braced herself for a round of protests, but Di did as she asked without a word of complaint.

During the drive back to town, Di remained silent, much to Jade's relief. She imagined her younger cousin was working on a decent explanation to tell her mother. Not that she had to worry. Auntie Em loved her only daughter to distraction and would fuss over her, ecstatic she'd come home safe. There would be no lectures or tearful recriminations. Di's mother would welcome her with open arms and joy that her daughter had come home unharmed. Jade bet her aunt would even take the pregnancy news with happiness.

Di knew this, too. She'd spent her entire life sheltered and spoiled by her mother. When they pulled up to the house, she jumped out of the car as soon as Jade put it in Park.

"Thanks for the ride." Di tossed the words over her shoulder as she hurried up the sidewalk. "You don't need to come in."

"Oh, but I do," Jade muttered. "I'm right behind you." She felt dizzy—and slightly ill. So much for Libby's idea that traveling to another dimension wouldn't make her sick.

She'd made it only halfway up the sidewalk when Di slipped inside. A loud squeal—Auntie Em—greeted the appearance of her daughter.

Jade got there just in time to see her aunt wrap Di in a massive bear hug. Triumph shone in Di's eyes as she peered at Jade over her mother's shoulder. Jade merely shrugged. "I'm used to it," she mouthed, even as beads of perspiration broke out on her forehead. Then, as Auntie Em turned around, Jade managed a grin. "As you can see, I found her."

Her aunt grinned back, opening up one arm so she could include Jade in the massive hug. "And it only took you four days."

Stunned, Jade hugged her aunt back before stepping away. Four days when it seemed like four hours. No wonder she felt ill.

"I told you," Di said. "You kind of lose track of time."

"Where was she?" Auntie Em asked. Before Jade could speak, she turned and asked the same question to Di. "Where were you?" Since it would only be a matter of time before Auntie Em noticed her daughter's pregnancy, Jade figured she'd better get out of there before she did.

"I'll let you two talk about everything." Jade began backing toward the door. She wasn't exactly sure how much information Di would share with her mother, and she really didn't want to know. "I need to go check on my business and my family." And Libby, though she didn't mention it. She'd never been away from Forestwood this long, at least not since she'd become Guardian. She sincerely hoped Libby hadn't needed her. She couldn't help but wonder what might happen if she had.

That thought worried her, even though Libby had been the one to order her to go and rescue Di, saying her cousin was in danger. Which, if Jade had read the situation correctly, Diamond hadn't been. Another oddity, since Libby was never wrong.

Maybe she should drive out to the lake and see if Libby could do anything about Jade getting sick. She yawned, stifling a gag, and reconsidered. Nope, she'd better wait. She'd be lucky to make it home. If she felt better, she'd pop out there first thing in the morning.

Frequent yawns combined with her stomach's rumbling impeded her driving, so she opened the windows and cranked up the radio, deliberating whether to go straight home or check on her job. Though she worried she might be sick, she couldn't ignore the business she'd worked so hard to make successful, especially since she'd been away longer than she'd intended.

Driving carefully, she stopped at Dogs Off Leash. Her employees gathered around her, happy to see her, a few of them assuming she'd taken a vacation. Only Sue, who'd known that Jade had gone to the lake, stood back and didn't join in when the others peppered Jade with questions about where she'd been. Holding on to the front counter to steady herself, Jade responded in kind, teasing them with words like *exotic* and *out of this world*. She tried to broaden her weak smile since they had no way to know she was actually telling the truth.

After informing them she needed one more day off to recover from her "vacation," Jade had a private word with Sue.

"Everything okay?" Sue asked. "You look really…beat."

Which meant Jade must look a mess. Hopefully not as bad as she felt.

"I'm fine," she lied. "Just tired. Once I get some sleep, I'll be back to normal." At least she certainly hoped so.

The other woman nodded. "Why don't you sleep in? I'll open up in the morning."

Grateful, Jade nodded. "Thanks."

"Can I ask you something?" For whatever reason, Sue seemed oddly hesitant.

"Of course."

"That man, the handsome one. Rance something-or-other. He came here looking for you. Somehow, he knew you'd gone to the lake when I didn't even say anything."

Battling a wave of nausea, Jade nodded and then immediately regretted it. "He found me." Great, now her head was pounding.

"He's a reporter, isn't he?" Expression concerned, Sue laid her hand on Jade's shoulder. "I know it's not my place, but do you think it's wise to date him? What if he finds out something about...?"

Jade sighed, praying she wouldn't lose the contents of her stomach in front of Sue. "First off, I'm not dating him. Secondly, he's not a reporter, he's a photojournalist. He tells stories with pictures rather than words. It's okay, I promise."

"But..." Sue searched Jade's face. "What about Libby? Can you keep her safe with someone like that around?"

Suppressing a groan, Jade started to nod again, and then thought better of it. "Of course I can. And I'm Guardian. Believe me, I know how to take care of Libby."

"Okay." Sue didn't sound convinced.

Which hurt more than it should. "Is there anything else?" Jade asked. If not, now all she had to do was make it home.

Dropping her hand, Sue shook her head. "No. Have a good night's sleep."

Feeling even wearier, on top of queasy, Jade headed

home. As usual, the sight of her family home perched on the hill lightened her heart.

"Family meeting tonight," Amber declared the instant Jade walked in the front door. Watching from the stairs, the twins snickered and nodded. While Jade wondered what on earth was going on, Opal appeared in the kitchen doorway holding a wooden spoon. "An *emergency* family meeting," she declared, glaring at Jade. "Mandatory attendance for all Burnetts."

Her pronouncement made, the elderly woman disappeared back into the kitchen.

"Well?" Amber crossed her arms. "You look terrible. Where have you been for the last four days?"

"Finding Di." Though exhaustion and dizziness made her sway, Jade managed a wry smile. "She's safe at home with her mother."

"Thank you!" Amber exclaimed, wrapping Jade up in a quick hug. "Is she all right?"

"I think so. But she's pretty mad. She didn't want to come home."

"Where—" Amber began.

Lifting her hand to silence her mother felt rude but necessary. "Call your sister. I'm sure she can explain everything. I'm sick and beat and need to go lie down. I'm not even sure I'm up for a meeting, even a mandatory family one."

"Humph." Amber narrowed her eyes. "Your grandmother is making lasagna," she finally said. "The special kind, with spinach and mushrooms added."

Though at first even the thought of food made her feel worse, Jade actually perked up at the thought of her grandmother's special lasagna. This was the one item Opal cooked without Amber's help. Maybe some food in her stomach would help. "Why the family meeting?" she asked. "Didn't we just do this?"

"True, we did." Amber gestured with her hands. "But something has come up. And you know as well as I do anyone can call a meeting."

Beyond drained, Jade sighed. "Call me when I need to come down. Right now I'm going to catch a quick nap. I feel a bit queasy."

"Queasy? A nap?" Amber eyed her up and down. "You're not pregnant, are you?"

Jade recoiled. "What? No. Of course not. Where do you get these crazy ideas, Mother?"

"Well, you *are* dating that handsome photographer. Even though we don't know what kind of shape-shifter he is, at least he's not human. Have you two done the...?"

"Mom." Face flaming, Jade cut her off. "Seriously. You know we're not dating. I'm doing my duty, nothing more. I had to leave the area to find Di, and you know how that affects the Guardian. Now if you'll excuse me, I really need to get some rest." She hightailed it up the stairs before her mother could say another word.

But before she could make it to her room, the twins stopped her. Great. Again she broke out in a sweat. "Jade, are you in trouble?" Pearl asked.

"Trouble?" Looking from one to the other, Jade sighed. "Not that I know of. Why do you ask?"

"Well, first you disappear for four days with no reason," Pearl said. "Which we all know you can't do."

"And then we heard that Libby called this meeting," Sapphire continued.

Libby. Crud. Hoping she hadn't heard correctly, Jade bit back a curse and stared, her illness momentarily forgotten. "Seriously. How? She only talks to me."

Pearl shrugged. "Well, I guess that is changing. This time, I heard she spoke to Mom."

"Are you sure?"

"Yes." Sapphire studied her fingernails, clearly working

on perfecting her this-is-boring voice. "She's displeased about something. I heard Mom and Grandma talking in the kitchen."

"Is it something you did?" Pearl asked again, the concern in her voice in marked contrast to her sister's affected nonchalance. "I mean, since you're in charge of her and all."

Pretending indifference, Jade yawned. "First off, I'm not in charge. Libby's a real person. I'm more her friend than anything else. And as far as being in trouble, not that I know of. Now if you'll excuse me, I really need a nap."

Both twins' mouths dropped open.

"Really?" Sapph asked. "A nap?"

"Yes, really. I don't feel well. As you just pointed out, Guardians get sick when they leave."

"True, but how can you sleep at a time like this?" Pearl stared at her as if she'd grown two heads.

"I can sleep because I'm really tired." Once again, Jade turned away.

"Wait." Sapphire grabbed her arm. "At least tell us where you disappeared to."

"I had to go searching for your cousin Di. I found her and brought her home. End of story." Even though it wasn't, she hoped this would at least discourage the twins from peppering her with questions.

The two younger girls exchanged looks.

"Okay," Sapphire finally said. "I'm guessing you don't want to talk about it."

"No. I want to sleep."

"But aren't you even a tiny bit curious to find out what's going on?" Pearl persisted. "I mean, Libby's going to be here and everything. Most of us have never met her."

Stunned again, Jade took care not to show it. As far as she knew, Libby had never attended a Burnett family meeting. Or even been inside Burnett House. At the realization, she felt ashamed. For far too long, this town—and her family—had treated Libby as if she truly was some sort of beast. That needed to change.

"I'm sure we'll find out at the meeting." Jade gently pushed them out of her way. Refusing to overthink this, Jade knew she had to rest if she wanted to be even remotely coherent later that night.

Once in her room, she kicked off her shoes and sat down on the edge of her bed. Praying a bit of rest would be all she needed to feel better, she took a deep breath. Fully clothed, she let herself fall back onto the comforter. In less than five minutes, she was fast asleep.

Her cell phone ringing woke her some time later. Groggy, she reached for it on the nightstand and answered, figuring it would be her mother with a time-to-get-up call.

"Jade?" The deep sexy drawl made her inner wolf whimper. Rance. "Did I wake you?"

"No," she lied, grateful that the room no longer seemed to be spinning. "Not at all. What's up?"

Though she no doubt sounded half-asleep, thankfully, he let it go. "Your mother called and said you had something to tell me. She said it was important and couldn't wait."

Mystified, Jade struggled to clear her admittedly still-sleep-fogged mind. "I'm sorry, but I have no idea what she meant," she admitted. Then, horrified, she remembered Amber asking her if she was pregnant. For the love of... "Um, I'll see if I can find out tonight at dinner."

"Dinner. About that..."

Her heart skipped a beat. Was he about to ask her out? "We have a family meeting tonight," she said, before he could. She sat up and swallowed. Mercifully, she no longer felt as if she could upend the contents of her stomach at any moment.

"Another one? How often do you have those things?"

"I didn't call this one," she admitted. "Libby did. It seems she's upset. I'm reasonably sure it's because she needed something while I was in Fae."

"Unless she somehow knows you agreed to let me meet her," he said, amusement coloring his voice.

Would she ever get used to his sexy Southern accent? Still, despite Libby asking to meet him, Jade wasn't ready yet. She wasn't sure exactly why, just a gut feeling she had. When the right time came, she'd know. Then she'd set up the meeting.

"I hadn't thought of that," she said. "Libby does often know things ahead of time."

"Well, when you see her tonight, why don't you ask her? I'd be interested to know the answer."

She murmured something she hoped sounded like agreement and hung up. Though she really just wanted to lie back down and pull the blanket over her head, she forced herself to get up and head into the shower.

Whatever the reason for Libby calling the meeting, she figured it would be about her.

One hour later, cleaned up, hair dried, makeup applied, Jade put on one of her maxi dresses. She felt the need to wear something other than her usual jeans and T-shirt.

When she got downstairs, she saw that almost everyone in the family had apparently experienced the same urge to dress up a little. Everyone except the twins, who wore what they always did—unrelenting black for Pearl and psychedelic seventies attire for Sapph.

The instant Jade walked into the dining room, all conversation ceased. Silent, everyone openly stared, their faces wearing mixed expressions ranging from trepidation to curiosity. As usual, the buffet had been set up and the table groaned under the weight of the food. Briefly, Jade felt thankful that tonight her mother and grandmother hadn't gotten together and made their usual inedible offering. Instead, she had that delicious lasagna to look forward to.

A quick glance around showed that Auntie Em and Di were the only ones not in attendance. Of course, Jade imagined they had a lot to catch up on.

"Oh, come on now," Jade said, looking around. "This is ridiculous. You all need to act normally."

"Do we?" Her grandmother studied her, one perfectly painted eyebrow raised. "Do you have any idea how unusual this is?"

"That Libby would call a family meeting," Amber clarified, in case Jade missed the point.

"I'm aware Libby doesn't call meetings very often…"

"Never," Amber interrupted.

Jade stifled a huge sigh. "Fine, Libby never calls meetings. Thank you, Mom. Now if you'll just let me continue, have you ever considered this might not be a bad thing? I imagine it gets very lonely for her sometimes, living all by herself in a cabin up by the lake. Maybe, just maybe, she's making the time to get to know the family from where her Guardians come."

Though Amber gave a loud snort and rolled her eyes, several others were murmuring among themselves and smiling.

"I'd really like that," Sapphire enthused. "I think Libby is the most interesting thing about this town."

"Me, too," Pearl put in, not to be outdone by her twin.

The doorbell rang, the deep melodic chimes echoing through the house. Since no one in the family bothered ringing the bell, this had the effect of causing everyone to go silent again. A few people—probably the teenage crowd—tittered nervously.

Jade started toward the door. "I'll get it," she announced, in case it wasn't obvious.

Opening the heavy oak door, she found Libby standing on the front porch. Looking small and determined and somewhat nervous. And as beautiful and otherworldly as ever.

"How did you get here?" Jade asked.

"I called a cab."

Giving in to impulse, Jade hugged her. "Come on in."

Instead of stepping into the foyer, Libby tilted her head, her amethyst gaze searching Jade's face. "That's the second time you've done that. Why?"

Jade smiled. "Because both times you looked like you could use a hug. Now come on in and meet the family."

Though she stepped forward, Libby gripped Jade's arm. "Stay close to me. There is something I want to talk to you about."

As they walked into the dining room, once again an awkward silence fell. Ignoring this, Jade led Libby over to her mother since they already knew each other.

"Amber." Libby held out her hand gracefully. "It's good to see you again."

Even though both women knew this wasn't true, Amber of course responded in kind. "You look wonderful, dear Libby. Having my daughter as your Guardian has obviously agreed with you."

Knowing her mother, Jade suspected that this last statement was meant as a slight dig. If so, Libby didn't acknowledge it as such. Instead, she beamed at Amber. "You did a good job raising Jade, my dear Amber. She and I have become really close."

Trying to not bask in the glow from the compliment, Jade finally decided what the heck. She liked Libby, liked her a lot. As a matter of fact, Jade actually considered Libby her best friend.

Expression sour, Amber excused herself to go check on something in the kitchen.

"Who do you want to meet next?" Jade asked.

"Where's your cousin Diamond?" Libby asked, scanning the room. "I know you rescued her."

"I don't know. I'd assumed she'd be here with her mother. Libby, I have a question. When I found her, she seemed fine. Yet you told me she was in danger. Grave danger."

Libby shook her head. "Did you not see what Prince Cai has done? He's using his Fae powers to ensnare young women and then he gets them with child. Did Diamond not believe she carried the heir to the kingdom?"

"Yes. Yes, she did." Jade took a deep breath. "Libby, you should know I nearly got sick from that trip. Apparently your other realm theory wasn't true."

Regarding her, Libby sighed. "I'm sorry."

Pearl and Sapphire approached, each of them regarding Libby with blatant curiosity shining in their matching green eyes.

Clearly, this conversation would have to continue later.

"Girls, this is Libby. Libby, these are my younger sisters, Sapphire and Pearl."

Pearl dropped into a half curtsy, as if meeting a queen. Sapphire shook her head and rolled her eyes at her sister. "Stop acting like a dork," she said, holding out her hand instead. "Pleased to meet you, Miss Libby."

The two shook hands, Libby's expression impassive, though a ghost of a smile tugged at her lips. Pearl hung back, her eyes wide, apparently still in awe.

"Come here," Libby said, holding out her hand for Pearl to shake. Instead, Pearl rushed over and wrapped her arms around Libby and gave her a quick hug. When Pearl stepped away, her face had turned pink with embarrassment.

"She takes after you, I see," Libby said, smiling. "Please, Jade, introduce me to the rest of your family."

The rest of the evening passed pleasantly, despite everyone's worrying. Once they got used to the idea that Libby didn't want to be treated like royalty, the family relaxed.

When Jade gave the signal to eat, everyone mobbed the buffet line exactly as they always did.

Jade and Libby joined the end of the line, where Jade whispered to Libby how she'd lucked out. "Normally, I'd have to give you a warning about the deceptive appearance and terrible taste of whatever concoction Amber and Opal had cooked up. This time, Opal made lasagna, without any help from my mother. This means it will be delicious."

Libby frowned. "Does that mean Amber is the bad cook?"

"Shhh." Furtively, Jade glanced around. "We never say that out loud. But I think it has to be her. When Opal cooks alone, we all discourage Amber from making anything on her own."

"Did she tonight?

"I don't know. Hopefully not. If she did, believe me, you'll know."

"And no one has any idea which one it is?" Libby asked. At Jade's nod, she shook her head. "That's easy enough to fix. Amber," she called out. "Jade has been telling me what a marvelous cook you are. Please, which one of these delectable dishes is yours?"

Amber smiled coyly. "You'll have to try them all and then guess."

"Yes, be surprised like the rest of us," Jade murmured. "Don't think you're getting off that easily."

Libby laughed. "I guess it will be kind of fun to find out."

"That's one way to put it."

Later, after the meal had been eaten and the buffet cleared away, Libby said her goodbyes. Jade walked her outside, full and content. This had been a very enjoyable evening.

"Walk with me?" Libby asked, smiling fondly.

"Sure." Inhaling the pine scented air, Jade smiled back.

Once they were away from the house, Libby stopped. "There's something I need to discuss with you," she said.

"Ah, the real reason you called this meeting?"

One perfectly arched brow rose. "I called this meeting because I wanted to meet your family. I'm tired of living like an outcast, all alone with no one to talk to. I'm glad I did."

"I'm glad, too." Jade squeezed Libby's arm.

"Yes, well… There is someone else I'd like to meet."

Jade waited. When Libby didn't continue, she smiled. "Who?"

"Your man."

"I don't have a man." Jade's response came automatically. "But I'm guessing you mean Rance Sleighter."

"Yes. Ever since he arrived in town, I've been troubled."

Now this was news. "Can you use your psychic ability to find out why?"

"I've tried." Sadness tinged Libby's voice. "But for whatever reason, the answer remains hidden from me."

"I see." Jade considered, and then decided to tell Libby the truth. "He wants to meet you, too. As a matter of fact, I agreed to let him if he accompanied me to the land of the Fae. He did, so we need to set something up."

Pleased, Libby clapped her hands. "So he senses it, too."

"Senses what?"

"A connection of some sort. I haven't been able to determine exactly what kind."

A connection. Swallowing back mingled feelings of dismay and, yes, jealousy, Jade nodded. "Well, I guess you'll find out soon enough. When would you like me to bring him by?"

"Day after tomorrow." Libby's instant reply made Jade feel even worse. "How about the day after tomorrow, around one. Can you do that?"

Jade pretended to have to think. "You know I've been away from Dogs Off Leash awhile, right?"

"Yes, and I also know you frequently leave during the day." Libby broke up her firm tone with a soft smile. Clearly, she had given Jade an order.

Relenting, Jade smiled back. "Fine. We'll be there at one. Day after tomorrow."

The phone call woke him before dawn. Seeing Eve's father Jim's number on the caller ID made his stomach drop and he could barely catch his breath enough to answer.

"I've called in hospice." Jim's broken voice brought an answering lump to Rance's throat. "She's in a lot of pain and is in and out of consciousness."

It took a moment before Rance could make his voice work. "How long?" he asked, choking on the words.

"It's difficult to predict. But the doctors say it won't be long now. Days or weeks, at the most."

Brushing at his suddenly stinging eyes, Rance promised to get there as soon as he could. He called the airline, changed his plane reservation and packed his suitcase. As he was about to go down to the front desk to check out, his phone rang again.

This time, when he saw Jim's caller ID, he nearly fell to his knees. Not even thirty minutes had passed. Surely...

"Jim? What's going on?"

"She's gone," the other man said, openly weeping. "No need for you to rush home now."

Rance dropped his phone. Somehow, he made it to the bed, where he curled up and let the waves of sorrow carry him away.

The next few hours passed in a blur. At some point, he got up, grabbed the car keys and drove out to the lake. Parking near the cliffs, he climbed from the car, shedding his clothing as he went. For the first time he could remember, he didn't take his camera with him. For now, maybe forever, telling stories with photographs no longer appealed.

Near the edge, he lifted his face to the sky and silently screamed out his sorrow before stepping off the edge.

Chapter 10

On the way down, Rance changed. Swiftly, violently, his body going from man to Drakkor so fast the pain nearly made him lose consciousness. But the shock of hitting the cold water revived him. As dragon, he dove as deep as his grief, frightening fish and turtles with his powerful wings churning water out of his way.

And he swam. Moving through the lake until his muscles screamed with exhaustion. And still he kept on. Though it was dangerous to be in his dragon form in broad daylight, he knew if he kept to the depths of the lake, he'd be all right. No one would see him. At this point, he didn't really care if someone did.

He'd hoped the utter silence would soothe the shrieking inside his head. Instead, he could see nothing but Eve. Eve as she'd been when healthy and whole, a sweet, active child always ready to laugh and play.

Gone. Her light snuffed out by one gust, a single blow of fate.

He snarled, surfacing once for air, before going under again. Usually, even in his dragon form, he kept the man foremost, aware of the need to think rationally. Not now. Not this time. This time, the dragon would own the body.

Giving himself over to his beast, he pushed all human thoughts and emotions away, concentrating on the here and now. Only by living in the moment—that very instant of time, frame by frame—could he keep the pain from spiraling into madness.

Hours passed. Or so he thought. When he finally let the conscious part of him resurface, he saw he'd fed and fed well. Sated, the dragon coasted just below the surface, occasionally raising his massive head to eye the nearly full moon shining in the midnight sky.

A day, then. He dove once more, needing to escape the world a little longer, grateful for the quiet and grace of the underwater world.

And then...he saw her. A flash of scales, the water too murky to see more. Was this Libby? With a swirl of muddy water, she disappeared. Normally, he would have pursued her, but not today. Not with so much sorrow coiling inside him, ensnaring him as tightly as a fisherman's net.

So he spun in the opposite direction. Swimming fast, he took off toward the cliffs, hoping she wouldn't follow.

When he reached his destination, he turned. And found himself alone.

Launching himself out of the lake, he flew, shaking off the water, his body aching. Aware his shaky wings would not support a long flight, he landed at the top of the cliff, dropping to the ground and initiating the change back to man.

This time, the shape-shifting went slower, the change equally painful, but more excruciating as it took longer.

Still dripping, he found his clothes and stepped back into his jeans. On the way back to the hotel, he almost stopped at a package store and purchased a bottle of Patrón and a shot glass, but at the last moment, he continued on past. While he definitely didn't want to think at all tonight, he knew if he took that slippery slope, he might lose himself forever.

The next morning, head aching not from a killer hangover, but from a night of tossing and turning and what promised to be the beginning of a terrible migraine, Rance headed to Burnett House.

Despite the knowledge that he needed food and coffee, in that order, he didn't want to take the time to stop for breakfast. In fact, he probably needed Advil more than anything, but if he wanted to catch Jade, he'd have to hurry. He left his motel just as the sun came over the horizon. He knew Jade would head into her doggy day care early to meet the folks dropping off their dogs before going to work. He wanted to make sure and catch her before she left.

After all, he needed to tell her goodbye. He wasn't sure where he'd go after Eve's funeral or what he'd do. No doubt he'd eventually find another hot story to pursue the hell out of. Distraction might be the one thing that would help him with the pain. But right now, he didn't have the heart to touch his camera. Good photographs were nothing without joy.

He parked the Mustang around the corner at the bottom of the hill, eyeing the stately house Jade's family called home. As he started to walk toward the steps leading to the front door, he spied Jade on the porch, watching him.

The sight of her made his aching heart skip a beat. Heartened, he picked up his pace. More than anything, he wished he could share his sorrow with her, but old habits died hard. He'd always been a private man and kept his emotions close to the vest.

As a result, he'd do his best to pretend nothing had changed in his world.

"Good morning," he said, climbing the steps up onto

the front porch and trying to inhale deeply. Even breathing hurt. He needed to focus on something else, something good. "The scent of fresh hot coffee has to be the best thing about mornings." He tried for a smile. "I figured you always take yours out here in the morning. Am I right?"

She shrugged and took a sip. "Whenever possible. Of course, I can't in the winter. But the rest of the year, yes. Since it's covered, I can even sit here when it's raining, as long as the wind's not blowing."

Since his throat had closed up again and he didn't want to risk speaking, he simply nodded. The movement didn't help his pounding head any.

Jade eyed him. "Would you like to join me? Mind you, I have to be leaving for work soon so I don't have very long."

Grateful for small kindnesses, he took a seat next to her on the swing. The fragrant aroma of hot coffee made his mouth water.

"Would you like a cup?" she asked, noticing the way his gaze wandered to her mug.

"Sure. If it's not too much trouble."

"It's not." Pushing to her feet, she set her coffee down on a decorative barrel that apparently served as a table. "Do you take cream and sugar or black?"

"Black, please."

After she vanished inside, he kicked back a little, sending the swing in motion. There were very few places on this earth where he felt at peace, and this porch in the front of this house on the hill had been, oddly enough, one of them. He couldn't help but wonder how much of that had to do with Jade.

A moment later she returned with his coffee. She moved with a sensual grace, apparently completely unaware of her allure. Still desperate for distraction, he tried to imagine her other form; no doubt whatever kind of beast she became, she would retain her human beauty. At the thought, his own dragon stirred inside him. Sluggish, yes, due to the amount of pain building up behind his eyes.

"Thank you." Accepting the mug, he drank gratefully, squinting bleary-eyed at the rising sun. At least the sting of his burned tongue helped him stop thinking about how much he'd like to twine his fingers in Jade's thick silver hair and pull her close for a kiss. Sort of.

Realizing he was only looking for a distraction, anything to help him not think about Eve, he knew he needed to focus if he wanted to keep from breaking down. "I didn't have time to get caffeinated before I came here."

Nodding, she retrieved her own coffee. "Are you all right?" she asked. "You look a little green around the gills."

He started to nod, but stopped himself. "Not really. I've only had a few migraines in my lifetime, but whatever is building up in my head promises to be the mother of all headaches."

"I'm sorry. Maybe the coffee will help."

"Perhaps it will," he said, taking a sip.

"I thought possibly you were hungover. Like you might have gotten bored and hit up the pub last night."

Which would be the last thing he'd do, but she didn't know that. Right now, with his entire body aching with pain, he knew how easily it would be to drink himself into oblivion and just stay there. "No."

She watched him, her emerald eyes wiser than her years. "Why are you here, Rance? What do you need?"

You. The thought came unbidden, the sudden sureness of it making him drink too deeply of the hot coffee than he should have. He winced as he burned his mouth, swallowing quickly and trying not to choke as the pain continued down his throat.

One cough turned into two. Eyes watering, he looked away.

"Are you all right?"

No.

Wordlessly nodding, he swallowed again before forcing his gaze up to her face.

Glancing at her watch, she stood. "Well, I've got to go. I have to be at work before the first drop-offs of the day."

Pushing to his feet, he drained the last of his coffee and put the cup down on the railing. "I need to meet Libby as soon as possible. There are photographs I've got to take." Damned if he'd give up on his promise to Eve, just because she was... No. He forced his mind to go blank. He'd get through this, do what he had to do and then go to a place that would never again be his home.

"I haven't forgotten." Wrinkling her nose, Jade smiled at him, unaware of his inner turmoil. Despite Libby asking her to bring him around at one o'clock, she still wasn't ready. "I'm just trying to work out the logistics." Stalling, true. But something still felt...off.

"I've got to leave town," he blurted, trying like hell to keep his tone ordinary, normal. Though Jim had yet to relay funeral arrangements, he figured it would be in the next two or three days.

Her smile slowly disappeared. "Oh. When?"

"I'm not sure yet," he lied, not wanting to tell her he'd already purchased a ticket for a flight. "Soon. Within the next few days."

"I see." She looked away. "Libby had asked me to set up a meeting with you. You leaving changes things."

"Why?" he asked, crossing his arms. "That shouldn't make any difference." Slowly she nodded. He got the distinct impression he wasn't the only one withholding information.

"It shouldn't be that difficult. Just let her know and take me there. Unless you think she'd have objections..." He knew his saying this was like offering her an escape route, a way to avoid keeping the promise she'd made. While he knew he really shouldn't care, to his surprise he did. Taking a picture of a lake monster had been Eve's last request. Damned if he wouldn't do his best to honor it, even if the idea of using his camera still made him feel nauseated.

"No, she won't object. Like I said, she actually wants to meet you. She even set up a time. But Libby wants the meeting to be while she's in her human form, and you...from what you said about taking photographs, I think you want to meet her after she shape-shifts into the lake creature."

He couldn't say why, but this statement flummoxed him. Still, that aching, pain-filled part of him felt glad of the distraction. "Wait a minute. Libby's a shape-shifter?"

Jade stared back at him, her own shock plain on her beautiful face. "Surely you didn't think she stayed as a lake creature all the time?"

Put that way, he could see why she was astonished.

"I didn't really think about it," he admitted, his mind whirling. "Part of me supposed if humans could be nothing more than human, then a lake beast could do the same."

While Jade didn't outright laugh at him, he could see her struggling not to. To his shock, he felt an answering smile tug at the corners of his mouth.

"I'd like to meet her as human, then," he said.

She grinned. "Would you?"

"Yes. If that's what she wants to do, then I'm game. I'd like to ask her permission to take her picture and I don't imagine we'd be able to talk if I met her in her lake beast form."

Now Jade snickered. "No, you wouldn't. Just like when you or I change into our beasts. We can't talk to humans, only to our own kind."

"Of course not." He sighed. "I got it. Now, when can you set it up?"

"Give me a minute." Pulling out her phone, she sent a text. "She suggested a time and I want to make sure it's still all right." A moment later, a chime indicated an answer. "Okay. Libby says you can meet her later today."

As distractions went, this was a doozy. He nodded. "Fine. What time?"

Again she glanced at her watch, still watching him closely, as if she somehow sensed something was wrong. Unsmiling, she finally answered, "How about one o'clock? We can grab a bite to eat on the way."

As if he could eat. He took a deep breath as another wave of grief threatened to overwhelm him. Though meeting Libby would, under any other circumstances, be awesome, the encounter had come too late. Eve was gone.

Because his eyes stung, he looked away. He tried to clear a suddenly aching thoat. All he could think about was how on earth he'd manage to fill the time until then. He had to stay busy; otherwise, the hours would stretch out bleakly, ready to constantly remind him of his loss. And he wasn't sure he was strong enough to face it alone. Not just yet.

"Sounds good." He thought he succeeded at sounding casual. Normal. As if his entire world hadn't been shattered. Keep busy, that would be the key. "Jade, do you mind if I hang out with you until then? I can help at your doggy day care if you need an extra set of hands."

Tilting her head, she eyed him. "Sure. Let me go inside and grab a few things and then we'll go."

Out of reflex, he pulled his cell phone out of his pocket, meaning to call Eve and tell her he was finally going to meet a lake monster. With the phone in his hand, he froze. Eve could no longer take his calls.

Dizzy, he closed his eyes, riding out the wave of grief. Maybe in time, he'd grow used to this. Maybe not. But right now, the loss felt all too fresh, and way too painful.

"Are you all right?" Jade touched his arm. Somehow, without intending to, he turned into her and pulled her close, holding on as tightly as if his life depended on it.

"Yes," he managed. "Just fine." Even though, clearly, he was not.

Jade stood still, holding him and letting him take what he needed from her embrace. He blinked several times to clear his eyes, cleared his throat and, finally, when he thought he had himself under control, released her.

"Do you want to talk about it?" she asked, her gaze searching his face.

He shook his head and averted his eyes. "No. I don't."

"Come on," she said, taking his arm and steering him toward her car. "If you want to talk, you can tell me about it on the way to DOL."

Instead, he sat in the front seat as she drove, doing his best to pretend all was just hunky-dory in his world.

"Are you able to tell me what kind of shape-shifter Libby is?" he asked. He wasn't sure why the idea of a lake monster being a shape-shifter had never occurred to him, but now that he knew it to be truth, he sort of felt let down.

Suddenly he realized if he took photos, he had no idea what he would do with them now that Eve was no longer able to see them.

Jade flashed him an arch look. "No kind of shape-shifter I've ever heard of. Sorry."

Normally a mystery of this kind would have intrigued him. As it went, every time his mind went to Eve being gone, he circled it back around to Libby and her Guardian.

When they pulled up at Dogs Off Leash, two parked cars already waited for them.

Jade groaned. "Dang it. I'm not *that* late. Come on, you can help me get the place opened up."

The next several hours thankfully passed quickly. While he'd never had a dog, he'd always liked them, and he shepherded dogs from playrooms to outdoor play areas, where Jade's employees supervised their activities. The dogs seemed to like him, which he considered good, since occasionally other animals sensed his inner dragon and were put off.

Once the steady stream of clients dropping off their pets slowed down, Jade told Sue that she and Rance would be leaving for a few hours. Surprised, Rance glanced at his watch. It was barely ten.

Curious, he followed Jade out to her car. Once she'd backed from the drive, she glanced at him. "I think we need to talk before we visit Libby."

Usually, hearing those words from a woman was enough to make him shut down. This time, rather from sheer exhaustion or the basic human need to have someone understand his pain, he nodded.

Still, now that she'd given him the opening, he couldn't seem to find the right words.

"Don't shut me out." Her soft voice nearly undid him. Even so, he must have opened his mouth five separate times before closing it.

She took a turnoff that promised to lead to a camping area. When she pulled off the road, killed the engine and turned to face him with an expectant look on her face, he shook his head.

"I can tell you're hurting, and from more than just a headache. I can help," she promised, placing her graceful, long-fingered hand on his arm. "Please let me help."

"Why?" he finally asked. "You barely know me."

At his words, hurt flashed in her eyes. "True, though I feel like I've known you forever. I…care about you, Rance."

"Do you?" The harshness of his tone came from pain. Leaning toward her, he slanted his mouth across hers. At first, she didn't move, and then she opened her mouth to his.

Passion exploded. He let himself fall into the kiss, suddenly craving her, needing more than anything to feel alive. To push away his sorrow with passion.

"Wait." Even though her breathing sounded as ragged as his, she pulled away. "I don't think…"

"Don't." He claimed her lips again. "We don't need to think at all."

Again, desire blazed between them. And for a few moments, rational thought banished; nothing existed but the drugging taste of her, the sensual warmth of her curves under his hands.

"No." This time, she shoved him. Hard. "I get that you want me. As I want you. But I know pain when I see it. Tell me what's happened."

And just like that, reality came crashing down. Eve, her small flame snuffed out far too soon.

Something must have shown in his face. Jade watched him, the sympathy in her green eyes almost more than he could bear. "You aren't alone," she said.

"Ah, but I am." The bitterness in his voice made him sound like a stranger. "You see, I was like you once. Always seeing the bright side of things. Once upon a time, I also believed in fairy tales."

He maintained eye contact as he spoke, as if he could make her understand by the intensity of his gaze. "I was married, with a family. I had a wife, Violet. She had a little girl from her previous marriage. Even though she and her ex-husband shared custody, I loved my stepdaughter as much as if she was my own." Swallowing hard, he hoped like hell he could get through the words without his voice breaking.

Past tense. He couldn't help but realize that now he used past tense for all of them.

"I lost my wife to a horrible illness." True to form, his voice cracked. He'd been expecting it, so he simply swallowed and went on. "Two years ago. I didn't even get sick. At all. Yet it took her within hours. She died in my arms." He looked down. "So fast and so deadly."

She leaned over, wrapping him in her arms. "I'm sorry. Was your wife a shape-shifter, too?"

"Yes. Her ex-husband, Jim, he was human. Their

daughter... Eve is—was—a halfling. Half human, half..." He stopped just short of revealing what he couldn't. His species. "Half-shifter," he said.

Nodding, Jade continued to hold him. She held on with just the right amount of strength, and he almost let himself clutch on to her as if he would never let her go.

Almost.

But he knew better. There were no such things as fairy tales or happy endings.

"What about your stepdaughter?" Jade finally asked. "Eve. Is she all right?"

He lifted his head, squared his shoulders and looked her right in the eyes. "I'm not looking for your pity."

"And I'm not offering it," she shot right back. "I want to know what happened to her."

"Oh, she got sick, too. And while she didn't die as quickly as her mother did, her illness ran a different course in her small body." He took a deep breath. Halflings were different than full-blooded shifters. Ordinary diseases could kill them. Ordinary diseases were not supposed to be able to harm shifters. But this one, targeting only his kind, had. Very few of the Drakkor women had been able to survive this illness.

"When she was four, she was diagnosed with leukemia," he continued, unable to tell her the entire truth. "She had a bone marrow transplant and it seemed like she'd recover. She got too thin and weak, but she was a fighter." He took a deep breath. "But she somehow managed to keep her joy. Her smile could light up a room." Still, though he continued to use past tense, he couldn't quite bring himself to say the words. Not yet. Maybe not ever.

"After your wife died, who took care of her?"

Simple questions. Those he could answer. "Her father, my wife's ex. His name is Jim. He's a good guy. I've considered myself damn lucky that he let me see her.

"Anyway." He forced himself to continue. "I made my little girl a promise before she died. She wanted me to take a picture of a lake creature."

For the first time ever he wondered if Eve had wanted this because maybe, somewhere deep inside of her, she understood her heritage. Being human, Jim didn't know that when Eve got older she'd begin to demonstrate the ability to shape-shift. And Rance would be the one to teach her. Or he would have been.

Another wave of grief hit him. He took a moment, willing it to recede.

"I'm sorry." Jade smoothed her hand across his cheek. "You lost her, didn't you? Was this recent?"

He blinked, startled to realize she'd wiped away a tear he hadn't even realized he'd shed. "Yes. Yesterday."

Suddenly he couldn't breathe. Opening the car door, he got out. "Jade, she died before I could keep my promise. She was five years old." His voice shook with the pain he tried to conceal. "And part of me died with her."

Chapter 11

Watching Rance stride away, into the woods, Jade wasn't sure if she should follow or simply give him space. His grief had been palpable, his unconscious need for comfort making her entire spirit ache.

Tears stung the backs of her eyes. The magnitude of his loss made her wonder how he was even able to function.

Had she been wrong to push him away? She wanted him, in every way a woman could desire a man. She always had, from the very first moment she'd seen him in her dreams. But for her, she knew when she and Rance came together, it would have to be more than a rushed coupling in the car.

Still, everything inside her screamed that she'd made a mistake. Her body throbbed with need. They were both adults. And he'd experienced a horrible, life-changing loss. But he'd need comfort more than pleasure. How could she deny him this, when she cared so much about him?

He'd be leaving town soon. The knowledge squeezed her heart even harder. She had to wonder, now that he no longer had a reason to meet Libby, why he still wanted to. And she doubted he'd come back. No doubt he'd want distraction instead, to help him deal with his grief. He was a photojournalist, after all. He'd chase another story, somewhere exotic, something dangerous and fast-paced that would take his mind off his loss.

Restless, she got out of the car. No sign of Rance. Deciding, she took off in the direction he'd gone.

She found him on a bluff high above the lake. He stood near the edge of the cliff, and for one heart-stopping moment she thought he contemplated jumping. But then hearing her, he turned his head, his expression carefully blank. "I'm sorry. I'm not very good company right now."

"That's understandable." She went to him, wrapping her arms around him from the back and just holding on tight. He let her, though she got a sense he wasn't exactly participating, more or less tolerating her offer of comfort.

Again, she couldn't blame him. She couldn't even imagine how awful it would feel to lose a child. Placing her cheek against his back, she hoped whatever comfort she could offer would help him.

Again, as always happened whenever they touched, something changed. A peculiar catch in his breath told her he was no longer dwelling on his loss.

When he turned to face her, the intensity of his hooded gaze told her what he wanted. And she...this time she wanted it, too.

"Yes," she whispered, right before his mouth claimed hers. "Yes."

He touched her then, touched her in a way that made her feel both infinitely precious and desirable. Using his long and elegant fingers, he stoked the flames of her passion, until she quivered with need. When she went to return the favor, he captured her hands with his. "Not yet," he told her. "Let me see you without your clothes."

Nearly panting with desire, she nodded. "As long as I can see *you*." His wicked smile was answer enough.

They undressed each other, him moving so slowly and deliberately she thought he might be trying to drive her insane. He laughed at the impatient look she gave him, quieting her protests with another deep and passionate kiss.

When finally she stood naked before him, wearing only her necklace and trying not to shiver in the crisp autumn air, he let his gaze roam over her, dark and full of heat. She'd never really understood how someone could *swoon*, but now…now she did.

"It's your turn," she whispered, her tongue thick in her throat. "Let me undress you." Not surprised to see her hands were shaking, she tugged at his shirt, wanting to taste the bare skin of his chest. He helped her, pulling his T-shirt over his head. She gasped at the sight of an ornate dragon tattoo, long tail and elegant head wrapping around his heart. "I love it," she breathed, spreading her fingers over the design, loving his sleek skin and hard muscles.

"I want more," she declared, and she undid his belt, aching to touch the bulge of his arousal.

Again he stopped her, catching her wrists. "Not yet," he growled. "I want to make this last. We need to slow down."

Frustrated, she shook her head. "I don't want *slow*. I want fast. Hard and heavy, hot and deep."

His answering groan told her how her words affected him. Still, he continued to hold her hands. "Patience, little one."

Then, releasing her, he eased his zipper down over his engorged body as she watched.

Nearly panting, she tried to contain her need. Seeing this, he gave her a wolfish smile before pulling her to him.

The instant their bodies came together, she shuddered in ecstasy. When he slid his fingers into her moist heat, her tenuous grip on control shattered.

"Now," she urged, arching her body into him as she rode his hand. "I need you inside me. Right. Now."

When he finally entered her, the raw act of his possession brought tears to her eyes. The hard length of him filled her, and as her body clenched around him and she shuddered in ecstasy, he began to move.

With each stroke, electrifying waves of desire throbbed through her, searing her. For the first time in her life, Jade realized every sense had been awakened, and she let herself surrender to the storm, riding him to the height of passion, crying out with each deep stroke.

She let her hands explore his body, greedy to know the feel of him under her fingers. His muscular hardness, the perfect counterpoint to her curves.

And then, when her release came, pure and explosive, she shattered into a million stars as the world spun. He continued to push into her as her body clenched around him. And then, a few seconds later, he poured his essence into her.

Making her realize she'd somehow completely forgotten about protection. She'd never been this careless.

As a shifter, she didn't have to worry about disease. However, she made babies the same way as everyone else.

Horrified, she attempted to push him away. He held on, his expression fierce. "No regrets," he said, the rasp of his voice skittering along her sensitive skin.

"We didn't use protection."

At her words, he closed his eyes and bowed his head. "I'm sorry. We both got carried away."

Truth didn't make it better. She swallowed. When he placed a soft kiss on her cheek, she exhaled.

"What's done is done. If anything comes of this…"

"It won't," she interrupted, furious for no reason. "You have enough to worry about right now. Come on, let's get back to town. I'm sure you have some packing to do before you leave."

"Leave? No. I've got to go meet Libby first."

She'd started shaking her head before he'd finished speaking. Not only did Libby's wise gaze see everything, but Jade wasn't sure how the cloud of grief enveloping him would affect her charge. "Not today. We'll reschedule. You go back to Texas and take care of Eve's service. We aren't going anywhere. We'll be here when you get back."

Though he nodded, something flickered in his eyes, making her realize he hadn't intended on returning. Hurt stabbed her, which she promptly shoved deep inside, refusing to allow herself to feel regret. Reflexively, she fingered her necklace, though this time the simple action didn't give her any comfort.

Turning her back to him, she got dressed. Judging from the sounds behind her, he did the same. "Are you ready?" she asked, jingling her car keys in her hand.

"Yes."

Odd how such a simple word could break her heart.

The instant he stepped out of the airport terminal in Houston, Rance felt the heat and humidity like a slap in the face. Ignoring this, he caught the airport shuttle to long-term parking, where he'd left his pickup truck just one short week ago.

It seemed like it had been much longer.

As soon as he reached his vehicle, he paid the lot attendant and turned the AC up to blasting. While autumn had come full swing to upstate New York, here in Houston summer kept a stubborn grip on the weather. His dashboard thermometer read ninety-four.

Habit almost made him take the exit for the hospital. Instead, realizing Eve's body would have been removed already, he drove to Jim's house off the South Freeway.

The instant he pulled up in front, he knew something was wrong. The house appeared deserted, and not just recently. Rance counted back, trying to calculate the last time he'd been here. It had been well over a month; once Eve had gone to the hospital, he'd visited her there instead.

Worried, he tried the door anyway. Locked. He walked across the lawn, through the unkempt landscaping, and tried to peer in the dirty front window. As he'd suspected, the house was completely empty.

"Can I help you?"

Turning, Rance saw the next-door neighbor, a feisty elderly woman named Betty. She stood in her driveway, hands on bony hips, and watched him.

"Hi, Betty." He knew remembering her name would count for a lot. "I'm looking for Jim."

She continued to eye him suspiciously. "Are you a bill collector?"

"Nope. Just a friend."

"Hmmph. You mustn't be much of one. Jim moved out the night before last. He took off in the middle of the night, which usually means he owes money to somebody. I only know because I couldn't sleep that night and I was sitting out on my front porch."

This sounded so unlike the Jim he knew that Rance could only stare. "I just talked to him yesterday," he managed. "He didn't mention anything about this."

She cocked her gray head, her ancient eyes wise. "I don't imagine he's proud about what he's done. Especially pulling that sick little girl out of the hospital. Listen, when you see him, don't mention that I told you. I don't think he knows anyone saw him."

Immediately, Rance took a step toward her. "He had his daughter here? Eve?"

"He sure did. And that child was so ill she could hardly walk. He carried her from his truck to the house, and then back out again. He must have already moved the furniture, or he didn't have much to begin with. What he brought out that night didn't even fill up his truck bed."

Rance's head spun. Maybe the old woman had grown delusional. That would be the only explanation. Especially since he'd talked to Jim and, as far as he knew, Eve hadn't left Texas Children's Hospital before she died.

"Thank you, ma'am," he said, heading back toward his truck. Once inside, he called Jim. The call went straight to voice mail.

What the...? Suppressing the urge to kick something, Rance headed to the small apartment he rented. Halfway there, he changed his mind and drove to the hospital instead.

After parking, he strode into the lobby of the west tower, bracing himself for the antiseptic smell he'd always associate with illness. He rode the elevator to the ninth floor, aware he'd been a regular enough visitor that several of the nurses would recognize him.

In fact, the first nurse he saw appeared shocked to see him. "Mr. Sleighter? You do know Eve isn't here any longer, right?"

He found her choice of words interesting. Also the fact that she hadn't offered him her sympathy for his loss.

"Yes. Do you know where she is now?"

Slowly, the heavyset woman shook her head. "Her father took her out against the advice of her doctor. Simply picked her up and carried her off. We called security, the police and CPS, but he was gone before anyone could reach him. That little girl needs around the clock medical care. I'm really afraid she'll die if she doesn't get it."

Rance tended to agree with her. "Maybe Jim—her father—transferred her to another hospital?"

If anything, that statement made her look even more distressed. "Not in Houston. MD Anderson Cancer Center would refer a pediatric patient here, I believe."

Thanking her, he headed back to his truck. What the hell was Jim up to? Rance couldn't help but wonder if, in his worry and fear for his daughter, the other man had completely lost his mind.

Rance knew he had to find them, before it was too late and Eve really was dead.

Once Rance had driven off in the rental car, Jade prepared to settle back into her ordinary life. The one she'd been craving ever since he'd disrupted it with his arrival.

Yet something—everything—had changed. Not just because they'd shared amazing, transcendent, extraordinary lovemaking, but something else. She wasn't sure what exactly. She only knew she felt like a different person these days.

She went to Libby to see if the other woman had insight. When she'd postponed Libby and Rance's meeting, Jade had only said he was called out of town unexpectedly. It had taken her a full three days to be able to even say the reason why he'd left without breaking into tears.

"I don't understand how I can miss him so much," Jade said, pacing. "We barely knew each other. A few kisses don't make a relationship." No way did she plan to mention that she and Rance had shared a lot more than a few kisses.

To her surprise, Libby laughed. "Don't they? Stop pacing and sit down. I'll make a pot of tea and some snacks so we can eat while we discuss."

Jade nodded. Too restless to sit, she followed her friend into the kitchen. "Let me help."

"Okay. You put the teakettle on while I make little sandwiches."

The two worked together in silent harmony, which soothed Jade somewhat, to her surprise. When the kettle whistled, she poured the boiling water into a heavy china pot and added tea bags. Today they were having Irish breakfast tea and some kind of finger sandwiches.

"What are those?" Jade asked, eyeing the yellow-gold filling.

"Pimento cheese," Libby answered. "It's a Southern thing. Your man would probably like them."

Her man. A stab of wild longing filled her. Instantly, she pushed it away. "He's not my anything."

"Except you wish he was," Libby responded.

Since that was pretty much truth, Jade only shrugged and followed Libby outside. They settled in their usual chairs on the deck with the lake glinting in the distance. The vibrant colors of the changing leaves never failed to fill Jade with pleasure. Except this time, she found herself wishing Rance had stuck around long enough to see their glory in the peak of autumn.

Libby poured the tea, just as she always did, and Jade eyed the sandwiches, not sure if they looked appetizing or not. The bright yellow color didn't make it look edible.

"Just go ahead and try one."

Why not? Jade grabbed a napkin and reached for the smallest sandwich. If she didn't like it, surely she could manage to choke it down.

To her surprise, it tasted good. The creamy texture melted in her mouth. She had a second, then a third, finally looking up to see Libby grinning at her as she ate.

"I love these," Jade admitted. "Pimento cheese, you say?" At Libby's nod, she snagged another one. "You need to give me the recipe. I'll make them the next time there's a family meeting."

Helping herself to a couple of her own, Libby beamed and took her own bite. "How's your cousin?" she asked, after she'd swallowed.

"Diamond?" Jade shrugged. "I haven't seen her. But I

haven't heard anything, either, so that's good. My mother would tell me if Auntie Em was having a problem with her."

"And the baby? She's doing well in her pregnancy? I only ask as sometimes carrying those Fae children can be...tricky."

"Tricky?"

Slowly, Libby nodded. "There are inherent dangers in carrying a halfling-cross between Pack and Fae. Mostly health issues concerning the mother."

Jade hadn't considered that Di might be in danger. And with her stubborn nature... "I'll have to make a point to stop in and check on her."

"Please do that." Libby sipped her tea. "And keep me posted. Your family is the only connection I have left to the outside world."

Unable to keep from helping herself to another sandwich, Jade made a mental note to stop by and check on Diamond on the way home.

"Now that we've gotten that out of the way, tell me what's new with Rance."

"I don't know." Jade tried not to show her despair. "I haven't heard from him at all. Not one phone call or text or Tweet. It's like he's dropped off the face of the earth."

"Well, it's only been a week."

Jade sighed. "True. But I'd think he'd have at least checked in by now." Of course, he'd only do that if he ever intended on seeing her again. The way things stood now, she had a sneaking suspicion he had no plans to return to Forestwood.

Libby made a sympathetic face and took another sip of her tea. "I hope he's all right."

"Me, too." She told Libby about his stepdaughter, omitting only their lovemaking in the woods. "He's really grieving."

"Oh, my goodness." Libby set down her teacup. "That's heartbreaking. She was five years old, you say?"

"Yes. Cancer."

"So she isn't a halfling, then?" Libby sighed.

"She is. Her mother was a shifter and her father human, I believe. It's all so sad."

When Jade glanced up, she realized Libby sat ramrod straight, staring ahead with that otherworldly expression that meant she'd gone into a trance. Jade knew better than to disturb her, so she continued sipping her tea. There were two halves of the sandwiches left and she decided to take one and leave the other in case Libby wanted it.

Slipping into a trance felt similar to slipping beneath the cool surface of the lake. One minute, she was talking to Jade, the next—nothing but the deep, dark waters of her abilities.

Danger lurked close by. Though startled, Libby couldn't shake the sense of formless unease. She tried not to panic, aware her abilities could manifest themselves at any time.

But they did not. Instead, she twisted and turned, feeling blind and trapped in fear.

It had been decades since she'd felt darkness looming over her. Worse, for the first time in her life, her ability to foresee the future apparently failed her. Try as she might, she saw nothing. She had no idea from where the threat came.

She remembered what Jade had told her of her cousin Diamond and the Fae prince's child. Could this be the source? Or was she looking in the wrong direction? She considered Jade's man, Rance Sleighter, and wondered if she'd been wrong to feel a sense of kinship with one who'd left Forestwood without a second look.

Or could it be something else, something completely unrelated? It bothered her more that she had no idea.

The only thing she did know was that she needed to find out before something truly awful happened. Something like the last time she'd had this feeling and her entire family had been wiped out.

Terror zinged along her nerve endings, in her blood and in her veins. She blinked, suddenly desperate to break the trance. Trying to do so felt like trying to swim to the surface while tied to a large rock on the lake floor.

When she finally came to, her chest rose and fell from her rapid breathing.

"Are you all right?" Jade leaned close, her expression concerned.

"I think so," Libby managed, still panting. Then, as she tried to collect herself, she shook her head. "No. No, I'm not." Because the ominous dark cloud still overshadowed her, ruining the day.

Danger. She knew the feeling to be true. There could have been a hundred possible reasons, but her past told her there always was only one. She just needed to locate the source so she could put her anxiety to rest.

"Libby?" Jade again, placing her slender hand over Libby's. "Do you need to lie down and rest?"

Did she? Confused, Libby tried to think. Though she'd wanted to put this off for a bit longer, maybe the time had come to enlist Jade's help. Once Jade knew how to connect with her to strengthen Libby's powers, the two could join forces to vanquish whatever evil may threaten.

Of course, Jade had to agree. Libby wasn't sure she would, but she had nothing to lose by asking.

She placed her other hand over Jade's. "There's something I need to discuss with you," she began.

Rance tried every place Jim had mentioned. In two days of driving all around Houston, he learned Jim had quit his job, closed out all his bank accounts and virtually disappeared. Desperate to find him, Rance enlisted one of his buddies at the Houston Police Department. He learned Jim hadn't used a single credit card since the day he'd called to tell Rance that Eve had died.

Why had he done this? And why had he lied? Rance couldn't figure out what Jim would have to gain by claiming Eve was dead. Surely he'd understand such news would bring Rance back to Texas to attend her funeral.

Unless… The idea seemed so startling, Rance nearly discredited it. Unless Jim had wanted Rance to search for him.

If so, Jim certainly hadn't made it easy. Short of hiring a private investigator, Rance had run out of options. Still, he spent another week searching for his friend and Eve. No one—not Jim's friends nor his family—had any idea where he and his little girl had gone.

Rance spent close to two hours with Jim's sister, Chloe. The older woman had dementia and resided in a memory care facility. Though he remembered Jim talking about her, Rance had never actually met Chloe before. But since Jim had said she had occasional moments of clarity, Rance figured it was worth a shot.

The instant Chloe met him, she decided Rance was her husband, a man who'd died ten years earlier. She chided him for taking so long to come and get her and insisted he take her out of this place right now.

Twenty minutes in, Rance knew she had no idea where her brother might have gone. Heck, he wasn't sure she even knew she had a brother.

When the caretakers started rounding up the residents for lunch, Rance figured he'd slip away. But Chloe insisted he stay and eat with her, so he walked with her to the dining room. She introduced him to every person they passed as her husband, Hal. Guessing it'd be easier to play along, Rance smiled and nodded.

As soon as the food was delivered to the table, Rance

excused himself. Despite the fact that he didn't even know Chloe, his chest tightened when she begged him to be sure to come back.

When he hurried toward the door, his heart heavy, one of the attendants stopped him. "It's all right," she said. "Ten minutes from now, she won't even remember you being here."

Since that knowledge only made him feel marginally better, he nodded and waited for her to punch the code so he could get out.

Now what? He got in his truck and turned the ignition. He couldn't think of a single place he might have missed looking for clues.

He'd tried talking to Eve's doctor, but neither he nor his staff would tell Rance anything, citing privacy laws. During a second visit to the hospital, no one knew anything more than the fact that Jim had taken his daughter without saying why.

Which meant Rance was at a dead end. Nine days of searching and he was no closer at finding Jim and Eve than he'd been on day one.

And then he remembered something Jade had said. One of Libby's abilities was the gift of being able to find anything or anyone who has gone missing.

Did he really believe this? Was such a crazy idea worth a shot?

Uncertainty pulled him in every direction. He wasn't sure how much time he had, but then he realized he truly didn't know Eve's condition. If Jim had been willing to lie about his own daughter's death, then every time Rance had spoken to him by phone might have been false. Was she even critical or had her disease gone into remission? The latter would be the best explanation Rance could figure out for Jim pulling her out of the hospital.

Unwilling to admit defeat, Rance spent another three

days repeating the rounds he'd made before, with the same results. No sign of Jim or Eve. Not even a clue to tell Rance where they might have gone.

Finally, it came down to two choices. Rance could stay in Houston and continue spinning his wheels. Or he could fly back to New York and drive up to Forestwood to talk to Libby.

After all, Jade had promised he could meet her. Jade. At the thought, his heart squeezed and his breath hitched. He'd missed her, so much more than he'd imagined. With so much going on, every time he'd thought of her, he'd pushed it away.

He eyed his phone. He hadn't made a single attempt to contact Jade. Granted, he'd only been gone just under two weeks. He doubted she'd even expect him to touch base so soon during such a trying time. However, they'd made love and he'd taken off. She probably was furious with him and he didn't blame her. He'd been so focused on his own situation, he hadn't been very considerate toward her. At all.

In the end, he decided he'd simply go to her. Her and Libby both. The situation was too important to attempt to discuss over the phone. Plus, truth be told, he wanted to see Jade again.

Chapter 12

A s Jade waited for Libby to speak, guessing the other woman had seen something important in her vision, once again her thoughts drifted to Rance. Maybe she should call him, just to see how he was doing. But no, everything inside her rebelled at the thought. If he didn't care enough to keep her involved in what was going on with his life, then so be it. After all, he couldn't have made it any clearer. No phone calls or texts... nothing. It shocked her how much it hurt. Even worse, despite all that, she couldn't stop missing him.

"You're thinking of him again," Libby observed, her voice soft and her smile gentle. "You always get a dreamy look when you do."

And her necklace always grew warm. Keeping that fact to herself, Jade blushed. "Sorry. I'm a sap. What is it you need to tell me?"

"I need your help."

"That's new," Jade joked. "Usually I'm the one asking

you for help. Of course I'll do whatever you need me to do. Just say the word."

Libby didn't even crack a smile. "Perhaps you'd better find out what it is before you agree."

"I trust you. Without hesitation."

Libby's eyes misted over. "Thank you. I have a sense of terrible danger, but I don't know the origin. For once, my visions have failed me. This is why I need your assistance."

Though puzzled, Jade nodded. "Of course. I'm not sure what I can do, but I'll help in any way I can."

Libby hugged her. "If I could have had a daughter, I'd wish for one exactly like you."

Now Jade had to wipe at her eyes. While she loved her own mother, she often felt closer to Libby. "We have a wonderful bond."

"Yes, we do." Though Libby stepped away, her normally serene expression had gone serious, her face lined with worry. "I've had many Guardians over the years, but I have to say you're one of my favorites. Only one time have I asked any other what I'm about to ask of you. And then, it happened by accident as I wasn't even aware such a thing was possible." She took a deep breath. "Please know you are free to decline, of course, and there will be no ill feelings."

This was interesting. "Now I'm intrigued. Please continue."

Libby smiled, though her gaze remained serious. "There is a process where we can form a...bond. Apparently, this ability is unique only to me. My own form of magic, if you will."

"What kind of a bond?"

"Sort of a temporary joining of minds. This allows us to share each other's thoughts. And abilities. When we each wanted, we could see the world through the other's eyes."

"Ouch." Jade had to shake her head. "I'll be honest. That

makes my skin crawl. I don't want anyone—even you—inside my head."

"It could never happen without your agreement."

"You mean it's like a switch? It can be turned on and off? Or would you be there all the time?"

"More controlled," Libby's soft voice continued. "Your switch analogy is perfect. Most of the time, each of us would go about our normal lives, without anyone else aware of our thoughts or our actions."

Still puzzled, Jade crossed her arms. "But why? Why would you ask me to do such a thing?"

"Good question." Libby sighed. "Partly to help you if you needed it. I think it's the only way to keep you from becoming ill if you travel to Fae again. And partly for my own selfish reasons. I'll be blunt, Jade. I'm getting old. I've been alone the majority of my long life. I have regrets—a lot of them."

"I know, and I'm sorry." Jade swallowed. "I'm hoping we can change that."

Libby gave her a sad smile. "While I appreciate the thought, some things never change. Before I die, I'd like to experience life through the eyes of someone young and vital. A person I trust. Someone like you."

Stunned, Jade couldn't find the right words. "Die?"

"One never knows when their time on earth is over."

Libby's cryptic words didn't help. Still, she couldn't wrap her mind around what Libby asked of her. The idea of allowing Libby—anyone, actually—inside her head made her feel ill.

Part of her felt selfish, denying Libby. As she opened her mouth to say no, she couldn't deny the overwhelming feeling of relief.

"There would be a value to you also, of course," Libby said, before Jade could speak. "When something necessitated it, like grave danger, we could join forces and amp up my abilities," Libby continued. "Because of my strong sense that we are standing on the edge of a precipice, I have a feeling this will be sooner rather than later."

Still dubious, Jade shook her head. "But you'd be able to see through my eyes. That's really invasive. Even though I trust you, I don't think that I can…"

"I understand." Libby got up and walked to the edge of the patio, where she gripped the rail. Back to Jade, she stared out over the lake, her expression inscrutable.

"Please don't be upset," Jade began.

"I'm not. I told you that you can refuse. No hard feelings, I assure you." But still, Libby wouldn't look at her. "Jade, I want you to understand I have had a strong premonition. Whatever is about to happen isn't going to be good, I can tell."

"As long as you aren't going to die, I think we'll survive."

At this, Libby met her gaze. "I have no plans to die, dear one. I'm reasonably sure that whatever I feel doesn't involve my death. I just have a sense of time rushing past." Libby bowed her head, but not before Jade saw the sheen of unshed tears in the older woman's violet eyes.

"I…" Jade didn't know what to say. Suddenly, she saw quite clearly what she'd simply taken for granted. Forestwood—and especially the Burnett family—had treated Libby like an outcast, as if she truly was a beast rather than a living, breathing person.

"Why don't you take some time to think about it?" Libby said, clearly mistaking Jade's hesitation. "And please, if you don't mind, stop in on the way home and visit your cousin. I need to make sure this feeling isn't due to something that's going on with her and her unborn child."

The words sent a chill through Jade. "I will." She felt uncomfortable, more uneasy than she'd ever been around Libby, even the first time they'd met, though part of it was her own guilt over the way Libby had been treated. No wonder she was lonely. "I should be going. I'll stop and see her and then I'll give you a call and let you know."

"Sounds perfect." Still Libby didn't turn. "I'll wait to hear from you. Oh, and, Jade? Tell no one about this conversation. Not even your family or Rance. There are some secrets that can never be shared."

After murmuring her agreement, Jade left. She felt strangely hollow as she walked to her car. Once all this was over, she was going to make sure things changed. Libby would no longer be an outcast. Jade would make sure of that.

But this request? Was Libby right? Would doing this enable Jade to leave the immediate vicinity without becoming ill?

Climbing inside her vehicle, she sat in the driver's seat and tried to think. Never once had a vision that Libby had seen in a trance been wrong. If she said danger lurked around the corner, it did. And if Libby was worried enough to ask Jade to help... How could Jade refuse? Not once had her charge asked anything of her, yet she'd given without complaint every single time Jade had asked for her assistance.

And all Libby really wanted to do was protect the people Jade loved. If Libby wanted to experience the world through Jade's eyes, why not? As long as it was a temporary thing, and Jade could stop it if she felt uncomfortable.

In the end, Jade had to decide if she trusted Libby. Unequivocally, the answer was yes.

Just like that, Jade realized she'd been wrong. Selfish even. She got out of the car and headed back inside to tell Libby she'd changed her mind.

Tapping lightly on the door, she stepped inside without waiting for Libby to invite her. Which was good, because Libby still sat on the back patio, staring out over the lake. She looked up as Jade approached, her slight frown smoothing out into her normally serene expression. "Did you forget something?"

"No." Jade took a deep breath. "I've decided I want to help you any way I can. Tell me what I need to do."

"Are you sure?"

"Yes. Absolutely."

Libby smiled. "Thank you. You don't need to do anything. Your agreement is enough. Merely touch your necklace and say my name out loud three times when there's something you think I should see. I'll join you then."

"Will anyone else be able to tell?" Jade shifted her weight from foot to foot. "I guess I'm asking if it will be obvious that you're somehow inside my head?"

This made Libby laugh. Rising, she crossed to Jade and swiftly hugged her. "No one will know unless you tell them."

"What about—" Jade swallowed "—if I decide I want privacy. Once you're there, I mean. Is there a way for me to…?"

"Order me to leave?"

"Yes."

Libby chuckled as she hugged her once again. "All you have to do is say so and I'll be gone. I promise never to overstay my welcome."

Relieved, Jade hugged her back. "What now?"

"Would you mind checking on your cousin? I'm worried about her. I don't actually have a valid reason, but I'd feel better if you'd stop in and see her."

"Sure." Checking her watch, Jade nodded. "I can run by there right now. I don't have to be back at Dogs Off Leash for a couple more hours, until closing time."

"All right. Remember, if you need me, you only have to say my name."

"I'm sure Di is fine," Jade muttered to herself as she

drove to her aunt's house. Alone in the car, she found herself missing Rance with a visceral ache. The passion that had flared between them had burned hot and fast. It hadn't yet burned out.

At least for her.

She wondered if Di had heard from Prince Cai, the father of her unborn child. Somehow, she doubted it. If not, she knew her cousin wouldn't take it well.

Jade couldn't blame her. She struggled hourly with the desire to call Rance. But she didn't, mainly because she'd already called twice to check on him, and he hadn't answered or returned her call.

Maybe she and Di would finally have something in common, after all. She could certainly commiserate if Di hadn't seen hide nor hair of Cai. Of course, Jade privately thought the Fae prince was pompous and narcissistic. All he had going for him were his good looks.

Ah, but Rance had seemed different. She remembered how he'd reacted to her temporary fascination with the handsome Fae prince and how she'd thought he had to feel something for her. Clearly, she'd been wrong.

Twelve days had passed since he left to return to Texas to bury his stepdaughter. Almost two weeks, and despite the fact that she'd given him her cell phone number, he hadn't bothered to call or text.

Again the familiar ache. She'd been foolish to think a man like him could ever be interested in her. He roamed the world, reporting on interesting events while she was a small-town, stuck-at-home sort of woman.

Her cell phone rang, making her jump. For one tiny second she allowed herself to hope…but no. Caller ID showed her mother.

"Hi, Mom. I'm on my way to see…"

"There's an emergency," her mother cut her off. "How quickly can you make it to the hospital in Kingston?"

"Are you okay? What's happened?"

"It's your cousin Diamond. I'm here with my sister. We've just learned two of her friends are also pregnant and are seriously ill. Now it appears that whatever they have, Di has it, too. They're both in comas on life support. As of right now, Di is still conscious. But we're afraid it won't be long until she's in the same state as them."

"What?" Stunned, Jade pulled into a gas station, aware she needed to focus on the phone call rather than drive. "What's causing this? What do the doctors have to say?"

"No one seems to know anything." Amber's voice contained both anger and sorrow. "Emerald is beside herself. She and I have talked and, besides Libby, she knows you're the only one who can help. Please, how quickly can you get here?"

Help? "I'm on my way," Jade answered. "Um, Mom? I can lend support, but you do know there's little else I can do, right?"

"Oh, that's where you're wrong, my darling daughter." The grim note in Amber's tone sent a chill down Jade's spine. "With Libby's assistance, you have a few other abilities as Guardian. So far Libby has never saw fit to bestow them on any of her Guardians. Maybe this time, she will."

A chill snaked down Jade's spine. How did her mother know? On top of that, she'd just given her word to Libby not to reveal anything they'd just discussed.

"Where did you hear this, Mother?" Wary, Jade rubbed her suddenly aching temples.

Silence. Then Amber sighed. "There are books. I swear, I put them away and forgot about them, until recently. That's why I've never shared them with you. These books are a history of our family's role as Guardian, dating back to when Libby first appeared in Forestwood Lake."

"Mother, I've been Guardian for nine years. How could

you not have given me them then?" Stunned and outraged, Jade gripped her phone.

When Amber spoke again, her tone was quieter. "Honestly, I didn't think about it. I only skimmed through them once or twice, several years before you took over as Guardian."

Deep breaths. "Ok. I'll try to let that go, Mom. I will never understand, but I can't dwell on it now."

"You're right and I'm sorry." Amber sighed. "But you and Libby seemed so close, while she and I... well, we never clicked. I was jealous, so I put the books away. I know I was childish, but over time, I convinced myself that you didn't need to see them. The two of you clearly connected, so I assumed you had everything under control already."

"Under control?" A wave of sadness choked Jade up. She gave herself a mental shake. "This is crazy."

"I agree. I hope you can forgive me someday, but right now we've got bigger worries," Amber said, a pleading note in her voice. "Your cousin is in trouble. I need you to use your extra abilities to save Di."

Aware of her oath, Jade swallowed. Libby hadn't granted her any healing powers. Heck, she didn't even think Libby could heal herself.

"Well, if I have any extra abilities, Libby hasn't told me about them." Unless she counted Libby being able to go inside her head. Jade didn't think that would count as an ability.

"Call her," Amber urged. "Tell her what's going on and ask her if you can help. I know Libby and there's no way she'd simply let Di and her unborn child die."

Jade agreed. Anything she could do to help her cousin, she'd try. "I'll do that," she said, and ended the call. Maybe this—whatever it might be—might be what had caused Libby's sense of foreboding.

Phoning Libby, she outlined the situation in a few short sentences.

"Oh, honey," Libby commiserated when Jade had finished. "You know—and so does Amber—that my abilities don't include healing."

"Yes, but from what my mother is saying, the doctors are stumped. They have no idea what this illness is or what's causing it. Can't you use your abilities for that?"

"I hadn't thought of that. But it's possible. Actually, since we've become linked together, I should be able to do it through you. Go to the hospital, visit your cousin and then call my name. Together, we'll figure something out."

Relief flooding her, Jade agreed and hung up. Then she headed toward the hospital, dialing Amber as she drove.

Eve. Knowing she still lived brought Rance a bit of relief. Not much, since he had no idea what the hell Jim was planning. Why the other man would take his seriously ill daughter out of the hospital, Rance couldn't fathom. He pictured her the last time he'd seen her, blue eyes too big in a wan face, valiantly trying to smile so he wouldn't look so worried. She'd told him so, telling him to stop it because he was scaring her.

When he'd learned she'd died, he'd thought he would die, too. But he'd shored up, braced himself and headed home for her funeral, only to learn she wasn't dead, after all.

Joy filled him at the knowledge Eve still lived, but for all he knew, she could be in mortal danger.

He missed her with a wild pain akin to the grief he'd felt when her mother had died. He wanted a drink, as badly as he ever had, and resisted the urge with every fiber of his being.

The craving for a drink never left him. Every beer commercial, or restaurant advertising its drink specials, made his mouth water. Still, he'd persevered, and he'd done it without attending a single meeting and declaring to anyone that he was an alcoholic. Of course, he wasn't foolish enough to completely rule out the possibility that he would need to find a group of supporters someday, but he hadn't needed them yet.

Now, though, he sorely did. This was almost worse—not knowing if Eve was dead or alive, safe or sick and terrified, ate away at him the way a glass of rotgut whiskey once had.

The Burnett family had taken over the hospital waiting room. The instant Jade walked in, Pearl and Sapphire ran to her. Grandma Opal had even brought Sam, Jade's grandfather. Due to his dementia, he hardly ever left his room and right now he appeared overwhelmed and confused.

"Where's Mom?" Jade asked the twins.

"In with Di," Pearl answered, her expression solemn, her huge green eyes welling with tears. "The doctors are acting like she's going to die." The plea in her voice broke Jade's heart.

"It's okay, honey." Jade shook her head. "Doctors don't know everything. I'll go see what I can find out. Which way?"

In unison, they both pointed past the nurses' station toward a set of double doors. "She's in there. Room 12."

"Thank you." Nodding a greeting at the rest of the family, Jade pushed her way through the doors. She straightened her spine and tried to prepare herself for the worst.

Right before she reached Room 12, she remembered Libby's instructions. Grasping her necklace, she took a deep breath. "Libby," she said out loud, feeling slightly foolish. "Libby, Libby." She waited a second or two, to see if she felt any different. When she didn't, she then had to wonder how she'd know if it worked.

It did. Libby's voice, very faint, inside her head.

"Okay," Jade muttered.

You don't have to speak out loud, Libby told her.

"Thanks." Jade took a deep breath and entered the room.

Both Amber and Emerald looked up when she entered. Amber had her arm around her sister and judging from their reddened eyes and blotchy complexions, they'd both been crying.

Di lay unconscious in the hospital bed, hooked up to three different machines.

"Where is Uncle Jack?" Jade asked. Di had been the apple of her father's eye ever since she'd been born.

"He went outside to get a breath of fresh air," Amber answered.

Em nodded. "This is very difficult for him," she said. She appeared to have aged ten years overnight. The anguish in her expression tore at Jade's heart.

"I imagine it's difficult for you, too." Jade went to her aunt and hugged her. "Have the doctors come up with anything concrete?"

"No. Only that it's somehow related to the baby. Di has two other friends who are pregnant. They're both here in ICU with the exact same symptoms."

Jade swallowed hard. "What I have to ask you is very important. Has Di told you anything about the father of her baby?"

"No." Em's mouth tightened. "All she would say was that he was a prince. Sure he is. Some prince. Dumps her once he's gotten her with child."

"What about the other girls? Do you know who the fathers of their babies are?"

For a second, Em appeared startled. "No, I can't say I do. When they each got pregnant in such a short time, so close to each other, this seemed to cause a rift in their friendship. I would have thought they'd have grown closer, so they could lean on one another through the pregnancy. Instead, they're not even speaking."

Jade wondered if she should tell her aunt about Cai. From the deepest portion of her mind, Libby asked her to wait. She wanted to touch Di and see if she could use her powers to see what exactly might be wrong with her.

Moving carefully, Jade went to her cousin's bedside. She reached out and placed her hand on Di's swollen belly, hoping Libby would be able to tell something.

If she did, Libby didn't comment on it.

"I'd like to see the other two girls as well," Jade said. "Do you mind if I talk to their parents?"

"Not at all. They're both here in the ICU. The nurses claim only family can visit, but they don't seem too strict in enforcing it."

"I'll say I'm family," Jade said.

"Why do you want to talk to them?" Amber's sharp gaze missed nothing. "Do you think this has something to do with their illness?"

"I don't know," Jade answered honestly. "But it doesn't hurt to explore every angle."

The scenes in both of the other rooms felt eerily similar. Comatose patient, worried and grieving parents. Once Jade explained who she was, both of the other girls' mothers said something similar to what Emerald had said. Their daughter refused to talk much about the father of their baby and would only say he was a prince.

Which might explain the sudden friction between them. Judging from what Jade had seen, Prince Cai apparently took pleasure in charming women, making them believe they were special and then, once he'd impregnated them, sending them away.

Not to mention carrying a Fae child requires a special kind of fortitude, Libby informed her. *These changelings are different than your ordinary halfling. Not only are they able to shape-shift, but they have Fae magic. They're able to accelerate their gestation period if they decide to be born sooner. This can wreak havoc on the mother's body.*

"But both Di and her friends are shifters," Jade argued silently. "Only a silver bullet or fire can kill us, you know that."

I didn't say they'd die. But what use is a ruined body? Once the child is through with them, they might wish they were dead. Your cousin—and her friends—might be left in a vegetative state.

Jade shuddered. "This is why you spoke of danger."

Libby considered. When she finally answered, she sounded as puzzled as she had before. *I don't know. This is part of it, for sure. Right now, that doesn't matter. We've got to concentrate on saving both mother and child. While I can't actually heal, there's got to be some way to stop this.*

Jade kind of liked this method of communication. Like talking on a cell phone, only inside her head.

"Any ideas as to how we accomplish that?" she asked.

Unfortunately, I do. It won't be easy. And you can't do it today. You'll need to go home, regain your strength and wait. I'll make everything clear later.

Though Jade wasn't a fan of mysterious statements, she had no choice. She headed in to tell her mother and aunt goodbye, promising she was working with Libby on a solution.

And then, feeling even more bereft, she headed back to Dogs Off Leash to help close up for the day.

Chapter 13

Aware he'd reached a dead end in his search for Eve and Jim, Rance once again suppressed the urge to head into a bar and drown his sorrows. Instead, he headed back to Bush Intercontinental and purchased a plane ticket to fly back to New York. From there, he'd rent a car and drive up to Forestwood. He missed Jade, an admission that shocked him to his core. Yet he couldn't deny that through this entire ordeal, he'd found himself turning to tell Jade something, only to find she wasn't there. Several times a day, he'd grabbed his phone with the intention of calling her, but he'd held back. Intellectually, he knew the last thing he needed at a time like this was a relationship. Emotionally? Well, that was another story entirely.

Part of him craved Jade the way he'd once craved alcohol. He felt as if he'd known her his entire life, even though he knew better. He also knew a woman like her would never want a life with a man as broken and battered as him. Once the sizzling attraction between them had faded into the easy comfort of a stable relationship, she'd see him—*really* see him—without the haze of desire.

Which meant he'd have to give up his desire for her the same way he'd quit drinking. Cold turkey, all at once, without stopping to think too much about it.

Not yet, though. He needed her to help him find Eve.

The flight from Bush Intercontinental to LaGuardia passed uneventfully. He tried to sleep, but he alternated between worrying about Eve and picturing Jade's reaction when she saw him. He had to admit his heart took a skip or two when he let himself imagine her greeting him with a sexy grin and a kiss. Hell, he even indulged in a fantasy or two of a much more passionate reaction.

Jade. Again and again, it came back to the way she made him feel. If he wasn't so cynical, he'd allow himself to believe she might be able to heal him, which was sheer and utter foolishness. Seeing her once more could be dangerous. The last thing he ever wanted to do was hurt her. Yet he had no choice but to give in to the longing he tried to ignore, and contact Jade again. He needed Libby's help if he wanted to save Eve. As for himself, he knew he was beyond saving. Any hurt that came his way out of this, he had no doubt it'd be well-deserved.

The rental car he'd reserved was ready. This time, he hadn't been able to get a sporty Mustang and had to settle for a run-of-the-mill sedan. Driving out of the city went like it always did—traffic and horns and crazy taxi drivers. But once he'd left civilization behind, things calmed down. Heading northwest, he relaxed and prepared to enjoy the drive.

The car rental agent had warned him the Catskills would be crowded this weekend as it apparently was prime fall foliage viewing time, or "leaf peeping" as she'd called it. Rance had to admit the color of the trees was pretty spectacular. Constantly, he itched to pull over to the side of the road and take some photos, but he didn't. He couldn't afford to waste any time. His stomach churned with both worry and fear, anticipation and, yes, desire.

The closer he drew to Forestwood, the more impatient he grew for the sight of Jade's beautiful face. Once he told her his stepdaughter had not died and filled her in on what had actually happened, he knew she'd promise to help any way she could. She had a big heart, which was one of the many things he liked about her. If only he could convince himself to consider her a friend rather than the woman he craved. If he could manage to keep his desire under control, he'd be all right. They'd both be better off.

Dusk had fallen by the time he reached Forestwood. The soft glow of the setting sun gave the town a surreal light, broken up only as the streetlights came on.

Checking the time, he headed straight to Dogs Off Leash. Jade would most likely still be there, meeting with her clients as they arrived to pick up their pets. If he was lucky, most of them would have come and gone and she'd have sent her employees home for the night. He hoped he'd catch her alone, locking up the place for the night.

As luck would have it, the sight of her lone green SUV in the parking lot kicked his heart rate up to high gear. He parked next to her, mentally rehearsing what he'd say, then decided the hell with it. He'd wing it.

Opening his car door, he got out and headed for the door. As he stepped inside, he smelled the strong odor of antiseptic, which he figured meant Jade was somewhere cleaning up. So he went in search of her. At the end of a hallway he saw her, back to him, while she scrubbed at something on a small platform.

The sound of his footsteps on the concrete floor alerted her and she turned. Shock and then a brief flash of pleasure lit up her face before she shut down. "Rance," she said, her voice faint. "I didn't know you were coming."

Then, despite telling himself he wouldn't, he went to her and pulled her into his arms. Covering her mouth with his, he kissed her as if he were starving—and maybe he was.

And she—she opened her mouth to him just as hungrily, wrapping her arms around him tight, as if she never wanted to let him go.

When they finally broke apart, both were breathing hard. Jade eyed him, her gaze glazed with desire. "You came back," she said, sounding as if she didn't really believe it. Lust surged through him at the joy in her voice and it took every ounce of willpower he possessed to keep himself leashed.

"Yes." Trying like hell not to show how much he ached to kiss her again, he smiled instead. "I came back. Jade, I have a lot to tell you and I'm going to need your assistance. Is there someplace we can go to talk?"

"Definitely," she instantly agreed, her color still high and her pupils remaining dilated. "And you should know I also have stuff to tell you. We're in a bit of a crisis here. I'm going to need your help, too."

"How about we talk over dinner," Jade suggested. "I don't know about you, but I've got to eat something."

He nodded. "Mother Earth's Café?"

Shaking her head, her smile contained both exhaustion and wickedness. "No, I'm thinking more like the Brew and Chew Pub."

The place where other guys had bought him drinks and Earl had told him why.

They got in his rental car.

"No Mustang this time?" she asked.

"Nope." Instead of starting the engine, he turned to face her. "Listen," he began. "Before we go there, there's something you should know." Briefly he outlined what he'd been told about her supposed magical powers and sex.

The grimness of her unsurprised expression told him she'd heard it all before. "They've been saying that about me ever since I became Guardian. Before that, when I was in school, they said it about my mother. That was worse. Don't pay any attention to those fools."

Partly relieved, he shook his head. "Your matter-of-fact acceptance doesn't make it any better."

"What am I supposed to do? I can't take on every single idiot who believes nonsense."

"You need a champion," he heard himself say, wincing at the old-timey word. "Someone to stick up for you."

Her wry smile made his heart ache. "That would be a full-time job. Now come on, let's go eat. If it makes you feel better, we can go to Mother Earth's. But after the day I've had, I really could use a drink."

About to punch the ignition button, he froze. But then, what was one more temptation in an endless parade of them? He'd manage. He always did.

Earl's grin stretched ear to ear when they walked into the pub. Instead of taking seats at the bar, Rance steered Jade toward a booth. Once they were seated, Earl hurried over with menus.

"Here you go," he said, still beaming. "Glad to see you two are finally taking things public."

About to respond, Rance closed his mouth. They had too much other craziness to deal with tonight without taking on Earl and his gossip.

"Do you know what you want?" Earl continued. Jade ordered a seasonal pumpkin beer and looked at Rance.

"Ginger ale," he said.

Nodding, the bartender hurried away.

"Ginger ale?" Jade asked.

"I'm an alcoholic," Rance told her. "I don't drink."

Immediately contrite, she squeezed his hand. "You

should have told me. We could have gone to Mother Earth's."

"No need. I had an excellent burger in here the other night. And you said you wanted a drink, so…"

"But…"

"Seriously, Jade. I can handle it. There are far worse things in this world." Covering her hand with his, he told her about Eve. "I can't find even the slightest trace of where Jim might have taken her."

Expression dazed, at first she didn't respond. "You mean she's not dead?"

"No."

She exhaled. "You're telling me your daughter is alive and you never once thought to call me and tell me that?"

Slowly, he nodded. "I'm sorry. I meant to. But I was searching for her, for Jim, and time got away from me."

"Save me from the excuses." Voice cold, she eyed him.

"Jade, I'm really—"

Lifting her hand to stop him, she looked away before gathering up her purse and standing. "I'm going to go."

"Wait. Please, I know you're mad at me," he said, reaching for her arm. "But a little girl's life is a stake. I'm desperate."

Though she shook off his attempt to grab her, she didn't leave. "This guy, her father. Do you and he get along?"

He nodded. "We always have. Jim got custody after Violet died and never minded sharing Eve with me."

"Despite that, Jim lied to you, for some reason known only to him. Then, knowing full well you'd travel to Houston for her funeral, he took off with her before you got there."

"That about sums it up."

She sat back down. "And you don't have any idea why?"

Before he could answer, Earl showed up with their drinks. "Did you decide on anything?"

"Yes." Jade grabbed her menu, opened it, before closing it with a snap. "I'd like a double cheeseburger with fries."

"Make that two," Rance said, relaxing slightly now that Earl had begun acting professionally.

"You got it."

After Earl sauntered away, Rance gave her an answer. "I have no idea why Jim would do such a thing. I don't know if he thinks he's trying to save Eve, or if she's in grave danger."

"That's crazy."

"It is. Now you see why I need Libby's help. You said she can find things. I need her to find my little girl."

A shadow crossed over her face. "Libby." Fingering her necklace, she spoke the name as if summoning the lake creature. "Yes, Libby is good at finding things. I'm sure Libby will help you out."

Relieved, though he wondered why Jade kept repeating Libby's name, he took a deep breath. "Now what's been going on with you? You said you had a lot to tell me."

"After all you've been going through, I almost hate to bother you," she began, just a trace of cynicism in her voice. "Except I'm really going to need your help, too. Di is in the hospital—ICU—and in danger of losing her life. Two of her pregnant girlfriends are in the same condition. We know Prince Cai is the father of all the babies. And Libby—" she took a deep breath "—Libby believes the babies are harming their own mothers in order to be born earlier."

Dumbfounded, he stared. "We need each other," he said. As he made the pronouncement, he had a fleeting sense of meaning much more than for a temporary situation.

Foolish, he told himself.

"Yet I don't know which is more urgent," Jade continued. "Finding Eve or helping Di."

Every fiber of his being wanted to answer, *Eve*. But actually, he didn't know the truth about her medical condition.

He knew she was ill, but realized every single telephone update he'd been given by Jim probably was a lie.

While Jade's cousin could actually be dying.

"We'll help Di first," he answered. "And then, as soon as we have an answer, promise me you'll take me to Libby to see if she can help me find Eve."

"I promise."

"What do you need me to do?" he asked, glad she hadn't yet pulled her hand away.

"No questions about what I just said?" She couldn't hide her relief. "I know it sounds pretty fantastical."

"Hey, the whole Fae thing is strange by itself. I don't doubt you—or Libby. Just tell me how I can help."

She gave him a lopsided smile. "We've got to go back to Fae and confront the prince. We need to find out if there's some way to stop this."

"No problem. If you want, let's go right after we eat. The sooner we can get this resolved, the quicker I can ask Libby to help me find Eve."

When the burgers arrived, Jade lit into hers with single-minded fervor. Not only did she need the protein for strength, but she didn't want to think about the actual reason *why* Rance had come back.

It certainly hadn't been because of her. As the undeniable knowledge washed over her, she pushed it away. Now was not the time to face the pain of knowing he hadn't returned for her, but only to enlist Libby's help in finding his stepdaughter.

What had she expected? He'd made no promises, no declarations of undying love.

Love. Did she love him? Stunned, Jade realized she might. She certainly could, given enough encouragement.

One thing at a time. Libby's voice, serene and calming, inside her head. *Not everything is right there, visible on the surface.*

Whatever that meant, it still made Jade feel better.

For some reason, it struck her as important that Rance never know how she felt. Therefore, she needed to act as casually as possible so her feelings didn't show.

"These are so good," she enthused to Rance. "Thanks for agreeing to come here."

Her over-the-top cheeriness must have been obvious to him, judging by the sidelong glance he gave her. Still, he merely nodded, intent on scarfing down his meal.

After they'd paid, she followed him back outside to his vehicle.

"If you don't mind, can we make this quick?" He swallowed hard. "I know I'm always asking for your help, but I'm desperate. I'm worried Eve's in danger."

Though she felt a quiver of uncertainty, she managed to remain firm. "I understand. Right now there are a lot of lives at risk." She glanced sideways at him, her green eyes unreadable. "I never mind helping you, you know that. But right now, this has to be my priority."

She was right.

"Where to?" he asked.

"The woods. We need to find the portal, the same one we used before."

He nodded and then started his engine. "Before we go, is this dangerous? If Fae children are killing the women who carry them, wouldn't Prince Cai know?"

"To be honest, I don't know. It could be. Of course, someone as arrogant as he might simply scoff at us. My intent is to ask him if he will help."

Rance nodded, but still made no move to back out of the parking space. "What if he won't? What do you intend to do then?"

"I don't know." Libby made a tsking sound inside her

head, momentarily distracting her. "I guess we'll have to take it one step at a time."

Rance waited another second, as if he thought she might have more to say. Then, when she didn't, he backed the car out and began to drive.

When they reached the place they'd parked last time, they got out of the car and headed into the forest.

"If I remember right, it's a bit of a hike," he said.

"It is," she agreed. "And please, if it looks like Prince Cai is trying to work a spell on me, grab my hand."

She felt a thrill of pleasure when he immediately captured her fingers with his. "How about we hold on to each other until we get back home? It'll be safer that way."

Hiking together through the forest hand in hand brought its own set of challenges, but she found she relished them. Together, they kept to the path until they couldn't, and then Rance went slightly ahead, pushing through and holding the underbrush back for her.

The sense of rightness that had settled inside her might have been foolish, but for now she wanted to nourish it. Somehow, she thought this feeling of unity with him gave her strength.

Finally, they arrived at the clearing where, earlier, they'd stashed their belongings. Since she'd merely left her purse in the trunk of his rental car, she watched as he reverently placed his camera bag on the ground using only one hand, since he continued to hold on to hers with the other. "Are you ever without that thing?" she asked, only half teasing.

"Not if I can help it." Expression serious, he took great care to ensure the bag was nestled snugly in the hollow tree truck. Once he'd done this, he removed his cell phone and some change as well as a small knife from his pockets, and placed them next to his camera bag. "Quite honestly, I haven't touched it since I was told Eve had died. Now that I know she's alive, I'm trying to get back to normal, though it's been a while since I've taken any shots. I really wish I could bring it with me to the land of the Fae. That place and those people are seriously photogenic. Are you absolutely certain I can't?"

"Yes." She smiled to take the sting from her words. "Others have tried. Sometimes they never saw again whatever metal item they'd tried to bring. I don't know where it goes, but it doesn't travel to Fae. Believe me, you're safer leaving it here."

Though Jade had spoken Libby's name while at the pub, thus allowing her to enter Jade's head and see the world through Jade's eyes, Libby wasn't certain if traveling through the portal would change that. She hoped not. She'd never ventured to the land of the Fae, though she admitted to being intensely curious to see it.

Truth be told, she'd never seen much beyond her childhood home and Forestwood.

They passed what looked like an ancient burial mound.

"There." Jade pointed. "See the two slender birch trees?"

"How can you be sure they're the right two?" Rance asked.

Jade grinned. "Can't you feel the energy?" At her words, Libby realized little pricks of energy danced along Jade's nerve endings, electrifying her skin.

"No," Rance groused. "I didn't last time, either."

Experiencing the world through Jade's eyes, along with her wild rush of emotions, could easily become addictive. Libby had lived so long in isolation that the sense of completion Rance's and Jade's linked hands brought made her feel happier than she had in decades. Seeing the way Jade watched Rance and experiencing the thrill that skittered up the younger woman's spine each time their gazes met reminded Libby of everything she'd missed out on in her long life.

Jade loved him. Stunned, Libby was still trying to process this far too intimate knowledge when Jade and Rance stepped through the portal with their fingers still entwined.

Together.

The icy shock of the void made Libby queasy. Even worse, it seemed they were free-falling, spinning through what could only be described as the complete absence of light. Jade's brief jag of terror brought a rush of adrenaline. The only thing solid was Rance and Jade held on to him for dear life. Libby couldn't blame her.

And then it all stopped.

Still clutching Rance's hand, Jade opened her eyes, affording Libby a scene of such stunning clarity of color it took her breath away.

"We're here," Jade announced. Libby noted neither she nor Rance seemed in any hurry to unlink their hands.

And then, through Jade's eyes, Libby looked around. A meadow of lush emerald grass lined with a rainbow of vibrant flowers stretched before them.

"And I assume we just start walking toward the palace?" Rance asked.

Before he'd even finished speaking, they heard hoofbeats in the distance, heading toward them.

"I guess the prince is coming to meet us earlier this time," Jade mused. "Let's just wait right here for him."

Libby couldn't wait to see this prince. Or any Fae, to be specific. As a child, she'd often heard stories of their exceptional beauty and blatant trickery.

"I don't think that's the prince." A note of warning sounded in Rance's voice and five black-clad riders thundered toward them.

"They see us and it's too late to take cover," Rance continued. "Get behind me. If it comes down to a fight, at least I can cover you."

"We have no weapon." Already Jade had searched the earth around them, looking for a stick or a rock or anything they could use. She knew, Libby realized, that something about the riders approaching them wasn't good.

"This is bad." Rance's words echoed Jade's thoughts. "All we can do is stand our ground. Get. Behind. Me. Now."

Jade ignored the order, moving up to stand at his side and squeezing his hand. "We face this together."

Libby marveled at their combined strength and show of support as they stood tall and faced the riders drawing near.

Mere yards from them, the group reined to a halt, their steeds kicking up grass and dirt and flowers. For the first time, Libby realized they wore hoods and some sort of veils over most of their faces. Only their eyes were visible.

"Are you human?" the leader asked.

Jade exhaled, noting from the timber of the voice that the leader was a female. While Libby pondered this, Jade stepped forward. "No, but we come from the human land. We're shape-shifters and we need to have a word with Prince Cai."

"Not until you speak with us." Holding out her hand, the woman in front helped Jade up on her horse behind her. A second later, another one of her group did the same with Rance.

While Libby wasn't too sure about the wisdom of this, she trusted Jade's instincts.

And they were off.

As they rode, Jade and Rance shared a look. This was not the way toward the palace.

"Where are you taking us?" Jade leaned forward, her mouth close to the leader's ear.

"To our lair."

The word did little to inspire confidence.

"Are you our prisoners?" Jade persisted.

The leader laughed. "No. Not at all. Everything will be explained once we are safe."

Safe from whom?

As the trees thickened, the riders slowed their pace. The quiet felt absolute, broken only by the horses' feet striking the damp earth and their labored breathing.

No one spoke, though Libby could tell Jade didn't feel any sort of tension between the members of the group. Rance, too, appeared relaxed, though his posture revealed he wasn't about to let his guard down.

The more time she spent with him, even if only through Jade's eyes, the more she liked him. Plus, the sense of familiarity grew stronger.

Ahead, a small earth mound rose between the trees. As they approached, Libby saw a large gate had been cut in the middle of the hill. Hidden from above by a canopy of leaves, no one would even know the entrance existed unless they knew to look for it.

The gate swung open. They rode through without stopping. Stunned, Jade and Rance exchanged glances. What had appeared to be only a mound from the outside was the entrance to an underground labyrinth, complete with lighted streets and small houses. Libby couldn't help but notice the close resemblance to what she imagined a medieval town would look like.

"Are you still with me?" Jade asked, whispering, which caused the rider to turn and peer quizzically at her.

Yes, Libby answered, though no one but Jade could hear her. *You don't need to speak out loud. If you want to talk to me, just think it and I can respond.*

The riders reined to a halt. Several people, small of stature with swarthy complexions, rushed to take the horses.

Dwarfs? Jade wondered silently.

Possibly, Libby agreed.

Rance frowned, glaring at the still-masked rider who'd captured Jade. "Reveal yourself," he ordered. "Show us what kind of beings you are."

"With pleasure." Again the mellifluous voice. She signaled the others, before removing her head covering. Her white blond hair gleamed even in the dim light, and her delicate features had a patrician cast to them.

Jade had been right. Female. And clearly Fae.

Now the others followed suit. Slipping their black hoods from their heads, they turned to face their leader. Each one of them had similar, clear-cut features and exotic eyes.

"Are you part of the royal family?" Jade asked. Though she didn't say it out loud, each of them clearly bore a striking resemblance to Prince Cai.

Instead of answering, the leader gave a signal for someone to help Jade down from the horse. Seeing this, Rance dismounted instantly, without waiting for assistance. He crossed to stand next to Jade, his legs planted in a classic warrior stance. Jade glanced at him. Even now, she couldn't help but admire the way his muscles rippled as he crossed his arms.

"Please." The leader flashed a dazzling smile. "I am Breena, Prince Cai's sister. We mean no harm to either of you. But we must talk."

Jade nodded. Though Rance gave no outward sign of relaxing, he inclined his head to signal his agreement.

The grooms led the horses away. Once they'd gone, Breena waved a graceful hand. "Follow me."

She started off. Exchanging another quick glance, Jade and Rance hurried after her. Her people—soldiers or family—fell in behind them.

I'm curious. Libby spoke in Jade's head. *I don't know if this is just court intrigue or something more.*

Jade shrugged. This time, instead of answering out loud, she kept the conversation internal. *I'm thinking we're about to find out.*

Chapter 14

Jade didn't know what to think when Breena turned and entered one of the smallish houses. Not sure what else to do, Jade followed. Once they'd all filed in after her, she indicated an array of brightly colored throw pillows placed on the blue tile floor.

Rance took Jade's hand, sending a jolt of warmth through her. He pushed two pillows next to each other and they lowered themselves to the floor side by side.

Once they were seated, Breena and the others took their own seats.

"We brought you here because we need your help in stopping the prince," Breena began. "I know you've visited him before, but you're quite possibly the first female from the other realm that he has allowed to leave unharmed in some way."

Not true. He'd allowed Di and her two friends to return home. Of course, he'd gotten them pregnant, which might qualify as harming them. Still Jade held her tongue. Libby admired the younger woman's wisdom. Best to wait and see what the situation might be before offering any comment.

"Cai is my brother," Breena continued. "Though I am the rightful heir to the throne, his numerous—and clearly unsuccessful—attempts to kill me have caused me and my supporters to go into hiding."

Clearly interested, Rance leaned forward. He opened his mouth as if about to speak, but a quick squeeze from Jade's hand warned him not to.

"Cai's ego is enormous." Expression grim, Breena met Jade's gaze. "Lately, he's been luring human women here and, once they've been charmed, impregnating them."

Not just humans, Jade thought. Shifters, too.

"Several human females have died trying to carry his children. I fear there will be more, if he isn't stopped."

"But why?" Jade finally asked. "What does he hope to gain by doing this?"

"With each woman he ensnares, he gains power. Especially once they forfeit their lives because of his spark of life growing inside of them."

Now Rance spoke. "You are making him sound like some sort of faerie vampire."

A ghost of a smile flitted across Breena's beautiful face, quickly gone. "That may be more accurate than you realize. While he doesn't bite them and drink their blood, he does steal their life force."

"Like a demon," Jade put in.

"Yes. Maybe that's what my brother has become. A Fae demon."

"Why do you think we can help?" Rance again, his tone guarded.

"Because I saw you when you came for the last human female he got with child. He allowed her to leave with you."

Diamond. Except Breena apparently wasn't aware Di

was not human. Nor were her two friends. Which could be a good thing.

"How do we know you're telling the truth?" Jade challenged. "For all we know, this might all be political intrigue, pitting one sibling against the other."

Breena cocked her head, her expression unruffled. "Have you checked on the females who carry his seed? By now, most of them should be dead."

"That doesn't make sense," Rance interjected, before Jade could respond. "There are stories all through history of human women birthing Fae babies."

"Are there?" Breena's smile was without malice. "If that's the case, they are not factual. Sometimes the Fae will switch their infants with a particularly beautiful human baby if they're in the mood to make mischief, but humans cannot survive carrying a Fae baby to term."

"I don't understand how such a thing as Prince Cai getting women pregnant could enable him to steal their life force." Rance spoke matter-of-factly. "Because the last time I heard, demons and Fae never comingle."

"Black magic," Breena supplied. "Somehow, this Fae prince allied himself with the darkness."

"I doubt that."

Breena gave him an arch look. "What would you know about such things?" she asked. "You are but a mere human."

"Am I?" he countered, surprised she didn't realize he was Drakkor. "Can the magical Fae not see such simple things as auras? Do you truly not realize what we are?"

At his words, Breena frowned. Looking from one to the other and back again, her frown deepened as she concentrated. Libby could tell the Fae princess was scrambling to make sense of Rance's words.

"Look." Finally Jade took pity of the other woman. "We came here because my cousin Di and her friends are deathly ill. They're all pregnant. And yes, we do believe Cai is the father."

"See?" Breena didn't exactly crow, but she came close. "That's what I'm trying to tell you."

"Yes. Maybe you're right. And maybe not." Jade took a deep breath before continuing. "Because this group of women are not human. They're shifters."

Breena gasped. "That might be different, then. Though I don't know if better or worse." She looked at Rance. "Is that why you asked if we could see your auras?"

His quick nod made her eyes widen. "Are you two also shape-shifters?"

"Yes." The terseness of his reply told Libby he planned to volunteer as little as possible.

"Then there truly is a possibility you could help us take our kingdom back from the darkness." Breena actually clapped. Blue eyes gleaming, she turned to her entourage. "For the first time in ages, we have hope!"

Libby waited for Jade or Rance to caution her, but both stayed silent. Jade because she would do anything to help her cousin. As far as Rance, he had his own reasons.

The small group broke out into cheers. Libby began to actually worry. She'd hate it if Jade and Rance were bringing the princess and her supporters false optimism.

"First, before we talk anymore, is there anything you can do to help my cousin and her friends?" Jade asked.

To her credit, Breena didn't immediately answer. She dipped her chin and mulled over her answer. "Maybe," she said, her tone cautious. "Do you have time to stay?"

Again Jade and Rance exchanged a long look. Libby marveled at the emotions coursing through her Guardian as she met his gray eyes.

"Time passes differently here," Rance finally answered. "We don't have time to waste."

Jade and Libby knew he was thinking of his stepdaughter as well as the pregnant women.

"You have one hour, no more," Jade answered, surprising herself. "Plus, I'm wondering if we should go talk to the prince. He's the father. Surely he could help us."

At that, Breena narrowed her eyes. "Have you not heard anything I've been telling you? If you were to appear in his court now, he would never let you leave."

"Says you," Jade retorted. "I'm not entirely sure I can trust you."

Libby braced herself for the other woman's anger. Instead, Breena appeared to be considering Jade's words. Finally, she nodded. "I believe you might be right. I must prove myself to you."

Both Rance and Jade waited, curious to see exactly how she'd do that.

With her head bent, the Fae princess appeared lost in thought. When she finally looked up and faced them, the eagerness behind her smile made her blue eyes glow. "Ask your Seer," she told Jade. "She knows exactly what we need. We are old allies with her kind. It's all her history, if she will but remember."

"Seer?" Then as Libby gasped inside her head, she realized what Breena meant. "Just a minute, and I'll ask her," Jade said, bowing her own head so the others wouldn't see her internal dialogue mirrored on her face.

Well? What does she mean? Jade asked silently, her impatience clear.

Still shocked at the revelation, it took a second for Libby to formulate an answer. *I always thought it was a myth, but she must be speaking of the first magical wars, when the Drakkor and the Fae teamed up to vanquish the demons.*

The...what? How long ago was this?

Libby sighed. *A long time. Christianity was still new and hadn't yet made it to North America.*

While that's all very interesting, and definitely something I want to look into later, what does that have to do with us in the here and now?

Ask her if she is asking for my help specifically, or if she needs something else.

Jade did.

Breena smiled, her perfect face still alight with a serene joy. "Not of her precisely, but of her kind. As it was long ago, so it shall be again. Good will vanquish evil."

Sadness knifed through Libby so sharp and painful that Jade nearly doubled over with it. What Breena wanted wouldn't be possible. For all intents and purposes, Libby considered herself alone. No longer were there armies of her people available to assist the beautiful Fae battle the darkness.

Recovering, Libby told Jade to be noncommittal. *There's no sense in letting her know up front that we have nothing to bargain with.*

Jade nodded. "We will consider your words. Now tell us how to help my cousin and her friends."

"I can do that, but first I must personally visit them."

Rance shifted his weight from one foot to the other, making Jade take a quick glance at his beat-up sneakers. He practically vibrated with impatience. She understood the sense of urgency he tried to squash. As far as he knew, the more time that passed without him finding Eve, the more in danger she might be.

"I'll take you now," Jade offered. "But we must go quickly. They are very ill." She reached for Rance, taking his hand and squeezing to let him know she understood.

"This is your chance to prove yourself," Jade added. "Heal them, and I'll speak with Libby about helping you."

Breena dipped her chin in a nod. She clapped her hands,

and suddenly they were back in the forest, a few feet away from the twin birch trees that marked the portal.

"Take me to them," Breena demanded.

Jade eyed her. With her black pants and shirt, Breena could pass for human. An exceptionally beautiful one. Even the hooded cloak would seem like an offbeat sense of fashion. And it might help with not drawing attention to her perfect features.

"Okay. Let's go. We'll have to hike back to the car, and then drive there."

"Can't they go alone?" Rance stepped in front of Jade. "I know I agreed to help Di first and then search for Eve, but I can't shake the overwhelming sense of urgency. I need to locate Eve."

Unsure, Jade looked at Breena. Feeling Jade's torn emotions, Libby voiced her opinion. *Tell Rance it won't take too long to bring them to the hospital. After, you can come straight to my house and I'll do my best to locate his little girl.*

Can't you do it now? Jade's heartbroken plea hurt Libby's heart. *Leave my head and do what you have to do to find her.*

The fact that they both knew how dangerous it could be to attempt a trance alone wasn't lost on Libby.

I can try, Libby couldn't keep the hesitation from her voice, even if it was only inside Jade's head. *But my ability is strengthened by your presence. You know this.*

I do. But I'm so worried for Rance.

I'm leaving now. I'll see you later, Libby said.

With that, she exited Jade's head, disoriented to find herself back in her living room.

Meanwhile, Jade felt a twinge as Libby left, then a devastating sense of emptiness.

"Jade?" Rance squeezed her shoulder, making her realize she'd been standing frozen while having her internal dialogue with Libby. "Are you all right?"

As her gaze met his, she swallowed. The tense line of his strong jaw attested to the iron grip he kept on his emotions. She could only imagine how he felt—if she felt torn, everything that kept him from finding Eve must be ripping him apart.

All her life, Jade had become skilled at putting others first. She'd developed a knack for assessing the priority of a situation, but this time, uncertainty made her feel ill.

"We'll take them to the hospital, introduce them to my mother and my aunt and then we'll go to Libby's," she said, praying she was making the right choice.

His jaw tightened but he nodded. "Let's go." He strode off without waiting to see if they followed.

Though Rance drove way too fast, Jade didn't say a word. She kept sneaking glances at Breena, who had gone pale and appeared about to be sick.

"You've never ridden in a car before," Jade guessed.

Hearing, Rance eased off the gas pedal a little. "Sorry," he muttered.

They pulled into the hospital parking lot and found a spot right near the front door. As soon as Rance cut the engine, he jumped out of the car and headed around to Jade's side, opening her door for her. "I'm Southern," he said, correctly interpreting her look. "My mama taught me never to forget my manners."

Amused despite herself, she smiled at him. "To be honest, despite your Texas accent, your manners are rarely on display."

His eyes widened. "Then I have been remiss. In the future, I'll try to remedy that."

Charmed, she nodded, unable to tear her gaze away from him.

"Come on." He gave her a tug. "Let's go."

"And there go the manners," Jade quipped.

Breena cleared her throat, making Jade realize she'd managed to forget about the other woman somehow.

"Put your hood up," Jade urged, watching as Breena covered her shining blond hair. Now, with her face in shadow, maybe she wouldn't cause too much disruption.

"Right," Breena drawled. "Because no one ever notices *you*."

Startled, Jade drew back. "Did you just read my mind?"

"No. I didn't have to. Your thoughts are plain on your face."

Rance took Jade's arm. "We can talk later."

They rode the elevator up in silence. Jade nervously wondered how her mother and aunt would react to the beautiful stranger. Ah, well, they'd asked Jade for help, and that was exactly what she was doing.

She only hoped Breena really could so something for Di, her friends and their unborn children. What a miracle if Fae magic could make them well.

Amber looked up as Jade entered the room. "You're back. It certainly took you long enough." Worry colored her voice. "What did you find out?" she asked, falling silent as she caught sight of a hooded and cloaked stranger. "Who's this?"

"A friend." Jade stepped aside so Breena could see her unconscious and intubated cousin. Pushing aside her twinge of nervousness and hoping Breena hadn't misled them, she kept silent while the Fae princess laid her long-fingered hand on the side of Di's face.

When she did, Di's baby kicked so roughly they all could see her bump move.

"She recognizes me," Breena said, sounding pleased.

She?

Amber started to speak, but closed her mouth when Jade shook her head in warning.

"I'll need to soothe her. And—" Breena looked from Jade to the two older women "—I'll have to place the unborn child into a trance. Only if she sleeps will she stop fighting her human mother."

"A trance?" Emerald gasped. "That doesn't sound safe for an infant in utero."

Breena shrugged. "It's your choice. But please be aware, if I do not do this, your daughter will die. And most likely the infant, too. I don't think she's developed enough to survive on her own outside of the womb."

Both Emerald and Amber gasped.

Meanwhile, Breena looked at Jade. "Can you lead me to the other pregnant women who are ill? If they have family with them, it will be their choice. If they do not, I will leave it up to you whatever you want me to do."

"Wait!" Auntie Em stepped forward. "I don't want my daughter to die. Please, do what you have to do in order to help her."

Breena nodded. Moving swiftly, she crossed to the hospital bed and placed both hands on Di's stomach. "I'll need absolute silence." Her gaze locked on Jade. "Do not allow anyone to disturb me. There could be disastrous consequences if that happens."

Immediately, Rance moved to block the doorway. "In case any nurses or aides try to come in."

Grateful, Jade nodded. With his large frame filling the doorway, he'd protect her cousin and the Fae princess. She smiled slightly at the knowledge of how much she liked having him at her back. Before, she'd enjoyed her independence. She still did. But there was something to be said for having someone around who you knew would never let you down.

As long as he was here, that is.

She pushed away the sobering thought. No matter how much she might wish it were different, it wasn't meant to be. She had deep ties to Forestwood, to this land and this lake and her home. And to Libby, of course.

While Rance—she thought trying to tie him to one place might be akin to clipping the wings off an eagle. He'd survive, but he'd never be the same. She'd never want to be the one to cause a look of loss and yearning in his beautiful gray eyes.

Shaking off her thoughts, she watched as Breena continued chanting in an unintelligible language over Di's unconscious form. Amber and Auntie Em stared, too, both wearing nearly identical wide-eyed expressions.

"There." Straightening up, Breena smiled at the two older women. "All finished. Now when it comes time for her to deliver, you'll need to contact me to wake the baby up. Other than that, Di should be able to enjoy a relatively normal pregnancy."

"Will the baby—" Emerald cleared her throat "—will she still kick?"

"Yes. And her heartbeat will be normal. The accelerated growth rate will slow."

"In other words," Jade chimed in, "everything will go back to the way it's supposed to be."

"Correct." Breena exhaled. "Now if you'll take me to the others, I'll see what I can do for them."

Rance turned, glancing at Jade before directing his attention to Amber. "Do you want to lead the way?" he asked, his polite tone at odds with his shuttered expression. Jade understood he tried to rein in his impatience.

"Of course." Gathering her belongings, Amber kissed her sister on the cheek. "Will you be all right here for a few minutes?"

Emerald never glanced up from her sleeping daughter. "Of course."

"As a matter of fact," Jade put in. "Breena, is it all right if Rance and I go now? He's got another urgent matter he needs to tend to."

"Of course." Breena waved them away. "Amber and I will be fine with the others." Her bright smile made her entire face glow. "And I certainly know my own way home."

"How will we contact you?" Emerald asked, finally looking up from her daughter. "For when it's time for Di to deliver?"

"They know." Breena inclined her head toward Rance and Jade. "But in case they're indisposed, ask Amber to show you the portal in the forest."

"Okay." Emerald returned her attention to Di, as if she could bring her awake by sheer strength of will.

At least Amber had the grace to look guilty. Suddenly, she wouldn't meet Jade's gaze.

"Mother? You know where it is?" Jade tried to keep the accusation from her tone.

"Of course. Oh, honey, don't look at me like that," Amber pleaded. "There's so much that goes along with being the Guardian. Some things you have to learn for yourself."

Though Jade didn't buy Amber's explanation, she also knew her flighty mother had hated being Guardian and couldn't wait to pass that particular mantle off on Jade.

"It's okay," Jade said, even though it really wasn't. Still, she saw no sense in holding a grudge for something that had already happened. Being upset wouldn't change things.

She looked up to find Rance watching her, his expression understanding. "Are you ready?" he asked softly, though worry and frustration vibrated just underneath the surface of his calm tone. "I don't want to waste any time."

"Yes." Jade gave Amber a quick hug, did the same for her aunt and then waved at Breena. "We'll talk to you soon."

"I have no doubt you will," Breena responded. "I can

tell you are the type of person who always keeps their promises."

Dependable and boring. And that pretty much summed her up, Jade thought with a sense of fatality.

With his gut seriously twisted, Rance didn't feel much like talking as they drove out to Libby's. He'd been clenching his jaw so tightly his teeth ached. Though he knew he needed to relax it, he couldn't even begin to try until he'd learned if Libby could find Eve.

"Are you all right?" Jade gave him a sidelong glance, concern shining in her green eyes.

Unbelievably, something stirred inside him as he met her gaze. Despite everything, he found himself wondering what she'd do if he kissed her again. Made love to her once more.

Damn. He felt a flash of anger at himself. Sure, he might be in need of a distraction, but Jade wasn't the kind of woman who deserved to be hurt the way he would end up hurting her. Especially now, when as soon as Libby told him where to find Eve, he'd be leaving Forestwood. He didn't figure he'd be back.

Again, his fingers itched for his camera. If possible, before he left, he'd have to get Jade to let him take some stills of her. He could picture exactly where they'd take them, and the time of the day—right before dusk, or soon after dawn, up on the cliffs overlooking the lake—when the light would be best. Even with his considerable photography skills, he doubted the camera could ever do her justice.

"Yes, I'm fine," he answered, forcing his thoughts back on track.

Though they'd been driving over the speed limit, Jade eased off the gas pedal, slowing to slightly below. Rance glanced around, wondering if she'd seen a patrol car or if he'd missed the flashing lights of a school zone, but he saw neither.

"What's going on?" he asked.

"Sorry." She shot him a slightly embarrassed, apologetic smile. "See that house right there?" She pointed.

He followed the direction she indicated. A small stone house sat back among the trees. It looked, as far as he could tell, pretty old, though well-cared for. In front, an evergreen garden framed the front door, and he could see a lot of lilac bushes mixed with roses, though the flowers were now dormant. With the muted sunlight, the scene took on the feel of a Thomas Kincaid painting. "What about it?" he asked.

"That's my dream house." Once they'd gone past it, she sped up. "If I could live anywhere besides Burnett House, that's where I would live. I always look at it when I go this way. Whoever owns it isn't around much, and I think they might use it for a vacation rental. A place like that deserves more than to sit empty ninety percent of the time. It should have a family, someone who loves it the way it was meant to be loved."

He wondered if she realized she was talking about an inanimate object, a structure. "The owners seem to take good care of it."

"They do."

"Burnett House is pretty awesome too," he said.

"Yes, it is. It's been in my family for generations. As Guardian, I have no choice but to live there."

"And sometimes you wish things were different."

She shrugged, clearly ready to change the subject. "So, are you curious?"

"Curious about what?"

"Libby. I know you have to be wondering if she'll be able to help you."

"Oh, I'm definitely curious about that."

"There's so much more to her, you know. She's really special," Jade continued. "Not only because of her ability to find things, but because she's such a sweet person. I've gotten to know her well in the nine years I've been her Guardian, and she's really fascinating." Her earnest tone made him smile. "Despite being one of a kind, she's also down to earth. And nice." —

"Nice, huh? That's a bland adjective to use to describe a shape-shifting lake creature."

Smiling back, she shrugged. "Well, it's true."

"Does she have magical abilities, too? I mean, besides being able to find things?"

"Probably, but I don't really know. I was never able to do any of my little tricks until after I became her Guardian."

Little tricks. The odd bits of magical ability she occasionally used. Another subject for another time. Now he wanted to focus on Libby.

"About that," he asked. "Why does she even need a Guardian? Even if she's a rarity, I've never heard of a kind of shifter who needed a caretaker. I'll admit I'm curious as to what species she is. I didn't get a good enough look at her to really tell."

"I think she needs a Guardian because she's so alone. As to species, I actually believe she might be one of the last of her kind." Jade's voice contained a note of sadness. "That's why she chooses to live out here completely isolated from others and possibly why she spends so much time in the water. She says it's one of the few places she can find peace."

He felt a flicker of interest. "A mermaid-type creature?" he asked. "All I really saw was a flash of scales when I was underwater. I think it was her, but it was too murky to see, and then she disappeared." He'd heard these beings existed, but had never met one. Of course, until recently, he'd never laid eyes on a Fae.

Jade laughed and shook her head. "I don't think so. I've seen her when she's in her creature form. She's definitely not a mermaid."

"Then what would you call her?"

Jade considered. "I don't know," she finally admitted. "If dragons existed, I'd have to say she was that."

Dragons. Her words sent a chill through his core. Not many in the paranormal world knew about the Drakkor, his people. They were a dying breed and they were also known as dragons. The existence of another Drakkor—another *female* Drakkor—would be akin to a miracle. This opened up an entire new realm of possibilities.

Why Libby might have chosen to stay hidden here, in a remote area of the Catskills, living among others who were not her kind, to begin with.

No doubt she had her reasons. Once he met her, he'd do his best to find out what they were.

Chapter 15

The possibility of Libby being a Drakkor had never occurred to Rance. But then, he'd only gotten a hint of this when she leaped out of the water. Not enough to see more than a few glistening scales. But that would explain the other abilities. Drakkors, especially the females, frequently had special gifts.

"You're awfully quiet. Are you sure you're okay?" Jade asked, making him aware he'd been lost in thought for several minutes. Damn good thing she was driving.

"Fine," he answered, trying to pretend his mind wasn't reeling. Of course, his first priority would be finding Eve. Once he'd done that, he'd return to unravel the mystery of Libby.

With a sense of relief, he understood this wouldn't be the last he saw of Forestwood—and Jade—after all.

They pulled up to a cedar A-frame house, nestled back in the woods near the cliffs with a panoramic view of the lake. Rance whistled. "That's some prime real estate," he said.

Jade smiled. Again his insides twisted. He wasn't sure how she had such a strong effect on him. He'd never been so aware of a woman, not even his wife.

"I think she bought the land and built that house several decades ago."

This time, he didn't hide his surprise. "Decades? Exactly how old is Libby, anyway?"

Unbuckling her seat belt, Jade shrugged. "No one really knows. But she's pretty old, though she doesn't look it. Before me, my mother was her Guardian. Before her, her mother. My family has taken care of her for as long as I can remember."

Longevity. Another Drakkor trait. But still, it was a long shot. If this Libby had managed to survive the plague that had taken almost all of the Drakkor women and caused the Drakkor men to become sterile, was this why she'd gone into hiding?

"Come on." Jade opened her car door. "She's expecting you."

Rance followed her up the sidewalk. He marveled at the beauty of the spot, the complete privacy and breathtaking views. As they approached the front door, he pushed away the strange reluctance that had come over him. As a journalist, he could honestly say he could count on one hand the times he'd been reluctant to cover a story. He didn't understand why he felt that way now.

If Libby truly were one of his own kind, she would no longer be alone. And the world would have one more female Drakkor in it. The Drakkor council would have to be advised.

"Earth to Rance." One hand on the doorknob, Jade tilted her head and frowned at him. "Are you sure you're all right? Maybe we need to do this another time?"

"Eve doesn't have time," he said. He didn't know why, but he almost hung back. This felt out of character for him, the investigative journalist, but he thought he understood the reason for his hesitation. Because Libby was his last hope of finding Eve. If she couldn't help him, he'd have nowhere else to turn. Eve would be lost to him forever.

Which meant he needed to get over himself. Immediately.

So when Jade opened the door, he charged inside. And stopped short when he caught sight of the petite, doe-eyed woman standing near the fireplace.

Something about her… Whether the peace she radiated, or the ageless loveliness he saw in her face, he instantly felt at ease.

"Welcome," she said. Even her voice washed over him, rich and soothing.

Drakkor. He knew instantly, though he had no idea how. Maybe something in her aura, or just the instant sense of familiarity he felt.

He opened his mouth, but found he couldn't speak, unable to cover the awe filling him. The sure and steady knowledge that he had somehow found another of his own kind made him feel dizzy.

"Rance?" Jade took his arm. "I know I keep asking you, but are you sure you're okay?" She glanced from him to Libby. "I know how important this meeting is."

And just like that, urgency replaced the wonder. Eve. Would Libby be able to help him locate her?

"My apologies." Mustering a smile, he faced the diminutive silver-haired woman who continued to study him.

"I'm so glad to finally meet you," she said. "I admit to quite a bit of curiosity. You've always seemed very familiar to me, though I can't understand why."

Always? He wondered how that could be, since this was their first meeting. "I'm pleased to meet you, ma'am," he said, and held out his hand.

When she slid her cool fingers into his, he felt that connection, the magic all Drakkors shared. Her eyes widened and he knew she felt it, too.

"You're…" Appearing overcome by emotion, she couldn't finish whatever she'd been about to say.

He nodded. "Yes. And you are no longer alone."

Jade glanced from one to the other, frowning. "What exactly are you two talking about?"

The sweetness of the joy in Libby's smile had Jade smiling back at her charge.

"Libby and I need to talk," Rance said. "Do you mind giving us a few minutes of privacy?"

Jade's mouth dropped open in shock. "Seriously?"

"It's all right." Libby placed her hand on Jade's shoulder. "She can stay. She's my Guardian. She's earned the right to hear whatever you have to say."

Eve, he thought again, forcing himself to remain patient. This moment had to be earth-shattering to Libby. Yet what she was asking him to do, to reveal what type of shifter he was to someone who was not his mate… This would mean breaking ancient laws.

He debated whether or not to tell Libby about them, since clearly she wasn't aware. He considered the risk, especially since he had a favor of his own to ask.

And heaven help him, he also took into consideration the bewildered hurt in Jade's emerald eyes as she looked from one to the other.

"Before I start, there's a bit of urgency to my visit." And he outlined what had happened with Eve and his fruitless search to find her.

The joy lighting Libby's face vanished. "Of course. You know I've tried, several times, since we were at the hospital, with no luck."

"Can you try again?"

Libby looked down. When she lifted her head, she smiled. "Let me see what I can do." She glanced from one to the other, heaving a sigh. "But I warn you, I don't do as well when I'm distracted."

"It's worth a shot," Rance persisted.

"Wait." Jade's hand on his arm stopped him. "She has to go into a trance to use her abilities. Whatever information you might give her is important, too. As is her state of mind. A few more minutes won't hurt. Please. Tell her what she needs to hear."

Never before had her love for her charge been so plain. He understood, and she was right. He'd spent days searching for Eve. Jade had given him a choice earlier and she'd been willing to put off helping her cousin for him. Surely he could rein in his impatience for a few more minutes.

"You're right," he finally said. "Jade, Libby and I are family. After all these years, Libby is no longer alone."

Libby beamed hearing his words. "We are," she happily agreed, her eyes glowing with joy again. "After so many years of believing I was the only one."

"I still don't understand." Jade looked from Rance to Libby and back again. "How are you related?"

He waited to see if Libby would elaborate. When she did not, he tried. "We are both the same species of shape-shifter. Our kind is extremely rare, so it's easy to understand how Libby could think she was the last of her kind. She nearly is."

Slowly, Jade shook her head, as if trying to negate his words. "That's not possible. Libby is a lake creature. While you... Are you telling me you're a lake creature, too?"

"The proper name is Drakkor," Rance said. "And there are so few of us left, most other shifters have no idea we exist."

"Drakkor is a word I'd thought I'd never hear again." Tears shone in Libby's eyes. "My people, they're all gone. I need you to tell me your story, your truth. How many survived the illness?"

"That's a long story." He glanced at Libby. "Is there someplace we can sit and talk?"

"Of course." Libby's voice still rang with joy. "Let me get some lemonade and we can sit on the deck. Jade, why don't you show him where. I'll join you both in just a minute."

"Follow me." Back uncharacteristically stiff, Jade led the way through the house to a back door. She opened it and they stepped outside onto a beautiful wooden deck that overlooked the lake.

"Rance." Her determined tone told him she had something serious to say. "I don't know what it is you're trying to pull, but I won't let you hurt Libby. As her Guardian, I take her well-being very seriously."

Again, he fought the urge to kiss her, to loosen the tight line of her lips with his passion. Instead, he swallowed hard and forced his unruly libido under control. Maybe all of that could come later, once he'd found Eve and made sure she was all right.

"Jade, I'm telling the truth. I didn't get a good enough look at Libby the one time I saw her in the lake, but once you started describing her to me, I knew."

"You're telling me you're a...dragon?"

"Yes. As is Libby. We're called the Drakkor."

"What about Eve, your stepdaughter? You said she's a halfling. Is she half-Drakkor?"

"Yes. Her mother, Violet, was killed by the illness, too."

"So recently? Libby lost her family decades ago. I would think by now someone would have come up with a cure."

"I wish. But this sickness, this plague, it's like cancer. One moment, a woman can be whole and healthy, and the next…"

Jade turned to stare out over the sparkling expanse of lake. When she turned back to face him, the sorrow darkening her eyes made his insides clench.

"What are you so afraid of?" he asked, reaching out to wrap a tendril of her hair around his finger.

She sighed, but didn't move away. "That Libby won't need me anymore. Truth be told, she hasn't needed me to be anything more than a friend, and I could do better at that. But she's always been the Lake Creature of Forestwood Lake. I don't begrudge her happiness, not for one second, but now that she has a family, she'll leave Forestwood and go to them. I'll never see her again." Her voice caught on that last statement.

"That will never happen." Libby appeared in the doorway, holding a tray with a pitcher of lemonade and three glasses. "This is my home. I also consider you my family. Please, Jade, sit down and let me tell you my story. When I've finished, I'd like to let Rance tell his."

Again, Rance felt the constraints of time. He struggled not to panic, even though part of him wanted to ask Libby to find Eve before she shared her history with Jade.

He met Jade's gaze and knew she was aware of his thoughts. "Patience," she whispered. In that instant, drowning in her eyes, he thought he might do anything she asked. Anything but put his stepdaughter in more danger.

"She's with her father," Jade said, stroking his arm. "Surely he will do what's best for her. He loves her, too."

Oh, how much he wanted to believe this. He thought this tiny sliver of truth might have been all that kept him sane through the worry of his fruitless search.

Finally Rance nodded. "Okay."

"Thank you." Jade kissed his cheek. "Come on." She followed Libby to a round, teak wood table and took a seat. After a moment, Rance did the same. Libby set down the pitcher and the glasses and poured the lemonade.

When Rance reached for his glass, he saw his fingers were shaking. Jade apparently noticed, too, because she covered her hand with his, squeezing to let him know everything was going to be all right.

"Libby, I know you've got a lot on your mind and I'm

dying to hear your story," Jade said. "But Rance is really worried about his little girl. Maybe you should go ahead and try again to locate her first."

Stunned and grateful, he sat up straight and met Libby's curious gaze.

"What happened?" she asked, her soft voice full of sympathy.

Trying to stick to the facts, Rance told her everything that had happened.

"She's with her father, whom you were friends with until she disappeared, and now he won't take your calls?"

He supposed her calm tone should make him feel better, but it didn't. "Yes." He felt his expression slip, revealing some of the starkness of his worry and pain. Though he instantly composed himself, he knew both women had seen.

"Of course I'll help you," Libby told him, leaning forward and patting his arm reassuringly. "But I need time to process this. Do you mind if Jade and I talk for a bit first? I promise not to take too much time."

Swallowing, he jerked his head in a nod. He didn't actually have a choice. Though everyone kept advising him to have patience, that wasn't possible when he wasn't sure if Eve might be in danger.

"She has to be in a certain state of mind to use her gift," Jade told him, almost as if she was aware of his thoughts. "I promise, she's not trying to delay. But if you'll just give us ten more minutes—let her tell me her story—it would give her a much higher chance of success."

"Of course." His smooth answer didn't fool her, but he saw from her sympathetic expression that she understood.

"All right." Libby sounded relieved. "I promise not to take too long."

"And this should be interesting." Jade glanced at Rance. "Though I've always wondered, you should know this is something I would never have dared to ask before you showed up in town."

"You already know part of it," Libby said. "Not the personal details, but the general history."

"No. No, I don't."

Libby stared, one perfectly arched brow raised. "I know your family kept some kind of written history of me. Have you never bothered to read it?"

"I never knew about it. I just now learned there were books," Jade answered. "When Mother passed the Guardianship on to me, she never said anything about them. She only told me when Di got sick and she needed our help."

"Of course she didn't," Libby muttered. "Not that there was anything in them but history." She took a deep breath. "All right, then. What would you like to know?"

"Everything. Start at the beginning."

Again Libby glanced at Rance. "I'm going to tell my version of it, based on my history. You may know more or something different, so if you do, please feel free to jump in."

Rance nodded.

"Once, my kind were as numerous as your Pack. These days we'd be considered an endangered species. The few females who survived were sent to live in remote locations, all near lakes. Something about the cold, deep water keeping the disease at bay."

Jade reached for Rance. He took her hand and captured it in between his. "What happened? What caused your numbers to shrink?"

"First we were struck by an illness. It killed off many. Those who didn't die were left sterile. Since no new babies were born…" Lifting one slender shoulder in a shrug, Libby sighed. "Some of us—myself, Nessie and a few others—managed to survive. We stayed in our homes near the lakes, aware the water was the one place we could retreat where the illness couldn't follow."

Hearing the starkness of the pain in Libby's gentle voice made Rance's throat ache.

"We will always have our history." Libby continued, "Centuries ago, we took to the skies in numbers. Humans both feared us and revered us. If you ever get a chance to see the books your mother has, you'll marvel at the medieval artwork."

"I imagine it was quite a beautiful sight. Were they your books?" Jade asked.

"Yes. I always entrust them to the Guardian. Amber was supposed to pass them down to you."

"But she didn't." Now Jade turned to study Rance. "What about you? Do you have something to add to her story? You said there are more of your kind."

He nodded. "There are. But only a few. And that illness still shows up at will and without warning. My wife died from it. And my stepdaughter is battling it now."

"How many are left? You say a few. What does that mean? Ten? Twenty? A hundred?"

"I wish I had better news." Swallowing hard, he met her gaze. "There are four females left that we know of. The illness has rendered our males sterile…" Now he quickly glanced at Jade. "Or so our doctors believe. No new children have been born in years. Until recently. Three of the four remaining Drakkor women are with child. We hope for successful births."

"Four?" Incredulous, Libby repeated the number. "Are you certain there aren't more females tucked away in hiding somewhere, like me?"

"I would love it if that were the case."

"What about halflings?" Jade asked. "You say Eve is one. Are there many Drakkor halflings out there? Maybe their constitution is better able to fight off this plague?"

"I don't know." Though Rance hated to admit it, he'd been kind of focused on his own, immediate reality until Violet became ill. "Eve was doing better, getting better. But then, according to Jim, something happened and she took a turn for the worse."

"And you don't know if Jim was telling the truth," Jade finished.

"One last question, though I fear I already know the answer." Libby glanced from Rance to Jade and then back again. "After all these years, no one has managed to find a cure for that plague? With all the brilliant scientists and doctors this world has to offer, and still nothing has been done?"

Grimly, he nodded. "It's like cancer in humans, though far more deadly. They haven't found a cure for that, either."

One silver tear rolled down Libby's cheek. She brushed it away. "I feared as much. Now, let me see what I can do about locating your little girl." She pushed to her feet. "Jade, will you help me get ready?"

"Of course." Pulling her hand from his, Jade stood also. "She has to go into a trance. It takes a lot out of her."

Heart rate increasing, he followed the two women inside. In a few minutes, he might finally learn where Jim and Eve had gone, and if his stepdaughter was all right.

Though happy for Libby now that she was no longer so utterly, totally alone, something about the dark circles under her eyes and the fine lines at the edge of her mouth worried Jade. Especially with all this talk of a fatal illness destroying the females of her kind.

Family had always been everything to Jade. She considered Libby part of her family. She'd always known she could count on any of the Burnetts, no matter what. Except now Jade felt betrayed by her own mother. Amber had known. All along. She'd mentioned reading the books when she'd asked Jade to get help for Di. And yet she hadn't bothered to fill Jade in. She'd let Jade be Libby's Guardian without having full knowledge of all the risks.

Inside the living room, Libby took her usual place on the overstuffed chair next to the fireplace. She waved toward the couch. "You two make yourself comfortable," she said, smiling. "Jade knows this can take me a minute or two."

Restless, Rance began to pace. Striding the length of the room in front of the wall of full-length windows, he clearly didn't see the look Libby gave him.

Jade jumped back up and took his arm. "Come on, let's sit."

He grimaced. "I need a minute."

"Then let's go back outside. Libby can't relax if she's surrounded by negative energy."

His bright gray eyes darkened. "I'm worried. Libby's my last hope of finding Eve."

"I know." Instead of squeezing his arm, she slipped her own arm around his waist. She liked touching him, loved the solid muscular feel of his body and the way his height made her feel protected.

He was the first man she'd ever felt this way about. Oh, she'd once thought she loved her fiancé, Ross. But that emotion had been shallow compared to the way she felt about Rance. She wanted to take every minute with him she could, hold it close to her heart and savor it. Because once he found out where Eve had been taken, she'd likely never see him again.

To her surprise, he put his arm around her, too. They stood side by side, with the dazzling lake spread out below them, framed by the brightly colored leafy display.

This. Jade knew this moment would be one of those memories she'd take out and keep close once he'd gone.

Gone.

"Do you think she's ready yet?" Rance asked, making her jump.

She smiled at his questioning look. "Sorry, I was deep in thought. Let's go inside and see. If she is in a trance, don't speak to her or make noise. If you do, you run the risk of pulling her out of the trance."

"I understand."

Quietly they entered the house. One glance at Libby sitting motionless in her favorite chair and Jade knew she'd gone into a trance.

Rance touched her shoulder. She nodded, indicating they should take seats on the couch. She'd never left Libby alone to come out of a trance and she wouldn't now.

They sat down, knees touching. For a brief second, Jade considered giving in to impulse and scooting over so that their entire bodies were touching.

Libby made a sound, which chased that notion right out of Jade's head. Sounds meant the trance would soon be ending. Judging from the way Rance had stiffened, he'd figured this out.

The main question—had Libby located Eve and her father?

Jade held her breath as Libby began to stir. When she opened her eyes, her unfocused gaze drifted around the room, finally settling on Rance.

"I know where Jim has taken his daughter," she said immediately, her voice weak, but certain. "He believes he's doing this for her protection. Someone…" Her voice cracked before she took a deep breath and steadied herself. "Prince Cai has learned what she is. He has convinced Jim to travel with her to the land of the Fae."

Chapter 16

Incredulous, Jade swallowed. Whatever she'd been expecting to hear, it hadn't been this. Judging from the stunned look on Rance's face, he felt the same way.

"How?" he asked, his voice hard and brittle. "How in the hell would a Fae prince learn about my daughter?"

Libby glanced at him before meeting Jade's eyes. "I'm afraid when the two of you went to Fae, he grew curious when Jade was able to resist his charms. He began to do research into you. When he learned you had a young daughter, he saw a weak spot."

Rance shook his head. "That doesn't make any sense. Why would he take Eve?"

"Because she's half-Drakkor. He has been searching for one for a long time. He plans to heal her and keep her there until he can use her."

Glowering, Rance's thunderous expression made a chill snake down Jade's back. "Use her how?"

"That I couldn't see." Libby spread her hands. "I'm

sorry. But she's not in danger. Cai won't allow any harm to happen to her. Jim finds this reassuring. He's hoping Fae magic will cure her."

"But Jim's human. He doesn't know about the Fae, or Drakkor, or any shape-shifter, for that matter. He has no idea what Eve is."

"Cai has enchanted him with Fae magic. Right now, Jim isn't asking too many questions. When Cai said he could heal Eve, Jim believed him."

Rance made a strangled sound.

"Cai considers her valuable," Libby continued. "Again, he won't hurt her."

While this should have made Rance feel slightly better, he continued to stand frozen, making Jade wonder if Libby's words even registered.

"Rance, she's all right." Jade tried to comfort him. "Maybe Breena will know what's going on. Remember, she said something about needing your help, too," Jade pointed out. "In the battle against her brother, Cai."

Rance had gone gray. She slipped her arm around his waist and held on, because she was afraid he might shatter.

When he looked down at her, a muscle working in his jaw, something twisted in her chest at the tormented look on his face. "We've got to go back to Fae," he said. "Now."

"I agree." Jade eyed Libby. She'd remained seated, and had curled her legs under her. Jade could tell she tried to hold her usual exhaustion at bay. "Will you be okay here without me?"

"Of course," Libby answered immediately. "But please, don't do anything foolish. You don't need to go rushing in there without a plan. Eve is not in danger. And Cai can be a formidable enemy."

"So we've heard. We've met Breena, his sister. Apparently, he's trying to steal the throne from her."

"I don't care about political intrigue," Rance growled. "I just want to make sure Eve is safe."

"She is." The certainty in Libby's voice appeared to calm him somewhat. "As a matter of fact, between Fae magic and her halfling genes, she's made significant progress toward vanquishing her illness." Sadness flitted across her expressive face. "If only that were all we needed to eradicate that illness once and for all."

"Maybe it is," Jade speculated, hiding her growing excitement. "Either way, it certainly bears investigating."

"Halflings have different immune systems, you know that." Rance sounded tired. "Though in the past, both Drakkor and halflings weren't spared." He eyed Jade. "Let's see if we can catch Breena while she's still here."

"I'll call my mother and see if Breena's at the hospital." Jade dug out her cell. Luckily, Amber answered almost immediately, relaying the news that Breena had left.

"We're going to have to go back to Fae," Rance said when she'd told him.

"Yes." Jade knelt down and dropped a kiss on Libby's cheek. "Are you sure you'll be all right? Do you want me to send Amber by to check on you?"

"No." Smiling, Libby waved away her concern. "I only need a little rest and I'll be just like normal. I let you pamper me because I enjoy it." The mischief in her smile had Jade smiling back.

"Come on." Rance fairly vibrated with impatience.

"It's going to be dark soon," Libby pointed out. "It'd be a lot safer to wait until morning."

"I'm going now," Rance growled. "I know you said she's not in danger, but I can't rest until I see for my own eyes that she's safe."

"You can't." The certainty in Libby's tone stopped him in his tracks. "Believe me. If you don't want to endanger the child, you'll wait until the Fae princess summons you.

You're going to need her help. Without it, you won't stand a chance against Fae magic."

After Jade and Rance took off, Libby sagged back in her chair and reached for her lap blanket to cover herself. While she'd spoken truth, she hadn't told them everything. For all intents and purposes, Prince Cai had taken Jim and Eve prisoner, though they didn't know it yet. They believed they were honored guests and wouldn't find out unless they tried to leave. She'd heard Cai discussing Jim with his inner circle. He'd actually voiced the opinion that the human man wasn't needed any longer. Which meant that unless Jade and Rance reached him soon, Jim's life was in grave danger.

Plus, she'd sensed some kind of sickness inside the human man. What it might be, she wasn't sure. But once he'd been rescued, she'd make sure he got to a doctor.

In all of this, Libby couldn't escape the notion that she'd missed something. Fae magic had, according to Jade, saved Di and her friends as well as their unborn babies.

And Fae magic might have helped Eve recover from what had mostly been a fatal illness.

Was this because she was a halfling, or something else? Was it possible the Fae could cure the devastating plague that had killed off the majority of Drakkor women and made the affected men sterile?

One thing Libby's long life and her voracious appetite for reading, especially history, had taught her was that the Fae did nothing for free. An old saying—magic always came with a price—certainly appeared to be true.

As excitement built in her, she reminded herself that all of this was only speculation, at least for now. She'd keep her eyes open and see what she could learn.

Who knew, but maybe, just maybe, a Drakkor named Libby who'd spent most of her life an outcast might figure out the solution to save her entire race.

* * *

Once they got in the car, Rance couldn't contain his frustration. "I really want to go right now," he said, trying not to clench his teeth.

"I understand." Jade touched his shoulder. "But Libby sees things. You know that. If she says we need to wait, then we need to wait."

"For how long?" The words burst from him. "Do you understand what it's like, knowing Eve and Jim are that pompous prince's prisoners?"

"I can only imagine. But we won't do any good bursting in there unprepared. You felt the lure of their magic. Without an ally, without Breena's help, we don't stand a chance."

Because most likely she was right; he finally nodded, hating the feeling of defeat.

They pulled up to Burnett House and parked. "Sit with me?" Jade asked. "You need to relax."

As if he could. No, what he needed was something much more physical, more distracting. He met her gaze, challenging her to read his desire in his eyes.

Her face colored. "Come on. Let's go sit on the porch for a while."

He followed her without commenting. As she settled in her swing and patted the seat next to her, he exhaled.

"Take a deep breath," she urged.

So he did. As she gently used her foot to send the swing moving, he felt some of the tension drain out of him, though desire still simmered in his blood.

A sense of peace stole over him, making him wonder if this porch swing had some magical properties of its own.

The entire house, in fact, but especially here, on the porch.

Jade's front porch had begun to feel like home. He'd rarely seen a more beautiful place and sitting on the swing, gazing out at the road and all the vibrant colors of the autumn leaves, brought him a sense of peace he'd never believed he could feel at a time like this.

And with it, a dawning sense of confidence, of certainty. He—they—would rescue Eve. For the first time in forever, maybe, just maybe, things would actually be all right.

With Jade beside him, he felt like he could conquer anything, be anyone, and this worried the hell out of him. The turmoil inside him felt like the opposite of how he believed life should be.

And Jade continued to look at him as if she thought him some kind of hero. After everything, he didn't really understand why.

He remembered the way her little sisters had warned him not to hurt her. Her mother, too.

Hurting Jade was the last thing he wanted to do.

He tried to figure out a way to warn her, to begin the process of getting her to become adjusted to the idea that he wouldn't be around much longer. "I'm thinking after I find Eve, if she's well enough, I'm going to take her with me on my next assignment. I'll make sure it's safe."

She went still, then smiled. "I'm sure she'd love that. But do you think her father would be okay with you taking her gallivanting around the world?"

A bit confused, he shrugged. "Why wouldn't he? He can come, too, if he wants."

The instant hurt flashed in her emerald eyes, he knew his mistake. He'd assumed Jade knew how he felt about her. What he wasn't sure of was if she felt the same way about him. He hoped she'd ask if she could come with him, too. He realized how much he'd truly enjoy showing her the world. Her delight in new experiences would make a road trip exciting in a way it hadn't been for a long time.

But she didn't ask. Instead, she simply nodded. "I see. That's a great idea. I hope she's well enough to travel."

"She will be." He didn't bother to keep the fierceness from his tone. Magic would make it so.

"Do you, uh…" Now Jade took a sudden interest in her fingernails. "Do you ever plan to come by this way again?"

He thought of his resolve, his intention of maybe trying to nourish the embers that sizzled between them. But he'd promised not to hurt her and he wouldn't. Making a promise he wasn't even sure he wanted to keep would be wrong. All he could give her was the truth. The truth as he knew it right at this instant.

"There's so much to see, so many places in this world I haven't yet explored," he told her. "Except for my home base in Houston, I don't usually make a return trip."

"You could make a new home base," she said. Though she kept her face expressionless, he saw from the telltale tremble of her lower lip how much it cost her to say such a thing.

Longing seized him, raw and like a visceral punch in his gut.

"I might have to think about that," he said, his tone deliberately light.

Her barely perceptible nod tightened his chest. "I understand. You'll think about it, and then you'll move on. For you, it's easier that way, right?"

Not sure how to answer, he swallowed. More than anything, he didn't want to mess this up. But he couldn't do this now, not yet, not until he knew his little girl was going to make it.

Now she met his eyes, the storm brewing in hers warning him he might not like her next words. "It's not always… Sometimes you might consider…"

Though he knew what she was trying to say, he wasn't sure he could handle her calling him a coward. If indeed that was her intention.

"I like life to be as uncomplicated as possible," he began.

"Really?" she shot back. "That must be pretty hard to do while keeping a relationship going with a seriously ill five-year-old."

And she had him there. The truth of what she hadn't said struck him. When something mattered enough, he went back. He made himself present.

Could he do that for her? Did she even want him to?

Or would one of them end up being hurt? Again, the promise he'd made her sisters—hell, the promise he'd made himself—wouldn't allow him to give her hope. Any kind, not even the smallest sliver, until all of this was over, and he knew for certain what he would be able to do. He knew what he wanted. Her. He'd do everything he could in his power to get there. But first, he had to take care of Eve.

Still, Jade gave no appearance of backing down. "I'll be fine," he said, his voice soft. "So will you."

"But it doesn't have to be like that," she insisted, with that stubborn tilt of her chin he had come to recognize and now found beautiful. "Sometimes the worst thing is to walk away. It takes more courage to stay."

He knew that. Damn, he knew that. If life had turned out differently, been simpler... But it hadn't and it wasn't and he refused to make any promises he couldn't keep.

"I'm not your former fiancé," he said. "So please don't treat me like I am."

The shock and pain in her eyes made him immediately regret what he'd said. "I'm sorry," he told her. "I didn't mean to...the way it came out. I just need you to understand."

"Understand?" she managed. "Who told you about Ross?" she asked, her quiet voice unemotional.

He sighed. "Can we just forget I said that?"

"No." Twin spots of color blazed high on her cheeks. "I want to know who told you."

"They had the best of intentions."

Before he'd even finished, she shook her head. "Those brats. When?"

"The second time I showed up at your house uninvited."

One corner of her mouth curled into the beginning of a wry smile. "I wonder why they'd even consider doing such a thing."

"I think they were warning me."

"Warning you against what? Me?"

He had to smile at that. "Hurting you. They told me you'd been almost engaged once and something along the lines of if I hurt you I'd be answering to them."

Now she laughed, the joy in the sound making him, absurdly, want to haul her up against him and kiss her senseless. He contained himself, barely.

There were women, he realized. And then there was Jade. She wasn't just the most beautiful woman he'd ever met, but one of a kind. Her strong sense of loyalty to her family, her dedication and love for Libby…and he'd seen how her customers—and their pets—clearly adored her.

As he did. Most of the extremely beautiful women he'd met over the course of his career—models, actresses and singers—were superficial, self-absorbed twits. Not Jade. Her beauty ran deeper than her appearance. He'd never met such a kind and sincere woman, which might sound boring, if she didn't have a body that made him think of sin.

Plus she had a way of looking at him as if she thought he stood ten feet tall. Around her, he felt like he did.

For him, the future had never been a source of worry, at least not until Violet had become ill and died, and then he'd nearly lost Eve. He'd taken solace in his freedom, comparing himself to the wind—here one day, and gone the next. He'd taken care to make sure he was always available for Eve and, to a lesser extent, her father, Jim. He never wanted Violet's beloved daughter to ache with missing someone the way he had.

And he vowed never to miss any woman again. He wouldn't risk that kind of agony. Once was enough.

Except Jade had somehow sneaked her way past his defenses. Her beauty intrigued him; her generosity of spirit captivated him.

His life would be much less beautiful without her in it. Lonely, even. He'd miss her once he'd left Forestwood.

Stunned, he froze. He'd also miss Libby, he told himself. And Sapphire and Pearl, Amber and Opal and the rest of the Burnett family.

He could definitely visit, right? Except since he'd lost Violet, he'd tried to make it a habit never to retrace his footsteps, other than the one exception he'd made for Eve. And he'd deliberately kept himself busy so he'd never been lonely since taking to the road. But now he felt the ghost of loneliness whistling around him like a specter, just waiting for him to strike out on his own.

Not many men were given a second chance. Many of his kind went their entire life without finding a mate, never mind two.

Torn, he swallowed hard. Eve had to come first. He needed to focus on his daughter until she got well. Then and only then, could he turn his attention to a relationship.

Jade would wait for him if he asked, he knew. But he never wanted to condemn such a vibrantly alive woman as Jade to a half-life, always waiting for Rance to brush through town on his way to somewhere else.

With a flush of heat, he realized that was exactly how he'd been living, halfway, always on the fringes of things, never jumping fully in.

Maybe the time had come to make more out of life. Maybe he should consider seizing what he and Jade had with both hands and holding on tightly, so tightly he'd never let go.

Again, he forced himself to stay on track. First, he

needed to rescue Eve. Assess her condition and get her well. Then and only then would he allow himself to take a second look at what he'd be letting go if he went back to his former life.

"Are you all right?" she asked, her voice breaking into his thoughts. Once again, she'd pushed aside her own hurt and what should have been anger to care about him.

He wanted to kiss her so badly it hurt. How could it be possible that he could ever deserve a woman like her?

"I sure am," he replied, standing up and holding out his hand for her to take. "Come here. Walk with me to the car. I want to tell you good-night and head on back to my motel so I can go to bed. It's been a long day and we've got a lot to think about. We can talk again in the morning."

She slipped her hand into his without a word, stunning him again with her generosity of spirit. Side by side, neither feeling the need to break the silence, they walked down the porch steps toward his rental car.

After he unlocked the driver's door, he turned and cupped her face with both his hands. A hundred words he couldn't say ran through his mind. Instead of speaking, he lowered his head and kissed her. She opened her mouth, giving him full rein to taste her sweetness. For a brief moment, he let himself drown in her and then he did one of the hardest things he'd ever done. He pulled away and smiled gently down at her. "See you in the morning."

Jade stood in the driveway long after Rance's taillights had disappeared in the darkness. Then, giving in to impulse, she turned and ran into the woods behind her house. As soon as she could no longer see the yellow lights from the kitchen, she stripped off her clothes, leaving her necklace on as she always did, dropped to the ground and initiated the change.

She didn't need to think, to worry. She needed to give

vent to her savage anger, and the best way she could think of to do this was in her wolf form.

Because she rushed the shape-shifting, it hurt. She didn't care; in fact, she reveled in the pain. As soon as she'd become fully lupine, she took off in a run, keeping low to the ground while her amazingly talented nose detected the presence of the small game she planned to hunt tonight.

Though she did her best, a couple of hours later Jade finally admitted defeat. She couldn't outrun her pain.

Plodding back to the spot where she'd left her clothing, she shifted back, slower this time.

Her entire body aching as much as her heart, she dressed and hurried back home. She slipped inside the front door, praying she didn't run into anyone. Her luck, at least in this, held, and when she reached her bedroom, she actually locked the door and kept the light off.

The last thing she wanted to do tonight was talk to anyone. She needed to be alone, to allow herself to wallow in the misery she couldn't seem to shake. Maybe that way, she could act normally in the morning. As if her heart wasn't breaking.

First thing after dawn, her cell phone rang. Libby. Calling to tell her the Fae princess was there and had asked to see both Jade and Rance. Which meant Jade needed to suck it up and call Rance.

Glancing at the clock—shortly after seven-thirty—she punched in his number. She kept her tone brisk, didn't apologize for waking him up. Instead, she told him what had transpired and asked him to meet her out at Libby's place in thirty minutes.

Then she rushed through her morning routine—a quick shower, not washing her hair, then brushing her teeth and applying some mascara before dressing.

Again she lucked out. In the kitchen, she managed to

snag a cup of coffee in a travel mug and get to her car without encountering anyone.

At this hour, traffic seemed lighter. Forestwood didn't exactly have a rush hour, but most people had to be at work at eight or nine, so there was a bit of traffic in the downtown area. This eased up as she left the outskirts behind her.

When Jade arrived, Rance had just pulled up. He got out of his rental car and waited for her to park.

Her heart rate sped up and she unbuckled her seat belt and opened her door. Eyeing him, his faded jeans low on narrow hips, his gaze shuttered as he watched her approach, filling her with such a sense of familiarity and rightness she nearly stopped in her tracks.

And then she remembered the dreams. She'd had them every night for several weeks in a row prior to Rance's arrival in town. In one of them, she'd actually been here, right at this spot, walking toward him with her heart full of longing.

Just like now. More than anything, she wished he'd meet her halfway, pick her up in his strong arms and crush her to him.

Right. Telling herself to get a grip, she managed to smile brightly up at him. "You made good time."

"Not much traffic." He didn't smile back. "As soon as I heard Breena wanted to meet with us, I rushed. I figure she found out what her brother has done. I'm guessing this meeting should have something to do with a plan to get Eve out of Fae."

For his sake, she hoped so. He'd been out of his mind with worry, and the delay only made him champ at the bit. She felt a swift stab of pain that she knew him so well, then pushed it away. Good old Jade, she thought. Nothing but practical.

"Come on." She took his arm. "Let's go inside and find out."

Breena stood in Libby's living room, looking as out of place as a rare flower in the middle of a woodpile.

"I'm glad you could make it so quickly," Libby said, greeting them both with her trademark hugs. "Please, come in and sit down."

As they made their way into the room, Breena spoke. "The hour has come."

Relief flashed across Rance's handsome face. "It's about time," he muttered under his breath.

"Time for what," Jade asked, causing Breena to fix her with an incredulous stare.

"I've helped you," Breena pointed out, including both Jade and Rance in her bright gaze. "Your cousin and the babies are safe. Now you must assist me. I claim my repayment."

"Payment?" Jade asked.

"The Fae do nothing for free," Libby told her, patting the younger woman's arm.

"Plus she told us she'd need our assistance." Rance continued to study the Fae princess. "Just as we also need hers."

"Again?" Breena arched one brow. "What now?"

"My stepdaughter and her father are being held prisoner by your brother. We need your help to free them."

"That can be accomplished," Breena said. "Once you help me complete my task."

"Which is?"

"Your aid to regain my kingdom."

Chapter 17

A battle? Not what Jade had been expecting to hear. After all, she and Rance had no magical powers. Libby had some abilities, but very little that would aid anyone in a fight.

"How?"

"In the days of old," Breena spoke carefully, "Fae royalty rode dragons into battle."

Jade stared, but Rance nodded. "I remember reading about that."

"Me, too," Libby chimed in.

"That's what we need now." Gaze skirting over Jade and Libby, Breena locked on Rance. "Not an army, but enough Drakkor that Cai's people will realize we are the rightful rulers."

"Are you?" Jade had to ask. "I mean, how do we know who is supposed to be on the throne?"

Breena blinked. For a second, Jade thought she might have angered her, but then the Fae princess laughed, a pleasant sound like bells tinkling. "Because I'm the oldest and my father designated me the heir before he quit."

"Quit? Like a job?"

"Sort of. Since Fae are immortal, when one of us decides they want a different life, such as a ruler who no longer wishes to be king, we can quit and use our magic to not only change our appearance, but our identity. The last I heard, my father is living somewhere in the South Pacific as a beach bum."

"Why wouldn't he help his family?"

Breena snorted. "He says not only does he not want to take sides, but he wishes to wash his hands of everything to do with the land of the Fae. He's a character, let me tell you." Still smiling at the memory, Breena waved her hands and a rolled-up parchment scroll appeared in her long-fingered hands. With its yellowed color and crackly edges, the document was clearly ancient. "Here." She held it out to Jade. "Read it yourself."

Accepting it awkwardly, Jade hesitated. She hated to try to unroll it and somehow damage the thing.

Her dilemma must have seemed clear to Breena. The Fae woman made another gesture with her long fingers, and the scroll unrolled itself.

"There." Breena pointed. "Second paragraph, lines three and four."

Sure enough, the flowery and archaic language named Princess Breena as ruler. Prince Cai had been named, but only with instructions that he assist his older sister in any way she needed.

"Satisfied?" Breena asked. At Jade's nod, she gestured and the scroll magically rolled back up before disappearing into thin air.

"Ok, but I still don't understand about your father," Rance put in. "If the document lists you as heir, even if he wants nothing to do with this land, why wouldn't he take steps to ensure his wishes are followed?"

"I asked him that exact same question." Breena rolled her eyes. "He says figuring out how to deal with conflict is part of what makes a ruler. Anyway, Jade, now you have confirmation. Is that enough for you?"

"Yes. Thank you," Jade said. She refused to feel foolish. It never hurt to check on the truth of someone's claims. Especially when that someone was about to ask Rance to join her in battle.

"Now, back to my request." Breena drew herself up to her impressive height—Jade guessed the other woman easily topped six feet. "I need just a few Drakkor willing to allow me and my supporters to ride them. We will enter the castle by flying. It's my hope the sight of the majestic Drakkor will be enough to make Cai's followers realize that they've backed the wrong person."

"I can get a couple of men," Rance said, voice thoughtful, his expression wary. "No women, as they are far too precious to risk. And most of them are pregnant."

"I can go." Libby spoke up, the firmness to her quiet tone telling them all she refused to take no for an answer. "Though I'm female, I'm far beyond my childbearing years. And I've spent way too long hiding in Forestwood Lake. I'd be honored to assist in your reclamation of your kingdom."

"No." Jade gasped, causing everyone to stare at her. "Libby, you can't risk yourself. I don't know what I'd do if something happened to you."

Libby crossed to her, wrapping her arms around Jade and pulling her in for a hug. She smelled as she always did, of cookies and vanilla, and home. Jade's eyes filled with tears as she hugged her charge back.

"Honey, look at me," Libby ordered. When Jade did as she requested, Libby gently wiped a tear off Jade's cheek. "You're my Guardian, and I understand your fears. But I can no longer live in a tree-lined bubble, hiding out from everyone and everything."

"But the danger…"

"Is slight," Breena interrupted. "Actually, I'd even consider it nonexistent. No Fae, not even ones as avaricious as my younger brother, would dare to attempt to harm a Drakkor. Our history with the dragons has made them precious to us. Even more so now that their numbers have dwindled."

The certainty in her voice made it difficult to doubt her. Still, the thought of losing Rance and Libby made Jade want to weep.

Except she wouldn't. She was much stronger than that.

The determined set of Rance's jaw told her he'd already made up his mind. And the steel in Libby's eyes spoke of her own resolve.

"Let me make a few calls," Rance said. "I'll see who else I can round up."

Breena nodded. "I appreciate this." Her crystal blue gaze found Jade. "And I promise, your cousin and her friends will survive their pregnancies. As will the babies. The mothers will need lots of support and understanding to deal with such powerful children."

Jade nodded, trying not to resent the beautiful princess. She didn't dare look at Rance, for fear he might see her emotions on her face or in her eyes. She didn't know how she'd breathe while he was off fighting a battle for the Fae.

To her shock, Rance moved to stand in front of her, lifting her chin with his large hand and making her face him. "Imagine what a beautiful sight it will be," he said, his voice quiet, the gray of his eyes darkened to the color of the lake after a storm. "I'd love for you to use my camera and capture some images for me to look at later."

Since his camera was his most precious possession, that registered first. And then, as she took in the rest of what he'd said, she swallowed, almost afraid to speak in case she understood him wrong. "Are you saying…that I'll be there?"

He kissed her, his mouth lingering on her lips. A quiet kiss, but one that seared her to her soul just the same. "Of course you'll be there. That is, if you want to be."

Now she lifted her head and gave him her truth. "I can't think of anywhere else I'd want to be than by your side." Of course, she didn't have the heart to remind him that he couldn't bring his camera into the land of Fae.

One corner of his sensual mouth quirked with pleasure. For a breathless second, she thought he might kiss her again.

"Good, then it's all settled." Breena spoke briskly.

"No." Rance turned from Jade to face the others. "It's not. I need assurance that Jim and Eve will be safe."

"Like I said, I can make no promises," Breena began.

"And by safe, I mean we get them out of Fae, away from your brother. And finally, you'll heal her."

"I…" Breena closed her mouth, biting back whatever else she might have been about to say. "Of course we'll attempt to liberate her from Cai. As to healing her, I will do my best."

"Your best isn't good enough." On this point, Rance's tone made it clear he wasn't going to budge. "From what Jade told me about the pregnant shifters, you have the ability to heal whatever this illness is that's killing Drakkors. Don't you?"

Breena bit her lip and didn't answer.

Now Libby stepped forward. "Do you understand what it will mean to the Drakkors if this is true? We are very close to becoming extinct. If you truly value us, revere us, as you said your people did in the past, then you will think very carefully how you answer."

Jade stared, amazed. In all the years she'd known Libby, she'd never heard her speak with such forceful authority.

"My magic isn't always foolproof," Breena finally admitted, looking like she'd swallowed something vile. "As queen, every spell I cast should be successful. But ever since Cai seized the throne…"

Before she'd even finished, Libby nodded with understanding. "I have the same problem," she said. "Though I don't cast spells, I have other abilities. Lately, I've noticed some stuttering. As if I'm having trouble starting and then sustaining."

"Exactly." The relief flooding Breena's face made Libby smile. When Libby enveloped the Fae princess in one of her comforting hugs, Jade watched as longing, amazement and finally gratitude flashed in Breena's exotic eyes.

"And you think I have an expressive face," she muttered to Rance. He chuckled and gave her a quick shoulder hug.

"Breena." Libby's soft voice seemed edged with steel as she continued to push for an honest answer. "Are you or are you not able to attempt to eradicate this awful plague that's taken so many of my kind?"

To her credit, this time the other woman carefully considered the question.

"I can make no promises," Breena finally answered. "All I can do is my best. I know I can help Di and her unborn child, as well as her friends, but only because I have done that before, with great success."

"What about my stepdaughter?" Rance asked. "I need a guarantee that she'll be safe if we attack Cai and his followers."

This time she shook her head and met his gaze full-on. "You know as well as I do that there are no guarantees in life. Again, I will do the best I can to make sure she is protected."

Rance eyed her with a narrow gaze.

This time, Libby spoke up, becoming the voice of reason. "Honestly, if Breena and her people fly at his castle on the backs of dragons, wouldn't you think the last thing Cai is going to be thinking about is some halfling child?"

"Good point." Breena laughed. Then, expression once again serious, she held Rance's gaze. "We need to act now. How long will it take you to get a couple other Drakkor?"

"Honestly, I have no idea. Let me make some phone calls." Rance stepped out onto the deck with his cell phone, leaving Jade alone with Breena and Libby.

"Do you really think this will work?" Jade asked, curious. "I only met your brother once, but he doesn't seem like the type of person too impressed with a few dragons."

Tilting her head, Breena smiled. "I'm not worried about Cai so much. It's his people. My people. I need them to see me on the back of a majestic dragon, and realize it's my destiny to lead them."

The plan still sounded far-fetched to Jade, but she kept her mouth shut. Instead, she pulled out her own cell phone and busied herself checking her email and Twitter.

A few minutes later, Rance came back inside. The defeated resignation on his face told them that he'd had no luck. "I can't get anyone else," he said. "Libby and I will have to do. Are two Drakkor enough to accomplish what you want?"

"They'll have to be." Breena's grim voice matched her expression. "How long does it take you to shape-shift?"

Now Libby and Rance stared, both wearing identical amazed expressions. "You want to do this right now?"

"Yes."

Ever practical, Jade took charge. "We'll need to get closer to the portal. If they were to change into dragons here, it'd be too dangerous. Someone might see them."

"Point taken." Breena gestured, and they found themselves back in the forest, the two birch trees a few feet away.

Again Rance and Libby exchanged glances.

"I need a minute," Rance said. He took Jade's arm and

drew her a few paces away from the others. "I know you're aware that you watching me change breaks every law of our kind," he began.

"Unless we're committed mates," she finished. Though she hadn't intended to sound like she was fishing for anything, the second she spoke she realized what her words sounded like. "I didn't mean..." she tried to explain, aware the more she talked, the more flustered she became.

"It's okay." He kissed the tip of her nose, sending a jolt of heat all the way to her toes. "Let me finish. Most shifters aren't even aware of the Drakkor. What you see might be frightening to you, but you know it's still me. Just like when you become... whatever beast you are."

Lifting her chin, Jade nodded. "I'm a wolf, as I'm sure you guessed. Part of the Pack, of course."

He nodded. "I figured. Anyway, remember when you see me after, it's just like when you shift into a wolf. All right?"

She nodded, wondering why he felt the need to explain this to her. "Once you're in your dragon shape, what do you want me to do?"

"I'll lower my head. There are some ridges on my nose and neck. Use those to get up on my back. And hold on. Once we're in Fae, I want you to get down and take yourself somewhere safe. I imagine Breena will have a few of her people she'll want riding me."

"A few?" Heart in her throat, she searched his face. "How many people can you hold?"

"I dunno. I've only seen others do it. They only carried a couple at a time. I'd imagine not more than three."

"Three." He'd sounded supremely unconcerned. She swallowed. "What about Libby?"

"She's a female, so her dragon will be a bit smaller. She can only carry one."

"I will ride her," Breena said, so close she made Jade

jump. "Enough of this nonsense. We need to get through the portal. Time is growing short."

Rance didn't move. "What are you not telling us?"

Breena sighed. "I've received word that Cai is working on a magical spell to attack me. We need to strike first."

Until now, Jade hadn't truly considered that this was a war. She'd tried to buy in to the picture Breena painted, of majestic and fierce dragons in the sky, and the awestruck population being so thunderstruck they fell to their knees in reverent acceptance. Doing so kept her fear at bay. Now she had to face the fact that Cai and his people might actually fight back.

"Keep Rance and Libby safe, you hear me?" Jade rounded on Breena. "They're much more than just some props for you to use as transportation."

Breena shook her head. "Enough." She gestured at Rance. "Do your shape-shifter thing. Libby has promised to get started once you do."

Instead of answering, Rance turned away and dropped to the ground. "Give me some space," he growled.

Jade let Breena lead her away, though she kept her gaze glued on Rance. She'd seen her own kind change a hundred times, witnessed numerous humans become wolf, but she'd never, ever imagined a dragon.

And this was Rance. Until now she could only wonder what kind of dragon he'd become.

He groaned, the sound echoed by Libby's feminine voice. Startled, Jade glanced from one to the other. They were both dear to her, and she didn't want to miss a thing, but if she had to make a choice, she'd watch Rance. As Libby's Guardian, she'd seen Libby numerous times in her other form, though she'd usually been in the water. All Jade had been able to see was part of Libby's other form, never her entire body.

And she'd never seen her change, either.

Yet Jade couldn't tear her eyes away from Rance. There were no dancing pinpricks of light surrounding him as his body writhed, just a puff and a swirl of smoke while his bones lengthened and changed.

And then, while she watched, a huge beast with a fierce triangular head and sharp teeth stood where Rance had been. Curious, fascinated, Jade moved closer. His scales were iridescent, gray one moment, pearly shimmers of multicolors the next.

He reared up on his hind feet and spread his wings. Those things were massive; the wingspan had to be thirty feet or more.

Turning his head, he fixed his gaze on Jade. Unbelievably, she could see Rance inside the alien eyes.

As he lowered his head to the forest floor, she remembered his instructions and walked over. Even though her heart felt about to pound out of her chest, she reached out her hand and stroked his muzzle.

His skin felt soft, not leathery as she'd expected. As she touched him, his giant eyes half closed and she could have sworn she heard him give a low purr.

"Get on," Breena urged. "I'm going to go mount Libby and take us through the portal. My people will be waiting for us on the other side."

Though she felt awkward, Jade held her breath and climbed up on Rance's massive neck. She gripped the finlike protuberances and used them to climb. When she reached a relatively flat area right between his wings, she sat, gripping a smaller knob that appeared to be designed exactly for this purpose.

"Now!" Breena shouted, and Jade realized the Fae woman sat astride the other dragon—a beautiful creature with misty multicolored scales who had to be Libby. As Jade stared, the dragon turned and looked directly at her with Libby's soft eyes.

Then, as Jade marveled, she took a deep breath. A second later they went plummeting into the darkness of the portal.

Wildness coursing through his veins, Rance spread his wings and dove into the air. He'd heard stories of this sort of thing all his life. He'd seen the old illustrated books, traced the intricate miniature paintings with his fingers. But until this instant, he'd never known what it felt like to fly with the weight of a rider on his back.

That the rider should be Jade made the experience much more intimate. Surreal, even. Despite the thickness of his hide, the heat from her body warmed him all the way to his heart. He swore he could feel every breath she took, every tremor that shook her small body as she clutched his.

In his dragon form he'd always been able to sense human emotions such as anger or fear. He knew Jade felt a bit uncomfortable, then stark terror as they blazed through the portal. But when they emerged on the other side, shooting up into the impossibly blue sky like a bullet, he shared her exhilaration; the pureness of her wonder and joy fueled him, warming him to parts of his dragon body that had never felt such heat.

This warmth, this sense of oneness, gave him a deeper sense of being alive than he'd ever felt. Right then, he knew. No matter what happened from this moment on, he knew he could never let Jade go.

As he and Libby wheeled high in the sky, skimming through clouds, he spied the pearly marble castle up ahead. Breena said something to Libby but the wind snatched it away and Rance couldn't hear.

Libby altered course, overshooting the castle and heading directly for the small village that lay beyond it.

As their shadows blocked the sun, people looked up. Those outside called for others, and soon it seemed as if every person there had streamed into the street. All looking up and pointing.

From this mass of Fae, Rance picked up a sense of awe-struck wonder. No animosity or fear, just amazement. He glanced over at Libby and saw Breena sitting straight and proud, her expression both regal and full of warm greeting.

They landed in the open meadow between the village and the castle. In a few moments, they were surrounded by the villagers. Love radiated from them, all beautiful Fae who placed their hands on Rance and Libby. No one hung back; instead, they all seemed eager to touch and exclaim over the dragons in that beautiful lilting Fae tongue that Rance wished he understood.

After several minutes of this, Breena finally spoke. Everyone stilled at the sound of her voice. Faces upturned, they took in the sight of her on the majestic yet docile dragon. Libby saw him watching and grinned, exposing her sharp pearly white teeth. A few gasped, but most continued to study Breena.

At her command, Libby lowered her head so the Fae princess could dismount. As soon as her feet touched the earth, flowers of every color began to spring from the green grass.

She continued to speak, her arms outstretched. Even among a people known for beauty, Breena glowed with a brilliant sort of radiance.

The villagers began to ask questions. Breena answered, and even though Rance could not decipher the meaning, her rich voice rang of authority and love.

Still on Rance's back, Jade shifted her weight. Like him, she understood nothing of what Breena or the other Fae said. From the intent way Libby listened, he wondered if she understood the language.

Breena spoke out—something that sounded like a command. The people cheered, their combined voices lifting to the sky.

Breena said something to Libby. At her command, Libby opened her immense mouth and roared a great cry of fire and smoke.

The crowd went silent. Then, one by one, Breena's people dropped to their knees in front of her.

Only then did Breena turn to face Rance and Jade. "They have agreed," she said happily. "They will march upon the castle. My people will approach from the other side. And we—" she grinned "—we'll attack from the air."

He felt Jade stiffen. Praying she didn't question Breena, he tried to adjust his own attitude. In the history of his people, war had never ended well for their kind. Still, he knew in order to rescue Eve, he'd have no choice.

From the castle, a horn blared. A second later, another. The village Fae shifted uneasily, but continued to stand their ground. Breena shouted out some sort of order, and as the people began to march toward the castle, Breena mounted Libby and they lifted into the air.

Figuring he should follow, a second later Rance did the same, praying Jade had a good grip and wouldn't fall.

As they soared over the pearly stone, the turrets mere feet beneath their wings, below them the startled soldiers pointed and stared. A few dropped their weapons. That was when Rance realized Breena's plan just might work.

Circling, Rance and Libby set down in the middle of the courtyard. They'd barely landed when Cai appeared, surrounded by his usual retinue of men.

"What's the meaning of this?" he called. Rance saw how, once the prince had glanced around and took in the reverence in the faces of his people, his own expression hardened.

"This isn't going to be easy," Jade warned Breena. She

nodded and looked at Rance. The sadness behind her brilliant smile told him she'd never thought it would be.

"I've come back to claim my rightful throne, brother," Breena called out, still seated on the back of her dragon. At her words, several of Cai's soldiers muttered to one another.

"Go ahead and try," Cai sneered. "Not only are you greatly outnumbered, but my soldiers are not afraid of your dragons."

At his words, Libby opened her mouth and roared again. A rope of fire flared out, tendrils licking at the feet of the soldiers and no doubt singeing some of the hair on their heads. The men—save Cai—jumped back. Feet apart, hands clenched into fists, he never wavered in his stare at his sister. If looks could kill...

While Rance didn't like Cai at all, he couldn't help but feel a grudging admiration for the way the guy stood his ground. The Fae prince was either brave as hell or really stupid.

As if Cai heard his thoughts, he turned and directed a swift glare at Rance before focusing back on his sister. "I don't know where you got the dragons," he said. "But soon I will have one of my own."

Rage filled Rance as he realized Cai was speaking of Eve. Shuddering, he tried to throttle the emotion, but a snort of fire escaped him. This time, the blast had Cai taking a step back.

Which pleased Rance inordinately.

"The one you have is not grown yet," Breena declared. "Not only has she not come into the ability to change, but she's gravely ill. I fail to see how she will be of any use to you at all in the current situation."

"How do you know this?" For the first time since they'd appeared, Cai appeared discomforted. "No one except my closest advisers..."

"Enough," Breena roared, sounding more like a queen

than she ever had. "It does not matter how I know, only that I do. The only thing that matters is how you want to do this, Cai? Because that's up to you. You can surrender gracefully and peacefully, or declare an all-out war."

"War?" He raised an elegant eyebrow. "With what army? All I see is you, a human girl and two mangy dragons."

This time, both Libby and Rance bathed him in fire, making sure the heat blasted him. This time, he staggered back, falling to his knees as he attempted to extinguish the flames.

"Consider this your final warning." Breena shook her head, her long tresses swirling around her as if they'd taken on a life of their own. "In fact, my patience has worn quite thin. You stole from me what is rightfully mine. Do you intend to give me back my birthright peacefully or must I take it from you?"

As Cai climbed slowly back to his feet, for a heartbeat Rance thought the fool would continue his defiance. As a demonstration of his support for Breena, Rance reared up on his hind legs, unfurling his massive wings.

Cai barely glanced at Rance, and his face revealed nothing. Staring at his sister, he finally nodded. "You win. You may have your kingdom. But be aware, this is not over."

At his words, all of his soldiers knelt and bowed their head in homage to their new queen.

Too easy, Rance thought. But a quick glance at Breena showed her apparent unconcern.

Now, at Breena's instruction, Libby lowered her massive head. Breena dismounted, striding over to her brother. "Give it to me," she ordered, holding out her hand.

Jaw tight, he reached into his pocket. Instead of whatever talisman Breena had asked for, a knife flashed in his hand. He leaped for her, either intending to stab her or hold the knife at her throat.

Chapter 18

Rance couldn't react—if he tried to burn the prince, the fire would also harm the princess. Libby had the same problem.

But Cai hadn't counted on his men. His own men, who had already dropped and sworn their allegiance to their new queen.

Two immediately disarmed him, ignoring as he screamed invectives at them. With his hands behind his back, some sort of Fae handcuffs were placed on him. Then, and only then, did Breena repeat her request.

"Where is it?"

Eyes defiant, Cai didn't respond.

Breena sighed. Waving one hand, she spoke a few words in that lilting Fae language. Immediately a hawk screeched from somewhere above them. One of the soldiers tossed Breena a heavy glove. She slipped it on her hand. Then she spoke again, holding her gloved hand out. The bird dove down like a bullet, slowing at the last minute to execute a graceful landing on her hand.

Fluffing its feathers, the hawk appeared pleased with itself. The bird wore a silken cord with a sparkling pendant around its neck.

"Here we are," Breena cooed, carefully removing the necklace. Once she'd done so, she placed it around her own neck.

The soldiers cheered. As they did, they were joined by the villagers, who streamed into the courtyard through the open gate.

"And now," Breena said, facing Rance, "we will find your Eve."

Rance wanted to change. To him, it would be imperative that he greet Eve and her father as the man they all knew. As he swung his huge head around wildly, looking for a place, Libby spoke inside his head, in the way of all Drakkor.

Not yet, my friend. They will need us to travel back to the portal. You'll have plenty of time to change back to yourself once we get them home.

Though he could barely keep his frustration inside, he nodded. *Fine.*

"Now." Breena spun to face Cai's soldiers. "Tell us where we can find the girl."

Eve. Rance could scarcely contain his impatience. Libby must have sensed this, as she swung her massive head around and fixed him with a clear look of warning.

Throttling his impatience, he waited, to all outward appearances calm. As long as Eve was all right, he would do nothing. But if Cai or his henchmen had harmed one hair on that little girl's head... Nothing would restrain him.

"What's she to you?" Cai spoke, his tone subdued and genuinely curious. Still, despite his lack of defensive posture—which might have been only because his hands were still bound behind his back—his sapphire eyes still blazed defiance. "As I'm sure you've learned, I have great plans for her."

Rance hoped Breena didn't tell Cai the truth about his relationship to Eve. He sensed if the Fae prince had even an inkling that the little girl was important to Rance, he'd hinder her ability to leave Fae out of spite.

"The girl doesn't belong here," Breena said, nothing more.

Cai's gaze narrowed. "So? Lots of humans end up in Fae and never leave."

"You know as well as I do that she'd not merely human. She's half-Drakkor. She and her human father need to go home."

"Her father?" Once again, Cai's lips curved in that sneer that made Rance ache to reach out a claw and wipe it right off that face. "I'm afraid that's not possible."

Rance froze. Breena, too. "What do you mean?" she asked in a deadly calm voice. "Why would that not be possible?"

Cai stared at his feet with studied nonchalance. "Because he died."

Died? This time, Rance could not ignore the flash of rage. He roared, sending a wall of flame toward the Fae prince. Breena quickly gestured, making an invisible wall to block it. Otherwise, Cai just might be dead, too.

Calm yourself, Libby ordered, her voice brisk and authoritative in his head. *Focus on what's most important. Eve. We've got to get her out of here first. You can't go around meting out retribution. Not yet.*

Yet. Clutching on to that word, he took heart. If someone had harmed Jim, they would pay. But Libby was absolutely correct. Getting Eve out had to be a priority. The only priority for now.

Stepping back, Rance refolded his wings. Cai looked from him to Breena and back again. "What is it that you're not telling me?" he asked, his narrow gaze full of speculation.

She ignored him. "Did you kill him?"

"Why would I do that?" Cai's indignant tone seemed fake. "He had a heart attack and his spirit left before we found him."

Breena cocked her head. "And the child? Did the child witness his death?"

"She was asleep in another room. Though they wanted to be together, we kept them apart as much as possible so the girl could rest." Cai spread his hands, his effort to appear sincere making Rance wonder what else he might be planning.

If Breena harbored any of the same suspicions, she gave no sign. "Where is his body?"

"In a grave." Cai shrugged. "We buried it. If I remember right, that's what humans prefer."

Though it took real effort, Rance forced himself not to think about the circumstances that must have surrounded Jim's death. He could only hope Cai had spoken the truth and Eve hadn't witnessed them doing anything to Jim.

"Do you wish to visit the grave site?" Cai's silky smooth tone contained more than a hint of mockery.

"No." Breena shook her head. "Bring out the girl," she demanded. "Now."

Immediately, several soldiers rushed off to comply.

Watching them go, Cai shook his head. "A waste of time," he said. "As you've already pointed out to me, she's of no use to anyone."

"She has family who love and miss her," Breena told him. "With their help, she'll be able to grow into what she was meant to be."

"If she doesn't die first." To Rance's disbelief, Cai laughed. "She's still pretty sick. My healers didn't have much luck with healing her. It's that same old Drakkor illness. As I'm sure you remember, it usually is fatal. I haven't seen any reason to think this girl will be an exception."

Rance bit down hard to keep from revealing his fury. Then, to his shock, he felt Jade's small hand stroking his hide. She offered her support in the only way she could without drawing Cai's attention, through touch.

Warmth filled him, along with a sense of calm. Women like her and Libby and even Breena were a rarity and he considered himself damn lucky to have them in his life. He'd make her aware of his gratitude later, when he could.

And also later, he'd need to consider the truth about how Jim had died. If he learned Cai had killed the other man, he'd plan how to avenge his friend and Eve's father.

As the soldiers reappeared, they brought with them a stretcher, one man supporting each end. On the cot, Rance could only see a motionless form under a blanket.

His senses prickled as a feeling of foreboding filled him. Eve had been pretty sick before. He didn't want to think about how much worse she might have gotten since she hadn't been under a hospital's care. He was all she had now, and he vowed no matter what it took, he'd get her the best medicine money could buy.

And then, as the soldiers carried her over to Breena, she opened her eyes and looked at him. Really looked at him. With a flare of hope, he wondered if she recognized him inside the Drakkor body, even though he knew that would be highly unlikely.

When she turned away without giving the slightest hint of recognition, he swallowed back his disappointment.

"A lake monster!" she exclaimed. "With wings!" Though her voice wavered from weakness, she pushed herself to a sitting position and stared, her blue eyes huge in her pale face. "Oh, my gosh! Not just one, but two of them!"

The excitement in her tone made Rance grin, even though as a dragon it looked more like baring his teeth.

Seeing her alive and well, his chest felt about to explode with love.

And then Eve caught sight of Jade, sitting motionless on Rance's back. "You can ride them?"

"Yes." Jade's voice clogged with emotion. "Maybe someday you can, too."

"Oh, I'd love that!" Sighing happily, Eve's bright gaze drank both Rance and Libby in before fluttering half-closed. She yawned, and lay back on her stretcher, tugging up her blanket to her chin before falling back asleep.

"I used a sleeping spell," Breena told him. "We don't need her panicking when she goes through the portal. That's scary enough when you know what's going on. Plus, once you're home, her slumber will give you both enough time to shape-shift back."

Rance dipped his big head in a nod of agreement.

Breena strolled around to stand by Libby. With her elegant hand she stroked Libby's nose. "Once I get things settled here, I'll come visit you." She looked up at Jade and smiled. "Don't forget to call me when your cousin and her friends are ready to deliver."

"I won't," Jade answered.

"Now, Rance." Breena's voice turned serious. "If you could contact the other Drakkor—or the ones you mentioned who are protecting them—and let them know the queen of the Fae would like to form an alliance, I would appreciate that."

Again, Rance nodded. He appreciated that she'd asked instead of attempting to dictate. Breena would make a good queen. The Fae had chosen wisely.

"Are you ready?" Breena asked.

"Not yet," Rance replied. "What about Eve? You agreed to heal her as part of our deal."

Breena nodded. "I have kept my agreement. Along with

the sleeping spell, I used magic. Her healing has already begun."

"Thank you." Rance swallowed, struggling to keep his composure.

"Now, are you all ready?"

Both Rance and Libby nodded.

"Jade?"

"I'm ready," Jade answered.

"Then here we go. Eve will be sent with you." She looked at Jade. "Hold out your hand."

When Jade did, a tiny crystal bell appeared.

"Use this," Breena said. "Whenever you need me, use it."

"Thank you."

"You are most welcome." Smiling, Breena waved her fingers. Everything spun. Rance blinked, and they were back in the woods near the portal.

After climbing off Rance's back, Jade gave his surprisingly soft hide one more lingering caress before moving away so he could change back into his human form. She crossed to where Eve still slept, though the stretcher had vanished and she lay on a pile of multicolored leaves on the forest floor.

Moving closer, she studied the little girl, admiring her curly golden hair and delicate chin. Perfect skin, too, which made her wonder what Eve's mother had looked like.

She looked up to see Libby watching her and smiled. Libby dipped her huge head, her almond-shaped dragon eyes soft.

Simultaneously, Libby and Rance initiated the change. Again, Jade watched for the dance of the pinprick of lights, missing their absence. She wondered why the shape-shifting process seemed so different in dragon and wolf.

And then Rance stood before her, his powerful muscular body completely naked, his mysterious and sexy dragon tattoo emblazoned on his chest. She sucked in her breath, feeling the slow burn of desire low in her gut. Noticing, Rance grinned before turning and scooping up his clothes.

Jade looked away while he dressed. No reason to torment herself any more than she had to.

Stepping out from behind a tree, a fully clothed Libby hurried over to inspect the still-sleeping little girl. She placed her hand on Eve's forehead and closed her eyes.

"No fever," she announced. "Let's get her to my house and I'll check her out thoroughly."

"I really think she needs to go back to the hospital," Rance began. He stopped when Libby fixed him with one of her patented, no-nonsense looks.

"Not yet," Libby told him. "She's halfling. I honestly believe the human side of her is helping the Drakkor blood overcome the disease."

Jade nodded. "I agree." And if Libby was wrong, Jade had every intention of calling Breena and seeing if Fae magic could help. Honestly, she thought it could.

"All right," Rance finally agreed. "We'll give it a shot. But, Libby, if you can't help her, I'm taking her straight to the hospital."

"Agreed." Libby's radiant smile had him smiling back. Heart full, Jade watched the two of them for a moment before turning away. She didn't want to take the chance that Rance might see her love for him blazing from her eyes. He had enough to worry about right now.

"Are you ready?" she asked, glancing back over her shoulder in time to see Rance scoop Eve up in his arms.

"Lead the way," he said.

Jade nodded and started forward. "Crud." She turned and eyed the others. "We don't have a car. Breena sent us through with her magic. There's no way we can walk all the way back to Libby's with you carrying Eve."

Jaw tight, Rance considered. "While I'd rather not have

to, it can be done. Why don't you see if you can contact Breena again and have her use her magic to send us back to Libby's?"

Hesitantly, Jade rang the crystal bell. It made a tinkling sound, like tiny wind chimes in the breeze.

No sooner had she done this when Breena appeared. Rance explained what they needed.

"Just say the word." Her grin included all of them. "I thought of this issue right after I sent you through."

Rance gazed down at the still-slumbering child in his arms. "Will she wake up once she's there?"

"I'll make sure of it. Here we go." Breena wiggled her elegant fingers again.

"My back porch," Libby said, sounding satisfied. "Perfect."

A chilly breeze blew, stirring up the leaves. Out on the lake, small whitecaps were pushed toward shore by the wind.

Jade blinked, still slightly disoriented. She looked for Rance, finding him right behind her. The dazed and worried expression on his face made her heart ache. "Let's get Eve inside. I don't want her to get a chill."

Once inside, Rance gently lowered Eve onto the couch. Her eyelashes fluttered and she opened her eyes, her forehead wrinkling as she frowned in confusion. "Papa?" She met his gaze and then looked past him. "Where's Daddy?"

Jade saw the effort it took Rance to keep his face expressionless. At least her question meant Cai had told the truth and the little girl hadn't witnessed her father's death.

"He's..." Rance took a deep breath, his big fingers moving the hair away from her tiny face. "He's in heaven with the angels, sweetie. Just like your mommy."

Eve tilted her head, studying him. "Did I make him sick?"

"Oh, no, baby. Never think that." A flash of sorrow

crossed Rance's face. "He had something wrong with his heart. It had nothing to do with you."

"It didn't?"

"Not at all. I promise. And your daddy wouldn't want you to feel bad, either. He knows you'll miss him and be sad, but he'd never want you to think it was your fault."

Despite his reassurances, Eve pushed to her elbows in an attempt to sit. "He worked too hard to take care of me. That's why his heart gave out." Expression troubled, Eve held Rance's gaze. "He didn't know I heard him, but he used to whisper to me all the time. He'd say if I died, his heart would break. He must have thought I'd died if his heart stopped working."

Tears streamed down her heart-shaped face. "I want to see my daddy," she wailed.

"And you will someday," Jade interjected. "He will always be with you, watching over you and loving you."

"That's not enough," the little girl sobbed. "I want him here with me, not up in heaven with Mommy."

"You have me," Rance rasped. "And I promise I will do my best to make sure you're never alone."

"That's what Daddy said too." Eve rubbed at her swollen eyes, still sniffling. "How do I know I can believe you?"

"Because I love you," Rance answered.

"Where's my backpack?" Eve asked, her voice plaintive. "Daddy gave me a letter to give you if anything happened to him and I ever saw you again."

Jade located a small pink backpack and brought it to her. She unzipped it, and handed Rance a sealed envelope.

Hands trembling, he opened it. Withdrawing a paper, he began to read.

"What is it?" Eve asked.

"He had an attorney prepare a document granting me legal custody of you." He handed it to Jade, clearly unable to speak again. Covering his face in his hands, he bowed his head, his shoulders shaking.

Immediately, Eve reached her thin little arms out and attempted to hug him. "I'm sorry, Papa. Don't cry." Looking past him, her teary gaze found Jade. "All I do is make people sad."

"No, honey." Jade moved closer. Giving in to impulse, she wrapped her arms around both Rance and Eve. "Your daddy loved you and so does your papa." She read the letter. Jim had relinquished custody of his daughter to Rance. The paperwork merely awaited Rance's signature. The little girl considered her. "How do you know?"

Wiping at his eyes, Rance turned and gave Jade a quick look of gratitude before turning back to Eve. "She knows because Jade understands love."

"She does?"

"Yes." Rance leaned into the hug, pulling Jade and Eve closer, though he was careful not to hurt Eve. "She's been helping me try to find you. So has Libby over there."

Libby smiled softly, though she still kept her distance. "Believe me, you are loved, little one. And you are not alone."

Eve finally nodded, though her expression still seemed far too grave for one so young. "I know, but I still miss him."

"And you always will. That will never change. And I promise, I will not leave you." Rance exhaled, clearly trying to find the right words to soothe his little girl's broken heart, even temporarily.

"You already did, once." Eve sniffled.

"When?"

"You left me at the hospital. When my daddy took me out of there, he said you'd disappeared."

"I most certainly did not disappear," Rance told her, his tone a mixture of hurt and shock. "You'd asked me to find you a lake creature, and I went looking. Your daddy knew that."

Apparently he'd found the right words to distract her. She nodded. "Is that why you brought the dragons to see me?"

Jade noticed she hadn't called them *lake monsters* again.

"Yes." Rance kissed Eve's forehead. "You always said you wanted to see a picture of them. So I did one better. I let you see the real thing."

"Can I see them again?"

This time when Rance glanced back at Libby, she laughed. "I imagine that can be arranged," she said.

"Now try and get some more rest." Gently, Rance eased Eve back, cradling her head with a pillow. "Libby's going to take a look at you and see if you've gotten a lot better or a little."

Eve's eyes had already drifted closed. "A lot," she mumbled. "I think a lot."

When Rance straightened, Jade stepped away, not wanting to intrude on the small family. She crossed the room to stand next to Libby, both of them riveted on Rance and his stepdaughter.

"You love him, don't you?" Libby murmured. "The question is rhetorical, since I've been inside your head, but Rance would have to be blind not to see it."

"Blind not to see what?" Rance asked as he moved away from a now-slumbering Eve.

"Nothing," Jade answered, her face heating.

"Darlin', you just blushed with your entire body." Rance let his gaze roam over her, clearly intrigued. "Whatever you two were talking about must have been more than nothing."

Averting her eyes, Jade shrugged. Chuckling, Libby went to inspect Eve. Both Jade and Rance fell silent as Libby passed her hands over the little girl.

"There's nothing…" Libby let her words trail off. "Just a moment. Let me try this again."

Just then, in a flash of insight, Jade realized this could be dangerous to Libby. If Eve had the Drakkor illness, Libby could catch it. "Maybe you shouldn't..." she began. Libby waved her to silence.

"She's fine." Libby raised incredulous eyes to Rance. "No fever, her heart and blood and lungs appear normal. She's a bit weak and has some minor digestive upset. But all in all, I'd say she's going to be fine."

"Are you sure?" Jade knew Rance didn't mean to reveal such depths of hope in his voice, but the longing was there nonetheless. The sound of it made her knees go weak.

"I'm sure," Libby answered. "Eve is going to be okay."

Still, Rance didn't appear convinced. "Maybe I should get her checked out at the hospital just in case."

Shaking her head, Libby shrugged. "That's up to you, of course. But you'd better come up with an explanation for how a supposedly fatal illness has just disappeared."

"Good point."

Unable to help herself, Jade hugged him, letting herself revel for a moment in the feel of his rock-hard body. "Let yourself believe. This is something that should be celebrated."

"I agree." Libby flashed a happy smile at the two of them. "I don't have any champagne, but I have some fresh apple cider. Will that work?"

"Sure."

"Great." Bustling off to get it, Libby hummed as she disappeared into her kitchen.

Though every nerve, every fiber of her being, was overly aware of Rance standing next to her, Libby kept her attention focused on Eve. "You're her family now," she said softly.

"Yes, I know. I want to have some kind of service for Jim, even if it's private. He didn't have any other family, so I was all he had."

She nodded, wondering if Rance had yet realized exactly how much his life was going to change. She hoped to be a part of that life, but Rance had never made any secret of his plans to leave Forestwood.

While she never could. Not as long as she was Guardian to Libby. Plus, while she had no doubt of her feelings for Rance, she wasn't sure exactly how he felt about her. They were friends, certainly. But whether or not he felt more for her, she hadn't a clue.

"You're going to make a wonderful father," Libby said, peeking her head out of the kitchen doorway, her voice soft.

"Thank you." Raising his head, Rance smiled at her, before turning back to Jade. "You know Jade, I've been a fool. The two of us can do anything. Eve is going to need a mother, too. Do you think you might be up to the task?"

Stunned, Jade stared. "What do you mean?"

"I'm asking you to marry me, darlin'." His smile widened. "You're such a giving, generous woman. One of a kind. I think you and I would make great parents for Eve."

He spoke like he was hiring a nanny.

Behind him, Jade saw Libby's eyes widen. Refusing to acknowledge the awful, gut-wrenching hurt, Jade shook her head before slowly backing away. At least now she knew how he felt. "No, thank you," she said, her tone as impersonal and polite as she could make it. "But I wish you the best of luck in your search."

Turning around, she managed to walk to the door. Not run, as her every instinct urged her to do. But a stately and hopefully dignified walk, giving no one a clue how badly her heart was breaking. Once she'd opened the door, she managed to close it quietly rather than slam it like she really wanted to do.

Giving. Generous. One of a kind. The words echoing in her head, she got in her car, started it and headed home. All the while refusing to even think about what had just happened. What Rance had said. How he apparently really saw her. Once she got home, she intended to head to her bedroom and lock the door. Then, and only then, would she let herself fall to pieces.

Chapter 19

Staring after Jade, Rance scratched his head. Genuinely puzzled and hurt, he eyed Libby. "What's wrong with her?" he asked, still feeling fairly confident he could fix things once he understood exactly what had happened. "I know she cares about me. And about Eve. I guess Jade doesn't believe in marriage? Is that why she has an ex-fiance?"

Rather than answer him, Libby only eyed him, her unsympathetic expression completely at odds with her usually warm personality. "You don't get it, do you?" she finally asked. "Think about what you just said, then tell me you don't understand Jade's reaction."

He did as she'd asked. After all, he'd been happily married before and he thought he had a good understanding about women. Violet had never been one for flowery words, but he knew all women weren't the same. Jade's down to earth attitude had clued him in on what he believed she'd want to hear.

"I complimented her. Called her generous and giving.

Both are true." Though he didn't want to face the rest of it, he knew he had to. "And then I asked her to become my wife. That alone should tell her how I feel about her."

"Really?" Libby shook her head. "Do you really think so?"

"Judging from your tone, I take it you don't agree with me?"

Libby muttered something under her breath that sounded like, "Men," and busied herself cleaning up the apple cider glasses.

When she returned from the kitchen, her usual pleasant expression had returned to her face. "You and Eve are welcome to stay as long as you need. I don't see any reason she should live in a hotel, but of course that's up to you."

Still feeling shell-shocked, he nodded. "Thanks. I'd kind of figured I'd buy a place here. Now, I'm not so sure that's a good idea. I thought Jade…"

"You thought Jade what?"

Embarrassed, he lifted one shoulder in a hopefully casual shrug. "I thought she cared about me."

"I'm sure she does. And about Eve, too. As you said so eloquently, Jade is a giving and generous person."

Was that a trace of mockery he heard in Libby's voice?

"Why is that such a bad thing?" he asked, suddenly fed up with all the innuendo swirling around. "She's your Guardian. You know how valuable those traits are."

"It's hard to believe you're a famous reporter." This time, Libby didn't bother to hide her disgust. "Tell me, were those two words honestly the best way to declare your feelings for Jade?"

"I'm better with pictures." He spread his hands. "Not so great with words."

"Obviously. Now tell me, do you love Jade?"

Love. He frowned. Of course, he hadn't mentioned love.

He'd just assumed Jade understood how he felt. Why else would he ask her to marry him, to share his life and Eve's?

But then again, why would she know how he felt? With dawning horror, he realized what he'd done. He'd gone away and never called her. Worse, since he'd been back, he'd kept reiterating he wouldn't be staying. He'd done nothing, absolutely nothing, to show her how he felt.

Eve moaned, distracting him. He hurried over to her and felt her forehead, worried the fever might be returning. She felt all right, at least as far as he could tell. And she still slept. Maybe she'd just had a bad dream.

Relieved, he looked up to find Libby watching him. "You have a lot on your plate," she said. "Why don't you take a moment or two and deal with Eve. Think this through. Then, if you're really sure you want Jade, you're going to have to fight for her."

Jade knew she shouldn't expect Rance to come after her. Clearly, after what he'd said to her, he'd only asked her to marry him so he could have a nursemaid and helper for Eve. She'd proven herself a great Guardian with Libby, after all. Too bad he couldn't see she was so much more than that.

She let herself mourn. Grieve, actually, since she'd lost someone she'd love forever. She couldn't remain friends—she'd never understood how some women could go from passionately in love to simple friendship. Her feelings ran way too deep for that. As far as she was concerned, she never wanted to see Rance Sleighter again.

He called. She didn't answer. She deleted every message he left without listening to his meaningless words. Once, she would have given everything to have him pursue her. Now it was too little, too late and for all the wrong reasons.

Over the next weeks, she went on with her life and got her wish. She got up, went to work, came home. She read the thick books Amber had kept from her, and took detailed notes. Once, the role of Guardian had been taken much more seriously. Libby had been regarded as a creature, a nonhuman entity, despite her ability to shape-shift in the same manner as the Burnetts.

Reading, Jade understood why Libby had kept to herself, why she felt so alone. What had started as a self-defense mechanism had become habit. Not once had any of Jade's ancestors appeared to realize how isolated Libby had become.

She also found it interesting that the books hadn't mentioned anything about the necklace and the need to pass it on to one's successor. Which made Jade wonder if Libby had been the one who'd initiated that tradition.

Another sunrise, another sunset. Jade changed into wolf with her family and hunted the woods. On Saturday, she went to town with Amber and Emerald and ate at Mother Earth's Café. She visited Di, who now appeared hugely pregnant, making Jade think the baby still was growing way too fast. Through all of this, Jade never saw any sign of Rance or his rental car. She couldn't help but wonder where he might be and if he was hiding for some reason.

Or worse, if he'd left town all together.

Finally, when she called Libby to suggest they have dinner together and Libby told her she thought it was best if Jade continued to stay away for a little while longer, she put the pieces together.

Rance and Eve were staying at Libby's. Stunned, Jade sank down on her front porch swing and wondered why she felt so betrayed.

The bright riot of autumn color had just about come to an end. Dead and dying leaves swirled in the north wind. Her necklace felt unusually heavy around her neck, the purple stone radiated heat. Which reminded her of the one person she no longer wanted to think about at all.

She stood, looking around at her beloved home, and knew what she had to do. Before she could talk herself out of it, she got in her SUV and drove to the lake, a spot directly across from the place where Libby's house sat. Walking out to the edge of a cliff, she took the necklace from around her neck, trying to study the purple stone with a dispassionate gaze. For the first time she realized the color exactly matched Libby's amethyst eyes. This made her feel a twinge of sadness, which she pushed away. Nothing would deter her from what she now felt she had to do.

Taking a deep breath, she flung the necklace as far as she could, watching as it hit the water with a satisfying plop. She waited, curious to see if anything else would happen, but nothing did. The lake didn't foam or bubble up; Libby or another dragon creature didn't rise out of the water. And she didn't fall down dead. In fact, she didn't feel much different. Maybe a little bit lighter, but that was all.

One thing she knew for certain—Libby would never be able to enter her head again now that the necklace was gone.

So she got back in her car and drove home.

Her cell phone rang as she turned onto her street.

"It's time." Auntie Em sounded worried rather than excited. "The doctor wants to induce labor. I'm doing everything I can to get him to hold off."

"It hasn't been long enough," Jade protested.

"I know. But all along these pregnancies have been weird. All of the babies have had some kind of accelerated growth."

"Are they all ready to deliver?"

"Yes." Em swallowed with an audible gulp. "Can you get a hold of your Fae friend?"

While Jade wouldn't go so far as to call Breena a friend, she understood the urgency in the request. Breena had told them the babies needed to be woken or there'd be disastrous consequences. "Yes. I'll get her and send her to the hospital right away."

At least since Jade had the charmed crystal bell to ring,

contacting her had become much simpler than running off to the woods and jumping into the portal.

When Jade rang the bell, this time the tinkling sound reminded her of Breena's laughter. A heartbeat later, the Fae queen stood in front of Jade, her blue eyes twinkling. "You rang?" she said, before dissolving into peals of laughter.

Jade smiled along with her. She really thought she and Breena would eventually reach a tacit understanding. In time, the two might actually be able to be friends, but as ruler of a race of magical beings, Breena had a lot to deal with. Meanwhile, so did Jade.

"The babies are about to be born," Jade told her. "We need you to wake them before they are delivered."

"Of course." She looked around the interior of Jade's SUV with interest. "How fast can you make this thing go?"

Libby thoroughly enjoyed having Rance and Eve for company. No longer alone, she found she had a skill for entertaining a young child while at the same time teaching valuable skills. She taught Eve basic food prep skills, nothing too complicated or dangerous, but the little girl could now make a sandwich with a plastic spreader for her mayo with ease. This pleased her so immensely she'd taken to insisting she be the one to prepare lunch every single day.

Eve's strength had grown over time and Libby judged she'd soon be back to 100 percent.

Rance, on the other hand, was restless. He spent a lot of time outside with his camera, photographing the sunrise, the sunset, the lake and the trees. Libby wondered if he missed Jade and if he had any intention of going after her, but she didn't want to butt in where she wasn't wanted.

The truth of the matter was, Libby missed Jade, too. But she couldn't invite her over while Rance stayed here. If she'd owned a car and knew how to drive, Libby would have gone and visited. She guessed she could order a cab like she had when she'd called the family meeting, but that would mean explaining to Jade what she was doing and why. She knew Jade would view this as a betrayal, as if Libby needed to choose sides—either Jade or Rance.

Libby loved them both. She'd lived long enough to understand if she was patient, things would eventually work out.

So in the end, she did nothing. Kind of like Rance, who looked more and more miserable every passing day.

Finally, one morning when she went downstairs to make breakfast and found Rance sitting at the kitchen table waiting for her, she realized he'd reached a decision.

"You made coffee," she exclaimed, pretending not to notice anything out of the ordinary. "Thank you for that."

"Once you've gotten a cup, we need to talk," he responded.

"Okay." She took her time adding cream and sugar, before carrying her mug over to the table and taking a sip. "What's up?"

"How is Jade doing?" he asked, his casual tone at odds with his intense expression.

"Okay, I guess." She carefully shrugged.

"She won't answer my calls. I've shown up at the house twice, and the second time, Amber threatened to call the police. She told me I'm not welcome."

"I can't say I blame them," Libby told him.

His eyes widened. "What do you mean?"

"You hurt her. Badly. I'm guessing you want to apologize so you can assuage your guilt."

"Not at all." He swore. "I need to convince her I love her."

She snorted. "Do you? You could have fooled me."

His frown told her he didn't appreciate her comment, but she'd had enough. "Rance, one thing I've come to know about you is if you want something, you go after it. If you really wanted Jade, you'd have found a way to get to her."

"I..." Then he closed his mouth and she knew he realized she was right.

"Fine." He placed his hands on the table. "What are you suggesting I do? She won't see me or talk to me. I can't become her stalker."

Libby said nothing, letting him work it out himself.

"Will you help me?" he finally asked. "At least get her to agree to meet me."

"I haven't really talked to her much lately."

He swore. "I've come between you. Believe me, that's the last thing I ever wanted to do."

"You didn't, I promise. Okay, maybe only a little. But Jade needed some alone time to figure things out." She looked down at her hands. "Burnetts don't stay Guardians forever, you know."

"You're not thinking of cutting her loose, are you? That would destroy her."

Since she hadn't truly decided herself, she couldn't give him an answer. "All good things eventually come to an end," she said. "I'd like to give Jade the freedom to have her own life."

Forcing a smile, she looked up. "Meanwhile, you have your own path to follow."

"You're right," he agreed. "I think the time has come for me and Eve to move on," he told her.

Concerned, she made an effort not to frown. She would never have pegged him as a quitter. "Where are you thinking of going?"

He looked up from his own coffee and met her gaze. "I'd like to buy a place here in town. Nothing fancy, a simple house with a couple of bedrooms and a garage. I know I can't afford lake view, but I'd like to live as close to the lake as possible."

This time, she didn't even attempt to hide her blazing grin. "I knew you wouldn't give up so easily," she exclaimed.

"I'll help you in any way I can. I hope once you find your own place, you and Eve will visit often."

"Of course we will." And then he surprised her and gave her a hug. "We consider you family, you know. Eve has no grandparents and I'd be honored if you'd consider filling that spot for her."

Delighted, she hugged him back. "Of course I will. You have no idea how happy that's made me. Now go on. I'll watch Eve while you begin your house search. I think one of the Burnett family is a Realtor."

Something flickered in his eyes at the mention of the name. "All right. But I'd prefer to work with a Realtor other than a Burnett. Can you tell me where another real estate office is?"

"Of course." She gave him directions, shooing him out the door before Eve woke up. Then she got busy making some homemade cinnamon rolls for her granddaughter.

As soon as they arrived at the hospital, Jade hustled Breena upstairs. Of course even with them rushing down the hallway, both of them garnered several double takes and outright stares. Jade guessed Breena was probably used to this. For herself, all the attention made Jade feel uncomfortable.

"Thank goodness you're here," Amber exclaimed, jumping to her feet so quickly the magazine she'd been reading fell onto the floor. "Em's doing her best to keep the doctors from starting a C-section. I think the other girls' mothers are doing the same. I even heard talk about inducing labor."

"Don't worry." Breena's tranquil smile instantly vanquished the panic in Jade's mother's expression. "I'm here now. I've got everything under control."

What happened after that, Jade would later go over again and again in her mind. Even she, who had a pretty good understanding of magic, was astounded. What Breena did boggled the mind.

First, she froze time. Everyone, from the nurses to the doctors, even the machines, became like statues. Even Amber, Emerald and Di were immobilized. Out of curiosity, Jade moved her arm, surprised to realize she hadn't been frozen like the others.

"They can't see anything," Breena told her softly. "But you can. I might need your help."

"Of course," Jade answered, though she wasn't sure what exactly she could do.

Next Breena went to Di, lying prone in the hospital bed. She passed her hands over Di's protruding belly, again speaking in that unintelligible Fae language. Immediately, Di's baby bump began to contract.

"What's happening?" Jade asked, fearing for her cousin.

"I woke the infant up and now she's wanting to be born."

"What?" Panicked, Jade looked around. The nurses and the doctor remained like statues. "Don't you need to wake them up so they can help?"

"I will once I help the other women." Breena's matter-of-fact tone helped steady Jade's nerves. "Come, we'd better hurry. There are going to be several babies all born at once."

Later, once Breena had done her work and the normal hospital hustle and bustle resumed, the nurses shooed everyone from the room except the pregnant women's mothers.

Despite having done nothing but watch, Jade felt exhausted. She sank down in a waiting room chair, managing a smile as the rest of her family trickled in. Somehow, she completely missed Breena's departure. The Fae queen must have slipped away while Jade had been occupied with greeting her two sisters.

The three healthy babies—one boy and two girls—were born minutes apart. Breaking family tradition, Di elected not to name her daughter after a gemstone, choosing instead an ordinary human name—Mary. Amber claimed to be appalled, but Emerald declared she was fine with it.

As usual, Jade's twin sisters were engaged in a private conversation. They went quiet as Jade approached them. Jade noticed Pearl had something sheltered in her hand, like she didn't want Jade to see it.

"What do you have there?" Jade asked, curious.

Sapphire and Pearl exchanged a glance. "You'd better show her," Sapphire said. "You know she's going to find out eventually."

Finally Pearl nodded. "I found this." Pearl held up a familiar silver necklace, sheltering the stone with her hand. "Lucas and I were walking on the shores of the lake and I found this washed up, stuck between two rocks. Isn't it beautiful?"

Though she already knew, Jade had to be certain. "Let me see the stone."

Still Pearl hesitated. "Okay, so it looks just like the one you always wear." She peered at her sister. "Or used to wear." Resignation settled in her young face. "Did you lose yours?"

"No." Jade took a deep breath and then pried Pearl's fingers away. The amethyst stone gleamed in Pearl's small palm. "I threw it into the lake."

Pearl gasped. "Why?"

"It's a long story." Slipping her arm around Pearl's shoulders, Jade hugged her close. "It looks like Libby has chosen my successor. I think it's time you and I had a long talk."

"Here?" Pearl squeaked.

Glancing around the still-packed waiting room, Jade shook her head. "No, not here. We'll talk when we get home. In the meantime, you'd better put the necklace on. You don't want to lose it."

Sapphire watched the two of them with a combination of barely disguised envy. "So Libby picked Pearl over me? Just because she happened to be the one to find the necklace?"

Crud. These two were the first twins in the history of the Burnett family. "I'm not sure," Jade answered, choosing her words carefully. "I haven't talked to her yet. Let me do that before either of you go jumping to any conclusions."

"Okay," Pearl said in a small voice, her expression stricken. "Because if Sapph can't do it, I won't, either. You can tell Libby I said that."

Jade sighed. "We'll talk later. Right now I think everyone is getting ready to troop to the nursery window so we can see Di's baby. Let's go check her out."

Leaving the real estate office, Rance caught himself whistling an old tune, something he hadn't done since Violet died. Though there hadn't been an abundance of available empty houses in Forestwood, there'd been one house in particular he wanted. The only house he could picture having a family in. Though the place wasn't for sale, the Realtor had located the owner and inquired if they would be willing to part with the place.

They'd been surprised, but once they'd heard Rance's offer—all in cash—they'd accepted. Rance was just waiting for the paperwork to be done so he could set a closing date. Of course, he'd need to buy furniture and appliances, but this felt good. Right.

His life had certainly gone through a lot of changes over the course of two years. He'd lost Violet and Jim, but Eve had regained her health. And he'd found Jade, the woman he knew he wanted to spend the rest of his life with.

The woman he loved.

Now he just had to prove it to her.

He didn't blame her for being angry with him. He hadn't been very considerate, staying out of touch for extended periods, not giving much of himself but then expecting and asking for Jade's help. He could offer up a thousand excuses, but he knew she'd see right through them to the truth.

He'd put himself first. No woman deserved that. And he knew words wouldn't fix this. Only actions could banish her doubts.

Assuming she'd still want him.

Driving around the town he'd come to think of as home, he pondered what to do. He'd done an internet search and learned lots of enterprising men had staged elaborate proposals, complete with props, but that wasn't his thing. Nor was it Jade's.

Plus, he had one other handicap to overcome. Due to his own clumsiness, he'd managed to make Jade think he only wanted her because she'd make a good mother to Eve. When in fact, he wanted her because he didn't want to live without her. Ever since his botched proposal, he'd found it hurt to breathe, as if he couldn't get enough air. He thought of Jade constantly. She was his first thought when he woke in the morning and the last when he went to sleep at night.

He even dreamed of her continually, which made him wake aroused and aching for her. The intimacy they'd shared had been unlike anything he'd ever experienced, even with Violet. Jade was like no other woman he'd met.

Mate. He remembered when the term had first occurred to him and he'd tried to convince himself that he was wrong. How foolish he'd been.

He'd taken comfort in his camera, the way he always did in the past, but found little solace in the thousands of photos he took of the lake, the trees, Eve and anything else that caught his eye.

One afternoon, flipping through the photos he'd stored on his laptop, he realized what he might be able to do to prove his love to Jade. All his life, he'd made a living by telling stories with pictures rather than words. He'd hit bestseller lists and won awards with his photography books. Why not make a book of pictures to show Jade how he felt?

Feeling more optimistic than he'd felt in a long time, Rance got busy. If he worked day and night, he should be able to pull this thing together in a few days.

Chapter 20

Jade spent a lot of her spare time avoiding other people and hiking in the woods above the lake. She took care to stay away from Libby's house, thus avoiding the possibility of even catching a glimpse of Rance. Her heart couldn't take it.

"Out of sight, out of mind" didn't apply. She couldn't stop thinking about him, remembering the spark that had blazed between them. How on earth could she have been so wrong about his feelings for her?

Of course, she'd been wrong before. When she'd been dating Ross, believing him when he declared his love, giving him the greatest gift of all—herself, her first time. After, he'd proposed. She'd accepted, giddy with joy, expecting him to show up with an engagement ring.

Instead, he'd disappeared. He'd dodged her, wouldn't return her calls, and she'd gradually understood once he'd gotten what he wanted, he had no more use for her.

She'd been young and thought she wouldn't survive.

Now, she knew she'd only been foolish and infatuated. Now, she finally understood what real love felt like.

And now, Jade counted on her strength to help get her through. She had to trust that the pain would recede with time. It had to, or she didn't know how she'd stay sane.

As fall disappeared into winter, the definite chill in the air invigorated her. Despite the nearly bare tree limbs clawing at the gray sky as if warning of the imminent approach of snow, she tried to keep her mood upbeat. She refused to allow the heavy depression she'd been battling to settle around her like a leaden cloak. Not only did she feel she'd lost Libby, but she'd lost the one man she could ever truly love.

As if she'd ever had him. Rance had made it clear how he saw her. Good old dependable, steady-Eddy Jade. She wondered why he'd bothered to kiss her, why he'd made love to her with an intensity as fierce as her own.

No.

She wouldn't think of him. If all the country music songs were to be believed, time would heal her wounds.

In the meantime, she hiked as much as she could, aware once the snow started she'd lose this avenue for exercise.

A stick broke behind her, making her spin around. Her heart lurched. Rance. With his camera hanging around his neck. So help her, if he dared to raise it to his face and try to take her picture…

"Hey," he said, jamming his hands in his pockets as if he knew her thoughts. "How are you?"

Though she should turn around and walk away without answering, the sound of his Southern drawl made her crave more of him, even if it would only hurt her. So she lifted her head and managed what she hoped was a casual smile. "I'm doing well. Clearly, you are, too. How's Eve?"

"Getting stronger every day. Libby's agreed to be her grandmother, which thrilled her."

"Now all you need is someone to be her mother." The words slipped out despite herself. Appalled, she covered her mouth with her hand.

Immediately he crossed the space between them, reaching for her. She evaded him, shaking her head. "Don't touch me."

"I didn't mean to hurt you," he began. Damn him.

"But you did. And the worst part of it is that it's not your fault. I thought you felt the same way about me that I did about you, but clearly you just wanted a friend with benefits. I get it. Now go away."

Instead, he cocked his head, his gray gaze blazing with some inner flame. "How did you feel about me?"

Crud. She felt her face heat as she realized what she'd given away. Then she realized it didn't matter. "I cared about you." Past tense. As if those feelings were gone.

"I still care about you," he said.

"Not the same way. Clearly."

Briefly, he bowed his head. "I'm sorry. Honestly, I meant what I said as a compliment. I was so happy, I didn't think. I should have gone about proposing to you in a different way."

"Don't bother." This time, she managed to put scorn in her tone. "I'll never marry someone who just wants me because his little girl needs a mother." She lifted her chin. "And don't get me wrong, I adore Eve. And yes, I'd make a damn good mother. The best. But there's more to marriage than just that."

He took a step closer. "Yes. Yes, there is." Reaching behind him, he lowered his backpack. "I made you something." Removing a book of some sort, he held it out to her.

"What's this?" She made no move to take it.

"I'm clearly not good with words. But I'm awesome with photographs. I made you this photo book to show you how I feel about you."

Curious despite herself, Jade accepted the book, but made no move to open it. How could she, when she couldn't seem to tear her gaze off him. His nearness felt overwhelming. "What's the point of this?" she asked. "I'm not really sure what you're trying to accomplish."

Reaching out, he fingered a tendril of her hair, winding it around his finger before releasing it. "I want to show you that there's more—so much more—to my feelings for you than what I said earlier." He cleared his throat, sending another smoldering look her way. "I want to show you how I feel. I want to prove to you that you're... Well, you're my everything."

Hounds help her, her knees went weak at his words. She turned the book around in her hands, suddenly afraid to open it. Her emotions, her feelings, felt way too raw. Yet hope, that traitorous beast, made her heart beat faster.

"Please," he whispered. "Open it."

So she did. The first photograph was of her, shortly after they'd met. She'd stuck out her tongue at him, impatient with the incessant snap of his shutter. Yet despite this, he'd somehow managed to make her look beautiful.

Turning the page, she saw more pictures of her, as well as things she loved. There was one of Burnett House, bathed in the setting sun, with Jade on the front porch sitting in her swing, gazing off into the distance. She'd clearly been unaware of the photographer, and while Jade didn't understand how he'd done it, his love for his subject shone as clearly as the sunlight setting fire to the horizon in the background.

Here, Dogs Off Leash. Her employees playing with their charges, and Jade, over in the corner of the photograph, kneeling on the floor petting a fluffy white dog who gazed at her with as much adoration as she did him.

There were others, many that she didn't remember his taking. Her from behind, laughing over her shoulder at something he'd said, her feelings shining in her eyes. She and Libby with their arms around each other, standing on Libby's deck with the sparkling jewel of the lake in the background.

As she slowly flipped through the remaining pages, her eyes filled with tears. When she reached the last page, she found he'd written a note.

I love you. Adore you, in fact. I knew you were my mate the instant I met you, though I couldn't admit it for some time. I can't do flowery words, but you're beautiful and sweet and kind and sexy. I want you to be mine.

Will you marry me, Jade Burnett? Let me love you the rest of our lives?

Now she cried in earnest, almost afraid to believe, definitely afraid not to. "I love you, too," she managed. When he pulled her to him, this time she didn't resist.

She buried her face in his throat, inhaling the masculine scent of him.

"You haven't answered me," he said, his voice shaking.

She kissed him, long and slow and deep. When she came up for air, she could barely stand. Gazing into his beloved eyes, she nodded. "Yes. Yes, of course I'll marry you. As long as you promise to tell me you love me every single day of our lives."

He laughed, the sound full of both joy and relief. "Of course I will."

Hand in hand, they went to tell Libby and Eve. Jade felt a little nervous, especially since she had to discuss Libby's choice of Pearl as Jade's replacement.

As Libby's house came into view, Jade realized Libby was out on her back porch with a cup of tea. She caught sight of them as they walked down the hiking path toward her. "Oh, thank goodness," she exclaimed, standing and waving. "I'm so happy the two of you managed to work things out."

Feeling oddly hesitant, Jade left Rance and went to give Libby a hug. "What about you and me?" she asked. "I've felt lost without you these past couple of weeks."

"And I you." Libby pulled back, her amethyst gaze searching Jade's face. "Is everything all right?"

"Yes." With a pang, Jade remembered the necklace she'd tossed into the lake. "I understand you're wanting my younger sister Pearl to take over my role as Guardian."

"What?" Libby frowned in confusion. "What makes you think that?"

"She found the necklace. The one I was given when I became Guardian."

"Found it where? Did you lose it?"

Ah, here came the tricky part. Jade looked down, grateful when Rance slipped his arm around her shoulders in an offer of silent support.

"I tossed it into the lake," Jade said. She hated how small her voice sounded, so she tried again. "I thought you were done with me. That we were no longer friends."

"Oh, honey." Eyes wide, Libby appeared shocked. "Why would you ever think that?"

Taking a deep breath, Jade knew she'd have to expose her heart. But this was Libby, and Rance. She should have known neither would ever willingly cause her pain. "Because I was really hurting after what happened with Rance. I could have used your support and insight. When you kept putting me off, I finally figured out Rance and Eve were staying with you. It felt like you were taking his side, especially since you didn't even tell me."

"I'm so sorry." Crossing the room, Libby enveloped both Jade and Rance in her own hug. "I knew Rance loved you—of that I've never had a doubt. I could tell he just needed time to figure out how to prove it to you. And I didn't want

Eve, who's still recovering, living in a hotel room. It just seemed like the best solution for everyone."

"Hey!" Eve hurried into the room. "I want to be hugged, too!"

Jade opened one arm so the little girl could join in the group hug. Happiness blossomed in her heart. This was everything she'd ever wanted. Or nearly everything. One day she hoped to have a baby of her own so Eve could have a little brother or sister.

After a few seconds, Eve started squirming. "I'm hungry," she announced. "Papa, can I have a snack?"

"Of course." Taking Eve's hand, Rance led her into the kitchen. Before he left the room, he paused. "I'll be right back, darlin'," he told Jade. "Don't go anywhere, okay?"

Arm still linked with Libby's, Jade nodded.

"There are a few things I need to discuss with you," Libby began. "First off, you do know that necklace was just a talisman, right? It only had magical powers when I wished it so, like when you held it and spoke my name three times. Now that we've finished with that, it's gone back to being just a pendant, nothing more."

Jade wasn't sure if she should be surprised or relieved. "I didn't know. I knew it had some kind of connection to you."

"It did." Libby peered earnestly at her. "As long as we both wished it."

Jade nodded. "I see. That's why I assumed when Pearl found it that meant you had chosen her to be the next Guardian."

"Nope. Not at all." Libby took a deep breath. "To be honest with you, I don't think I need a Guardian anymore."

Shocked, Jade froze. "Why not? I mean, you've always had a Guardian."

"Not always."

"Okay, maybe not your entire life. But since you came to Forestwood, a Burnett has been your Guardian."

Libby's warm smile invited Jade to understand. "Yes, that's true. Long ago, my father initially put that plan into place so I'd never be alone. And for years, I lived a life of isolation. My Guardian was my only contact with the outside world. My only friend and my family. Now…"

She glanced toward the kitchen. "Now I have a family. You and Rance and Eve." Her tremulous smile spoke of her deep joy. "Did you know he asked me to be her grandmother?"

"So I heard." Jade gave her friend another hug. "I'm all for whatever makes you happy. However, I'm not sure if Pearl will be disappointed or relieved."

Libby's smile faded. "True. Over the years I've had all kinds. Some were angry, considering their Guardianship— and me—an onerous task, almost unbearable. Others were resigned, doing the bare minimum possible in order to fulfill their duty. A few started out initially curious, until they became bored. And then there was you."

Puzzled, Jade waited for Libby to explain. "Which one was I?"

"None of those," Libby answered promptly, her amethyst eyes shining. "You were the first of all the Guardians I considered my friend."

Wow. Jade blinked, trying to keep from crying. "Well, now you're family."

"Yes. Yes, we are. However, I need to let you know that once you're no longer Guardian, you'll lose whatever magical abilities you have, however slight."

"Good." Jade didn't even have to think about it. "I just want to be normal. You should hear some of the things they say about me in town."

"Your mother hated that, too. It's always been like that. People assume the current Guardian is some sort of witch. Now maybe that nonsense can stop. And," Libby continued, watching Jade intently, "you can move out of Burnett House if you want."

Jade swallowed. While the idea had a certain bold appeal, Burnett House was her home. She couldn't think of anywhere else where she could live that would feel like home to her.

Eve wandered into the room, munching on a half-eaten apple, with Rance close behind. "If y'all have a minute, there's something I'd like to show you. We'll need to drive. It's a surprise." The meaningful glance he shared with Libby wasn't lost on Jade. Whatever this surprise was, Libby was in on it. Which made Jade happy.

"I love surprises!" Eve said, jumping up and down. Her energy level had improved so much that Jade couldn't tell she'd ever been ill. "Don't you, Jade?"

"Sure I do," Jade answered, smiling easily. She met Rance's gaze, her heart full. "We'll have to take your rental car. My SUV is parked down by the entrance to the hiking trails on the other side of the lake."

"I don't have a rental anymore," Rance explained. "I turned it back in when I bought my own truck."

Surprised, Jade stared. They all trooped outside where Jade had to admire his black crew-cab Chevy Silverado pickup.

"Jade, you sit up front with me." Rance grinned, his excitement palpable. "Eve, let me buckle you in your car seat. Your grandmother will keep you company."

Once they were all buckled in, Rance drove back toward town. As they neared a familiar location, Jade sat up straight, straining as always to catch a glimpse of her dream house.

To her shock, instead of continuing on past, Rance pulled into the driveway and parked. "Here we are," he announced, killing the engine. "Everybody out."

Wondering what the heck was going on, Jade climbed

slowly from the car. "Do you have the owners' permission to be here?" she asked, slightly nervous.

"Yes, darlin'. I sure do."

As she stared at the house she'd loved ever since she'd been a small girl, Jade realized he must have rented it. This house was the only other place she could live that would feel as much like home as Burnett House.

Rance took her arm, kissing her cheek, which sent a zing of heat all the way to her toes. Eve and Libby walked up, holding hands. "Well, do you want to see the inside?" Rance asked.

"I do, I do!" Eve said, jumping up and down from excitement.

But Rance only had eyes for Jade. "What about you?"

Throat tight, she nodded.

As they walked up the sidewalk, Jade held her breath while Rance unlocked the front door with a key. Inside, the empty house still managed to look warm and inviting, with the dark hardwood floors and matching trim around the interior windows.

"Wait until you see the kitchen." Rance kissed her again, his lips tracing a path from her cheek to her mouth. "It's been completely updated."

"Come on, Eve," Libby said, steering the little girl in the opposite direction. "Let's go explore the bedrooms."

Once they'd disappeared, Rance led Jade into a large, French-style kitchen. The stainless-steel appliances looked new and expensive. She loved the granite countertop and the huge window over the farmhouse sink. "Wow," she said, turning slowly to take it all in. "If I'd been renovating this, I'd have done exactly this."

Rance grinned. "It's pretty perfect, isn't it?"

"Yes, it is." She tilted her head, gazing up at him with her heart full of happiness and love. "How'd you get the owner to rent it to you?"

"Rent?" He laughed. "Oh, no, darlin'. This is ours. I bought it. Just closed on it this morning. Since I knew you've always loved it, I couldn't think of a better place to make our home."

Though she wasn't the squealing type, so help her this time she squealed. Loudly. Launching herself at him, she wrapped her arms around him and pulled him down for a long, deep kiss.

The sound of Libby clearing her throat from the doorway broke them apart.

"Where's Eve?" Rance asked, his husky voice attesting to the way the kiss had affected him.

"Playing in her new bedroom." Looking from one to the other, Libby grinned. "She picked out the one she wanted. She's talking about getting a dog. I think she's pretty excited."

"A dog?" Rance and Jade said at the same time.

"I've always wanted a boxer," Rance mused. Jade didn't immediately respond, so charmed by the idea of their little family having a pet in this house that she couldn't speak.

"Boxers are nice," she finally said. "But if we get a dog, I want to get one from a rescue."

"Agreed." Rance laughed and spun her around, pretending to dip her as if they were dancing. Laughing back, she dipped, and when she came up, they continued dancing to their own music. Neither noticed Libby leaving the room.

The wedding was held at Burnett House, of course. Initially, Libby had wanted it to be at her lake place, but when all the Burnett women got together, there was no stopping them. And with their large family, plus all of Jade's employees and friends, not to mention Rance's work colleagues who flew in from all over the world, there was no way her little house could hold them all. Neither could Rance and Jade's new place.

Now that she knew she didn't have to be Guardian, Pearl

and her twin, Sapphire, appeared to have lost their fear of her. Libby found she quite enjoyed chatting with the teenagers, especially when they both offered to help her babysit Eve when Rance and Jade went on their honeymoon.

The morning of the wedding dawned cloudy and cold. Snow had been forecast, but so far only flurries drifted down from the sky. Libby did everything she could with her limited powers to make sure the weather held. She wanted to make sure Jade and Rance were able to drive down to New York City to stay the night before flying out of La-Guardia to Puerto Rico for their honeymoon the next day.

The entire Burnett family had embraced Eve, welcoming her into the fold like a long-lost family member. Amber had announced to Libby that they would share grandparenting duties, to which Libby had happily agreed.

Jade had wanted a simple wedding, politely shooting down Opal's desire for a barrage of candles and incense. There were flowers, autumn colors despite the fast-approaching winter, and the twins had been given the joint compliment of being asked to act as maids of honor.

And now it was time for the wedding to begin.

Despite the wintry air, Jade had insisted the actual wedding be held on the front porch. As a result, the family had brought in freestanding gas heaters to keep the guests warm. They'd placed them at strategic intervals under the huge white tent on the front lawn where everyone would sit.

Libby and Eve had front row seats next to Amber and Opal. One of Jade's employees played the harp, and he'd offered to provide the music, which, Libby had to admit, was lovely.

With everyone in place, Rance stood next to the minister on the front porch, near the porch swing. Pearl and Sapphire, wearing identical rust-colored gowns, walked up the steps and took their places on the other side of the minister. Catching Libby's eye, Pearl grinned and winked. Libby grinned back, reflecting what a great and fun Guardian Pearl would have been.

Then Jade appeared and Libby forgot everything else. Her white dress floated around her ankles, the beaded bodice clinging to her body as lovingly as if it had been made for her. One look at Rance, seeing the reverent awe and love in his handsome face, and Libby's eyes filled with tears. Since she'd sworn not to cry, she dabbed at the corners of her leaking eyes with a handkerchief she'd brought just for that purpose.

Head held high, with her amazing silver hair that had begun to turn red in a perfect French braid, Jade kept her gaze locked on her groom. A light flush made her alabaster skin appear to glow. Once she'd lifted the hem of her skirt and climbed the steps, she took her spot next to the minister. The harp quieted and the minister began to read the vows.

With Rance's precious camera in hand, Lucas Everett snapped photographs. He'd been amazed and honored when Rance had asked him to serve as wedding photographer, and seemed determined to do the best job he could. He even managed to keep from staring at Sapphire, who did everything she could to catch his eye.

"Do you, Rance Sleighter, take Jade Burnett as your lawfully wedded wife, to have and to hold, in sickness and in health, until death do you part?"

Rance didn't hesitate. "I do."

Then the minister turned to Jade and repeated his question. "I do," Jade responded.

"Then I pronounce you husband and wife. You may kiss the bride."

Libby, along with everyone else, held her breath waiting for Rance to claim his new wife for the traditional kiss. Instead, the two of them moved over to the porch swing. Jade took a seat, demurely setting her skirt around her.

Rance joined her, tenderly cupping her face with his large hand. "Forever," he said.

"Forever," she replied. And then the two of them finally kissed, setting the swing in motion. The wedding party cheered.

And the snow began to fall in earnest, though neither the bride nor groom noticed.

* * * * *

MILLS & BOON®

nocturne™

AN EXHILARATING UNDERWORLD OF DARK DESIRES

A sneak peek at next month's titles...

In stores from 14th July 2016:

- **Enchanted Guardian** – Sharon Ashwood
- **Lycan Unleashed** – Shannon Curtis

MILLS & BOON®

Why not subscribe?
Never miss a title and save money too!

Here is what's available to you if you join the exclusive **Mills & Boon® Book Club** today:

* *Titles up to a month ahead of the shops*
* *Amazing discounts*
* *Free P&P*
* *Earn Bonus Book points that can be redeemed against other titles and gifts*
* *Choose from monthly or pre-paid plans*

Still want more?
Well, if you join today we'll even give you
50% OFF your first parcel!

So visit **www.millsandboon.co.uk/subscriptions**
or call **Customer Relations on 0844 844 1351***
to be a part of this exclusive Book Club!